TAKING CARE OF BUSINESS

Stephanie Bond

CHAPTER ONE

FBI SPECIAL AGENT Steve Berringer sat in a loaner SUV studying the Taking Care of Business wedding chapel, a fireball of apprehension in his stomach. He'd walked into some of the most seedy bars, basements, betting parlors and brothels in Las Vegas with his weapon drawn and expecting the worst, but none of those places had put a sweat on the back of his neck like this innocent-looking little white building across the parking lot with pink and yellow flowers on either side of its covered entrance.

Maybe it was the August heat, he reasoned, glancing up through the windshield at the afternoon sun from behind his polarized shades. But a cool breeze was blowing today, making the cute little trees in front of the chapel sway in the most depressingly precious way. Plus he had the air conditioner on full blast.

Steve rubbed his hand over his painful midsection. In thirty-four years, this was the closest he'd ever come to the whole marriage process. He'd never even *seen* a wedding. He had ducked countless requests to be a groomsman, had RSVP'd with regrets to every invitation he'd received, had sidestepped requests from girlfriends to attend weddings as an escort. To a commitment-phobic guy like him, a wedding chapel was the ultimate nightmare. Churches, after all, could be used for other things: religious services, christenings, funerals. But a wedding chapel—man, that was hard core.

The phone on his belt rang and he checked it. Karen, his partner. He flipped up the receiver with a grunt. "What's up?"

"Just calling to give you a pep talk."

He frowned. "That's not necessary."

"I saw you pop an antacid before you left—are you sure you're up to this undercover assignment? I mean, I know how you get when someone mentions the 'M' word."

He poked his tongue into his cheek. "You know I'd do anything to nab Lundy. This time he's not getting away."

"But our informant said it could be a week before Lundy shows up there with his child-bride-to-be. It's hard to say how many weddings you'll have to video, how many vows you'll have to witness, how many garters you might accidentally catch."

"Are you through being funny?"

She laughed, then sighed. "Actually, I wish I was with you, partner—hanging out at an Elvis wedding parlor sounds like more fun than pulling desk duty."

"That's what you get for being pregnant." Karen was expecting her first child with her husband Daniel, and the last few weeks were wearing on her. To be honest, Steve was relieved to have her tucked away where it was safe. He expected this undercover operation to end smoothly, with Mitch Lundy being apprehended quietly after he exited the chapel as an unsuspecting married man, but the fewer people—especially pregnant ones—on the scene, the better.

"I know," Karen said. "But I'd give anything to watch you squirm being around all those men saying 'I do.'"

"Did you need something?" he snapped.

"Not as badly as you do," she sang.

"I'm hanging up."

"Bye."

Steve closed the phone and clipped it back onto his belt, then dabbed his neck with his handkerchief. God deliver him from smart-alecky females. He'd rather deal with a hard-nosed criminal any day—they were more predictable.

Heaving a sigh, he turned off the engine and lifted his camera bag from the passenger seat. Who knew that his long-neglected hobby would come in handy on a work assignment? And taking photos of the chapel would be the perfect foil for making sure Lundy was covered from every angle.

As he strode toward the chapel, he noticed the abundance of neon on the sign and the building itself—in the daylight, the little white chapel looked out of place on the garish Las Vegas strip, but after sundown, this place would probably outshine its flashy neighbors.

It was a one-story building, narrow along the street front, but deep. Cordelia Conroy was the owner of the place, early sixties, a former showgirl who once had ties to the mob. She owed the FBI a favor for helping her out of a jam years ago, so she'd agreed to let Steve come in undercover as an employee to keep an eye out for Lundy, on condition that the arrest wouldn't take place at the chapel and that her employees wouldn't be in danger. In return, the FBI had demanded confidentiality—none of the regular employees could know Steve's real identity or why he was there.

So, dressed in casual clothes, having purposefully missed his regular haircut last week and sporting two days' worth of beard, he would be Steve Mulcahy, scruffy photographer. If the undercover position were in any other place, he might actually be happy for some downtime, but being surrounded by flowers and music and gushing couples—*damn*. Not counting the oddballs he'd likely be working with in an Elvis wedding chapel. Steve tucked his sunglasses into his shirt pocket, then inhaled and opened the front door. He was looking forward to cuffing Lundy, but this would definitely go down as his worst assignment ever.

He stepped inside a foyer of sorts, immediately enveloped by the strains of "Love Me Tender" floating from mounted speakers. Spin-racks of postcards and Elvis Presley memorabilia occupied every available space, leaving a narrow path to a counter surrounded by poster-sized menus of wedding packages and bulletin boards full of photos of happy couples.

The willowy woman standing behind the counter glanced up, her violet-colored eyes wide, her pink lips open in a welcoming smile. Her hair was platinum-blond and short, sticking up at spiky angles. Her unusual pixie beauty hit him like a punch to the chest, and he suddenly was feeling a little better about the um…the um…

Oh yeah—the assignment.

Steve took a step forward, tripped over something solid and went down hard. The hidden gun in his waist holster stabbed into his diaphragm, driving all the air from his lungs.

The blonde gasped and ran around the counter to where he fell. "H.D., are you okay?"

Steve rolled over onto his back and panted for air. "My…name…isn't…H.D."

"I wasn't talking to you."

She knelt and pulled the wrinkly face of the world's fattest basset hound close to hers until their noses touched. "Are you okay, H.D.? Are you okay, sweetheart? You were sleeping in a dangerous place—you might have been hurt." She scratched the dog's elephantine ears, murmuring mommy-to-dog nonsense, then seemed to remember he was in the room and turned toward him. "Are you okay, mister?"

Having dragged air back into his collapsed lungs and determining that nothing was broken, Steve sat up, then pushed himself to his feet and retrieved his camera bag, embarrassed as hell. He looked down at the woman crouched on the floor and pointed to the droopy blob of spotted hound that seemed to have melted into the red carpet. "That dog is like an anvil."

The woman frowned, then stood and crossed slender arms over surprisingly full breasts. "May I help you?"

Momentarily distracted, he glanced up to find her eyes piercing him like a laser. Getting off on the wrong foot wouldn't help matters, he realized. He extended his hand. "I'm Steve Mulcahy, the new photographer."

Her pink mouth rounded in surprise. "Oh…yes, Cordelia said that she'd filled the position. I just didn't expect…" She straightened and put her hand in his. "I mean, welcome to TCB, Steve. I'm Gracie Sergeant, the wedding director."

He noted her white eyelet sundress, rhinestone flip-flops, blue nail polish, black velvet choker and the tiny mole on the crest of one fine cheekbone. She looked… eccentric…and oddly appealing. He shook her hand, wondering idly if all of her was as soft as her long, slender fingers. His chest expanded with satisfaction as he noticed her assessing his build as well.

She abruptly withdrew her hand and looked at her Betty Boop watch. "You're just in time. We have a 4:00 p.m. booking—they'll be here in an hour. That will give us just enough time for me to show you the ropes."

Since she was already walking away and talking over her shoulder, he trotted to keep up with her. He looked over and saw that, to his chagrin, the basset hound was also scampering behind her. Steve glared at the dog and swore the squatty beast glared back. Despite the pleasing view of Gracie's backside swishing the white dress back and forth, Steve stepped up the pace and caught up to her as she walked through a door behind the counter and down a hallway.

"So, Steve, what do you know about Elvis?"

The question caught him off guard. "I don't know. The usual stuff I guess—he sang, he made movies."

She stopped so suddenly, he almost passed her up. Her brow wrinkled. "He *sang?* He made *movies?*"

Steve glanced from side to side. "Didn't he?"

Her chin went up. "The *man* is an *icon.*"

Steve started to smile, then swallowed it when he realized she was dead serious. "Right," he said solemnly.

She gave him a suspicious look, then continued down the hallway, her sandals flapping against her heels. "The Burning Love chapel is on the right," she said, pointing to a set of white double doors. "It seats fifty. The Graceland chapel is on the left—it's smaller and our most popular venue, the one we'll be using this afternoon." She tilted her head. "You do know how to take photographs?"

He gave a little laugh. "Yeah—that's the job, right?"

"And you can operate a video camera?"

He nodded—he'd certainly filmed enough crime scenes. A wedding couldn't be too different, he thought wryly.

She looked relieved. "Good—that's one less thing I'll have to do. It's been just me, Cordelia, Roach, Lincoln and H.D. for a couple of months now, and everyone's been filling in wherever they could."

"Roach?"

"He's one of our ministers."

"Ah. And Lincoln?"

"Another minister—they swap shifts with Cordelia. Oh, and Lincoln's also our florist—he'll be here soon. I'll take you back to meet Cordelia in a few minutes—she's working the drive-through."

"Drive-through?"

She nodded. "It's our most popular feature, open twenty-four/seven. That's why we need three ministers to pull shifts."

Steve pursed his mouth—hmm. He wasn't keen on marriage, but if a couple were hell-bent on doing it, a drive-through sounded less expensive and less painful even than a justice of the peace. With a fifty percent chance of failure, why not at least go the cheap route?

"We offer full-service packages in the chapels from 4:00 p.m. until midnight." She smiled. "As the evening progresses, we tend to get drop-ins."

As people became more inebriated, he thought. "How long do the ceremonies last?" He needed to get a handle on day-to-day operations as quickly as possible.

She shrugged. "It depends. The Love Me Tender package is our most basic, and usually takes about twenty minutes. The Aloha Las Vegas package is our most comprehensive, and takes about forty minutes— forty-five if they order a hula dancer."

His eyebrows shot up. "Hula dancer?"

She looked sheepish. "I, um, wear a grass skirt."

At the thought of her in a grass skirt, his sex stirred. He shifted and cleared his throat. "What happened to your photographer?"

"He met someone during a wedding, got married and moved to Alabama."

"Oh."

She shrugged. "It happens a lot. The turnover rate here is pretty high—a lot of people wind up getting married and moving on. I guess it comes with the territory." She seemed a little sad, then suddenly looked hopeful. "You wouldn't happen to be married already, would you?"

"No," he said, more emphatically than he meant to. At her worried frown, he held up his hand. "But don't worry—I have no intention of getting married, in the near *or* distant future."

One delicately arched dark eyebrow raised. "Oh? Confirmed bachelor?"

Her eyes were smiling—mocking? Her lips were as plump and pink as fruit, and he unwittingly moistened his own mouth. "Yeah."

She looked relieved. "Good. I'm tired of training people for this job—which happens to be the most important as far as the customers are concerned."

She resumed walking, and he followed, working his mouth from side to side. He assuaged the slight pang of guilt that Gracie Sergeant might be burdened with more work when he left, with the knowledge that she would be safer on the streets of Las Vegas with a slippery thug like Mitch Lundy behind bars. Then a question popped into his head—was the fetching Gracie herself already married?

He decided not to ask. It was none of his business, and it was best not to become involved with the employees. When it came time to finally take Lundy into custody, he didn't want to be distracted.

He glanced at her slender tanned legs and again felt a tightening in his groin. It didn't mean, however, that he couldn't enjoy the view.

She opened a door, revealing a deep closet with shelves on either side lined with dated camera equipment, shabby background cloths and a mind-boggling array of tacky props. He picked up a dusty pink lei and had a flicker of panic about his tolerance. "So what kinds of pictures do most couples expect?"

At his feet, H.D. sneezed violently, then shuffled toward Gracie, who was in the back of the closet, flipping through a clothing rack.

"Don't worry," she said, her voice muffled. "The cameras and tripods are already in the chapels and they're top of the line." She looked back with a grin. "If I can take decent pictures with them, then they're almost foolproof."

"So you don't need a *great* photographer."

"Well, the video camera is a little more tricky," she offered over her right shoulder, drawing attention to the tattoo of a four-leaf clover there. He'd never been fond of tattoos, but against Gracie's smooth skin, it seemed more like…jewelry. *Nice.* And a bit eerie, considering he carried a four-leaf-clover key chain.

"Of course, the most important thing is the suit."

He nodded, and it was a few seconds before her words sank in. "Pardon me?"

"The suit," she said, turning and holding in front of her a large white jumpsuit with a wide pointed collar and jeweled studs down the rather low-cut front. She sighed. "It's going to be a little big for you—Roach has been filling in since our last guy left—but it'll do until I can take it in."

Steve stared at the jumpsuit, realization dawning with horror. "*Me*…wear that getup?" He laughed. "No way."

She frowned. "What do you mean?"

He backed up, shaking his head. "I mean I'm *not* wearing that."

"But the customers want the Vegas Elvis package, and this is the suit."

He waved his hands. "Oh, no. I'm not dressing up."

She frowned harder. "Cordelia said you understood that this was part of the job. In fact—" she stepped over the dog and extended the vile suit toward him "—it *is* the job. You're our Elvis."

CHAPTER TWO

GRACIE SERGEANT watched emotions play over Steve Mulcahy's handsome face: shock gave way to denial, and denial gave way to controlled annoyance. His cobalt-blue eyes went from icy to molten in a blink as he straightened.

"I'm *not* an Elvis impersonator."

Gracie inspected his lean physique again—broad shoulders, narrow hips, long legs…the man was perfect—er, for the job. Top that with his blue-black hair, piercing eyes and—she swallowed—sensuous mouth, and she had a feeling she was experiencing a little of what women must have felt when standing next to the real Elvis. The man was knee-weakening gorgeous.

It was a good thing she'd recently sworn off sex…not that Steve Mulcahy, confirmed bachelor, would be interested, but still. She'd had enough of fly-by-night affairs with transients who lost their mind and promised the moon (and their heart) in the crazy Vegas environment. The next time she fell in love, she wanted forever and a ring. When she'd said as much to Cordelia, who had never married, her boss had looked sad and declared that Gracie had listened to "Can't Help Falling in Love" one too many times.

Ignoring the sexy vibes rolling off the man in front of her, Gracie tried to appeal to his ego. "You're the closest thing we've had to Elvis in the ten years I've been working here. We've had a Korean Elvis, a dwarf Elvis, *two* black Elvises, several obese versions, one bone-rack, one guy who was eighty-nine years old—even a female Elvis for a while."

He was still shaking his head. "I came to take pictures—and that's all."

Worried that she'd lose their best prospect in ages, Gracie decided to turn on the charm—and lie. She gave him a coy smile. "All you have to do is wear the suit, and if you're afraid someone will recognize you, we have sunglasses and a wig."

He opened his mouth, then stopped and seemed to mull her words.

"It's really easy," she added quickly. "You greet the customers, walk the bride down the aisle and give her away, then run the video camera for the rest of the ceremony. The pictures come afterward."

He squinted, apparently considering it. "I'd walk the bride down the aisle? *Every* bride?"

Gracie tried not to frown—obviously her womanly charms weren't as persuasive as the idea of mixing with every female who came through the door. "Sure—it's part of the wedding package."

He covered his mouth with his hand, then nodded curtly. "Okay."

She grinned, her disappointment about his motivation vanishing in the wake of his agreeing to be their Elvis. If he were good, word would spread quickly. She stepped closer to him, holding the extra large suit against his shoulders. The movement displaced the air between them, sending the male scent of him into her nostrils, igniting little firestorms all over her celibate body. Shocked at her reaction, she lifted her gaze to his—a mistake, she realized instantly, because a woman could fall headlong into those deep baby blues with their long, black lashes. But when his eyes became hooded, she saw a flash of danger there—danger to her resolution to hold out for commitment.

Worse, her nearness seemed to have affected him as well. Beneath her fingers, his chest rose and fell more rapidly, then his mouth parted slightly. She had the surreal sensation that he might kiss her and felt her lips part, her breath whisk over her tongue. He wet his lips and she unwittingly mimicked him. "Can't Help Falling in Love" played over the central stereo—her weakness.

"Some things…are meant to be…"

Her throat tightened with the desire to swallow, but she was afraid to move a muscle, afraid she would rise on her toes and press her mouth to his just to knock him as off balance as she felt. But when she felt his warm lips against hers, she realized that in her mind, she might have restrained herself, but in reality, she had gone for the gold.

And while Steve Mulcahy might have been as surprised as she for a split second, he seemed to warm up to the idea of kissing her rather quickly. He opened his mouth and slanted his lips over hers, flicking his tongue over her teeth. He tasted like mint and coffee, and smelled like grass and sandalwood. While Gracie's breasts and shoulders tingled, a small part of her panicked, driven to keep the kiss going so she wouldn't have to face him when it ended. She'd never done anything like this in her life.

H.D.'s forceful bark broke their kiss like a sledgehammer against glass. She started and swung her gaze down, then realized that H.D. wasn't barking at them, but rather at the black-robed woman who stood in the doorway looking, well…shocked.

Under her boss's gaze, mortification bled through Gracie. Stepping back, she murmured, "Cordelia…hi. This is, um…um—"

"Steve Mulcahy, the new photographer," he supplied.

Beneath the pouf of fire engine-red hair, Cordelia's expression changed, and she studied Steve intently. Gracie was surprised to see something akin to disapproval in the woman's kohl-lined eyes before Cordelia schooled her well-preserved features into a smile. "Ah, yes. Welcome to TCB, Steve."

He nodded politely, but looked uncomfortable. If he knew that pink lipstick smeared his mouth, he would probably feel even worse, Gracie decided. He gestured to the air between them. "Gracie was just…showing me the ropes."

Cordelia lifted one drawn-on eyebrow. "Gracie keeps this place running—I don't know what I'd do if anything happened to her."

Gracie blinked. She'd never felt unappreciated, but Cordelia had never gushed about her to a relative stranger. Then in a flash of comprehension, she realized that her protective boss might have thought Steve was taking liberties with her—little did Cordelia know that Gracie was the one guilty of setting a record for sexually harassing a new hire.

"I can see that," Steve said smoothly.

Cordelia nodded toward the white jumpsuit and pushed her cheek out with her tongue. "I see she wasted no time in showing you the wardrobe."

His mouth twitched downward. "Yes, I'm surprised you didn't mention that aspect of the job when we... talked."

Cordelia's expression turned innocent. "I didn't?"

"Er, no."

"Oh, well, you two seem to have worked out the details."

"We have," Gracie said quickly, her mouth still warm from the imprint of his. "And the costumes will have to do for now, but I'll make the necessary alterations." She was babbling, like a teenager caught necking in the living room.

Cordelia hesitated, then nodded. "Is Lincoln performing the ceremonies this evening?"

"Yes. He should be here soon."

Cordelia glanced at Steve, and Gracie once again detected a wariness in her boss. "I'm going to take a smoke break. Gracie, will you let me know if you hear the drive-through bell?"

Despite her own recent transgression, Gracie straightened. "I thought you quit smoking."

"I did," her boss said. "And now I'm starting again." Cordelia leveled her no-nonsense gaze on Steve. "When you're finished here, Mr. Mulcahy, please see me so that we can discuss...your duties."

"I will."

But Cordelia was already gone, her black robe billowing behind her as she strode down the hall. H.D. trotted after her, loping as fast as his low-hanging belly would allow.

Gracie turned to Steve slowly, her skin zinging with embarrassment. "I'm…sorry about…the kiss. I don't know what came over me."

Before the words left her mouth, she realized how lame they sounded. To save him from having to respond, she hung the white jumpsuit on a rack and removed a tissue from a nearby container. She stepped forward and reached up to wipe his mouth. He stood still, but his eyes narrowed cautiously as she dabbed at the shimmering pink gloss.

Gracie focused on removing traces of their kiss, still reeling over her behavior. "But don't worry—this kind of thing doesn't bother Cordelia."

He looked amused. "So you do this kind of thing often?"

Her face flamed. "No. What I meant is that Cordelia wasn't upset about…what we were doing." She cleared her throat. "About what *I* did. Which, by the way, won't happen again. It was just…curiosity." She was babbling again.

One dark eyebrow rose. "I wasn't complaining."

Ignoring the barb of pleasure in her chest, she pushed ahead. "Cordelia hasn't been herself for the past several days." And whatever her boss had, apparently it was catching, Gracie decided, since she herself had just kissed a virtual stranger. "She's usually very easygoing. I don't know what…has her on edge."

His eyes darkened. "It's probably nothing serious."

Gracie nodded thoughtfully and averted her gaze, tearing her mind away from their off-the-cuff kiss and toward more important matters. She knew that business had fallen sharply over the past few months and suspected that Cordelia—and the chapel—were in serious financial trouble. Panic gripped Gracie's chest—Cordelia, Lincoln, Roach and H.D. were all the family she had. Yet lately, in the wee hours of the morning, lying on the sleeper-sofa in her cramped apartment, she had felt unsettled. For the past ten years, the wedding chapel had been a refuge from the unbearable family situation she had left behind in Oklahoma, and Cordelia had been the mother she'd never had.

But suddenly everything seemed to be in flux.

"Hey," Steve said gently, breaking into her thoughts. "Don't look so worried—whatever is bothering your boss will probably work itself out soon."

She looked up and was struck anew by his dark, sexy looks. That restless place in her seemed to call out to him, and it made her uneasy. It was a good thing that Steve Mulcahy had already expressed his vehement opposition to marriage, else she might be tempted to see just where a full-body kiss would lead them. But another glance at his high cheekbones, flaring nose, square jaw and overall rugged good looks made her sigh inwardly. Someone as delectably masculine as Steve Mulcahy would definitely already be involved with a woman...or two.

His cell phone beeped. He glanced at the display, then back up, slightly flushed. "Um, where can I take this in private?"

Gracie gave him a tight smile—just as she suspected. It was the reminder she needed. "Take it here. I have work to do." She tossed the tissue into a trash can, then vamoosed. As she walked out, she heard him say, "Hi, Karen. What's up?"

Gracie puffed out her cheeks as she walked down the hallway, then slid into her spot behind the counter. Waves of shame washed over her—what must he think of her, kissing him like that? She closed her eyes and groaned, burying her face in her hands. Why didn't life come with a rewind button?

She lifted her head and gave herself a mental shake. One thing was certain: Although her mind said, "Hold out for a stable guy and a long-term commitment," her body obviously wasn't on the same page. Still…Steve had to accept some of the blame. How could a man go around looking that good and *not* expect to be kissed on impulse?

Gracie practiced a few deep breathing exercises—she had to get past her gaffe if they were going to work together. But she was antsy…as if a switch inside her had been flipped to "on."

She straightened the postcards and other souvenirs in the spinner racks, then dusted the counter and the shelves, trying to tamp down the sudden surge of adrenaline. Steve Mulcahy had affected her like no man had in…ever. Working at close quarters was going to be difficult in her sex-deprived state, but would be a good test of her endurance because this was exactly the kind of situation she was trying to avoid: a dead-end relationship. At least he was more forthcoming than most men—he had let her know right away that marriage wasn't in his cards.

So who was Karen?

She tried to push the man and his love life from her mind as she looked for the file for the upcoming ceremony. But she was suddenly distracted by the hundreds of photos collaged onto the bulletin boards all around the counter. Hugging the file to her chest, she surveyed the couples' beaming faces as they clutched each other, poised to begin their lives together. All shapes and sizes, beautiful and not, all races, all ages—proof that over and over again in the big, wide world, people managed to find each other and fall in love.

Gracie angled her head, studying their eyes, their body language. How did love work, and if it worked for so many people so often, why didn't it work for her? She sank her teeth into her lower lip, then shook off her self-indulgent mood—she had a wedding to prepare for and she owed it to the couple to make sure it was as perfect as could be.

But when she walked back to the counter where she stood most of the day, Gracie suddenly noticed the black, worn spot in the red carpet. She stopped abruptly in her rhinestone flip-flops and her stomach hitched. She remembered vividly that new carpet had been installed the first week she had started working at TCB. And since that time, she had literally stood in one spot until the rug beneath her feet was threadbare.

The analogy wasn't lost on her, and the timing was perfect. If she was going to get on with her life—do something with the degree in public relations she'd managed to finish, meet a nice, stable guy and settle down—she was going to have to…move her feet.

The phone rang and Gracie snapped back into business mode.

"Taking Care of Business Wedding Chapel, where Elvis lives in your heart. How can I help you?" She answered the man's nervous questions by rote as she referred to the appointment book. "Yes, we have some openings this evening. When would you like to schedule a ceremony?"

"The earlier the better," the man said, his baritone voice bursting with love and enthusiasm.

Gracie's heart swelled and with great restraint she fought a crazy impulse to ask questions of her own, such as how he'd met the woman he'd fallen in love with, how long it had taken before he'd known she was the one and what had been the turning point? What exactly had made him sure she was the woman he wanted to spend the rest of his life with?

How ironic that she'd witnessed thousands of weddings, yet still was clueless about lasting love.

"How about seven-thirty, sir?"

"Great. But this has to be really special. My fiancée is a huge Elvis fan. Does your Elvis look like the real thing?"

Steve's chiseled features and blue, blue eyes came to mind with startling clarity. "As a matter of fact, he does. Does your fiancée have a favorite Elvis song?"

"'Love Me Tender' gets her every time."

"Then we'll include it in the package."

"Does your Elvis sing, or lip-synch?"

Neither, she thought, but didn't say so. "Our Elvis is having a bout with laryngitis at the moment, sir. But if he's not feeling well enough to sing, we'll play a beautiful digitally mastered recording in stereo. You'll feel like you're at an Elvis concert." She winced at her own words, but they needed the business.

The man made a doubtful noise. "I don't know…the Elvis over at the Fools Rush In chapel sings."

At a noise, she glanced up to see Lincoln Nebraska, their florist and spare minister, walk through the door carrying two bouquets of mixed white flowers. She smiled a greeting, then resumed her sales pitch to the customer on the phone. "I promise you, sir, that you won't find another wedding Elvis in Vegas as good as ours. I'll even throw in a complimentary bouquet for your bride and a boutonniere for you."

Lincoln frowned, but she ignored him.

"Okay," the man finally said.

"Great." She took down his name and contact information. "We'll see you and your lovely bride at seven-thirty." She hung up the phone and grinned at Lincoln, who was bald and tanned and wearing funky horn-rimmed glasses. "Hi, there."

"Who is he?" Lincoln said without preamble.

"Who?" Gracie asked as nonchalantly as possible.

"You know who—the hunk of burning love who was talking on the cell phone when I walked past the closet."

"Oh. Him."

Lincoln smirked. "Yes—him. *Tell* me he's our new Elvis."

She hesitated. "Yes. But he *thinks* he's the photographer."

Lincoln scoffed. "H.D. could run the camera equipment if someone lifted him high enough."

"I know," she said. "But Cordelia hired the guy and didn't tell him the full story."

"Ah, the old bait and switch. Well, she probably took one look at him and knew he'd be perfect." He sighed. "At least what I could see of him from the back looked perfect."

She laughed. "He's also perfectly taken. Or at least, I assume so, since he needed privacy for the call."

"Man or woman?"

"Woman," she said emphatically. "Sorry."

He looked distressed for all of two seconds, then wagged his thick eyebrows. "If he won't take me away from all this, maybe he'll rescue you."

Since Cordelia had caught them kissing, the news was bound to get out. "We, um, did have a…moment… earlier." She held up her forefinger and thumb pinched together. "Just a little…kiss."

He gasped. "I was only gone for a few *minutes*— how…?"

"It was nothing big, and it won't happen again." She made a note on the calendar for the seven-thirty wedding. When she looked up, Lincoln was gaping at her.

"Are you *kidding* me? You kissed the man already? Was 'Can't Help Falling in Love' playing?"

She nodded, feeling like a fool.

He sighed. "Don't be too hard on yourself, sweetheart. No one can fight those lyrics. Besides, the man screams 'affair.'"

She held up both hands. "No way. I've sworn off affairs, remember?"

"Oh, right. Well, maybe he's the settling down type."

Grace shook her head. "He went to great lengths to explain that he was not interested in marriage—now or in the future."

He frowned. "Kind of presumptuous of him, wasn't it?"

"It was in the context of business, but I got the point." At least her brain had understood.

Lincoln scrutinized a rose in one of the bouquets he held. "What's his name?"

"Steve Mulcahy."

"Nice name." He frowned. "What's his story?"

"What do you mean?"

"I mean, why would someone who looks like him be working in a place like this?"

Gracie frowned. "Thanks a lot."

"You *know* what I mean. I love TCB, but wedding chapels aren't exactly a magnet for straight, great-looking guys. What kind of photographer aspires to this job?"

Admittedly, the same thoughts had crossed her mind. She shrugged. "Maybe he's between jobs, or is down on his luck."

"Right. Maybe he's a gambler," Lincoln said. "Maybe he lost his real job, and he's desperate."

Gracie somehow couldn't reconcile the description of a quasi-loser to Steve, even if she had only just met the man. Something about him radiated power and authority, but Lincoln had a point. For some reason, though, she wanted to think the best of Steve Mulcahy, and that alone troubled her.

Gracie made a rueful noise. "Desperate is what I'm banking on. No offense to Roach, but without a good Elvis, our bookings are way down. Somehow I've got to talk the man into singing and swiveling his hips."

Lincoln grinned.

"*Don't* say it," Gracie said, giving him a stern look.

"Okay," Lincoln said in an innocent voice. "I won't say it. But I can think it."

Gracie sighed. So could she.

CHAPTER THREE

STEVE'S PULSE ratcheted higher as he listened to his partner on the phone.

"So," Karen said, "our informant thinks that Lundy could show up sooner than we'd planned—maybe the day after tomorrow. The good news is she was able to give me a few more details about the wedding that Lundy's bride booked."

Steve removed a small notebook from his pocket. "Go ahead."

Karen cleared her throat. "Apparently, they booked the Aloha—" She stopped and giggled, then recovered. "The Aloha Teddy Bear package." Then she laughed out loud.

Steve pursed his mouth, waiting for her to continue.

Her laughter petered to a cough. "Sorry, Steve, but you have to admit that this Elvis stuff is hysterical. I'll bet the impersonator there is a real hoot, isn't he?"

Steve closed his eyes and decided to withhold the full extent of his undercover duties for now. "See if our informant can find out any other details about the Lundy wedding—what kind of car they'll be arriving in, how big the wedding party will be, that kind of thing. And of course, a name would be great."

"Will do. So, have you met all the players over there? We need a description of all the employees so we'll know who's who when the arrest goes down."

"You have the owner's picture on file, right?"

"Right."

Steve hesitated as Gracie's pixie face rose in his mind's eye…along with the sensory details of her shocking kiss. Just the memory of her pink mouth on his elicited a response from his body. He set his jaw, then said, "The only other person I've met is the wedding director. Gracie Sergeant, female, thirtyish, short platinum-blond hair, violet-colored eyes." He bit the end of his tongue as soon as the words left his mouth.

"Violet-colored, huh?" Karen made a thoughtful noise. "With little golden flecks?"

He frowned, disgusted with himself. "I'll call you later." He cut off her laughter by disconnecting the call.

Steve pulled his hand down his face and forced himself to concentrate. Karen's information meant that he might have even less time to prepare for Lundy's arrest than he'd thought. He couldn't afford to be distracted by Gracie Sergeant's eyes. Or legs. Or mouth.

Or tattoo.

Turning in the direction Cordelia Conroy had gone, Steve walked down the hall past an office and what appeared to be the drive-through window, to a set of double doors that opened onto a covered concrete patio at the rear of the chapel. Cordelia Conroy stood next to a birdbath that had been filled with sand to serve as an ashtray. The behemoth basset hound sat near her feet. In a corner of the lot, the rear fins of a pink Cadillac peeked out from under a cloth cover.

When Cordelia saw him coming, she took a last drag on a short butt, then snubbed it out. After a few seconds' hesitation, she withdrew another cigarette from a pack and offered him one. His throat itched, but he shook his head. He'd quit smoking six times and this time he meant it.

While he watched, Cordelia lit her second—or third?—cigarette and took a deep drag. Well into her sixties, she was still an attractive woman, albeit a little rough around the edges. Street smart, he realized. And wary.

He stopped a few feet away and leaned against a column that held up the metal roof over the sparse patio. The hound dog moseyed over and sniffed at his boots.

"Is Mulcahy your real name?" she asked finally, on an exhale.

"As far as you're concerned," he said.

"You're not what I expected."

He kept his expression noncommittal. "What did you expect?"

She leveled her gaze on him. "Not some good-looking buck who hits on my wedding director."

He blinked. "She kissed *me*."

The woman flicked ash. "I didn't see you putting up a fight."

Steve squirmed, feeling like a naughty teenager instead of an undercover agent. "I was simply going along."

Cordelia looked all around, as if she were afraid they would be overheard. "This situation is dangerous enough without you getting involved with my employees."

"I understand. But I have to interact with them for things to appear normal."

She took another drag, then nodded. "I know, but don't overstep your bounds. Especially where Gracie is concerned. She's…susceptible."

He pressed his lips together and nodded curtly, hoping to end the awkward conversation. Wasn't it enough punishment that he couldn't get his mind off the abbreviated kiss? "I just received more details from our informant, who says that the wedding might take place sooner than we expected, and that the bride booked a—" he pulled out his notebook "—an Aloha Teddy Bear package?"

Cordelia frowned. "We have an Aloha Las Vegas package and a Teddy Bear package, but not an Aloha Teddy Bear package."

He scratched his temple. "So it could be either one. Do you keep a record of what the customers request?"

"Of course—that's Gracie's job."

"I'll need to see the reservations for the upcoming week."

Cordelia nodded. "I'll get Gracie's book."

"I'd like photocopies."

"We have a copier in the office." She exhaled and ground out the half-smoked cigarette. "Mitch Lundy's been operating on the wrong side for years—why the sudden resolve to bring him in?"

"In the nineties the Bureau cut him some slack for testifying against an associate and putting him away—as long as Lundy stayed legit. But a few years ago, he slipped back into his old businesses—prostitution, drugs, money laundering. He's ordered at least eight hits. He's more arrogant and dangerous than ever." Steve frowned. "To Lundy, eluding the FBI is just a game, and I want to put an end to it."

Cordelia pressed her lips together. "So what exactly is going to happen?"

Steve was momentarily distracted when H.D. sat down solidly on his boot. He tried to maneuver his foot out, but the dog was a block of panting dead weight.

"Best-case scenario," he said, "we'll be able to figure out which reservation is Lundy's and alert our agents to stand by. He'll be apprehended after he leaves your property."

"And the worst-case scenario?" Cordelia asked.

"Worst case is that he sneaks in and I don't have enough time to call for backup."

Her eyes narrowed. "But you'll still wait to arrest him until after he's off my property."

"That's the plan," he said. "But I have to be honest with you, Ms. Conroy—Mitchell Lundy is a dangerous criminal who's played cat and mouse with the Bureau for years. If something goes wrong, we'll still seize the opportunity to arrest him."

"Even if it puts my employees in danger?"

"Civilian safety is always our first concern," he said, and stubbornly, a civilian with white-blond hair came to mind.

"Are you sure you'll recognize this Lundy fellow?"

"If I see his eyes—he sustained a wound to one eye that left a permanent and recognizable scar."

"What if he recognizes you?"

"We're operating under the assumption that he or his people have a file on all the agents in the state." He frowned. "That's why I agreed to wear the costume—I doubt if Lundy will suspect Elvis. I understand there's a wig and sunglasses?"

"That's right." The shadow of a smile played on her lips, then disappeared. "Are you carrying a gun?"

"Bureau policy, ma'am."

She nodded, then straightened. "Well, Mr. Mulcahy, you have a job to do, but so do we. If you want to fit in here at TCB, I suggest that you do whatever Gracie tells you to do." She frowned. "In regards to work, that is. Until you make the arrest, we need for you to be a convincing performer for our customers."

He nodded, but his stomach felt tangled. And he wasn't sure what bothered him most—the thought of impersonating the King, or working closely with Gracie Sergeant.

"Come along, H.D.," Cordelia said, and the hound lifted his fat rump from Steve's instep. Steve shifted his weight to send blood back to his foot, then glanced at the pink Caddy. "Ms. Conroy?"

She turned back. "Yes?"

"Does the Caddy run?"

"Not for a year now."

"Care if I take a look under the hood?"

"Be my guest," she said, then withdrew a thick ring of keys from her robe pocket. She removed two keys on a separate ring, tossed them to him, then reentered the chapel.

Steve strode toward the old car, burning with curiosity. As he rolled back the cloth tarp, his pulse spiked in appreciation of the four-door Cadillac, rust spots and all. The paint was faded, revealing lots of body filler along the side panels, but the chrome was intact and the white hardtop and interior were in amazingly good condition. All four tires were flat

and probably ruined, but it should have whitewalls
anyway. He lifted the hood and stared down at the
corroded engine, registering in one glance that two
hoses were disconnected and the carburetor lid was
missing.

"She's a beauty, isn't she?"

Steve looked up to see Gracie walking toward him, his
pulse spiking again but for a different reason. Did she
know that in the sunlight her white eyelet dress was transparent? She wore a lacy strapless bra and high-cut bikini
panties. The silhouette of her opposing curves—breasts,
waist and hips—stamped into his brain in the same place,
he suspected, that songs embedded themselves to emerge
as torture at the most inconvenient times.

His sex hardened, straining at his zipper, preventing
him from straightening to greet her. "Yeah," he murmured. "She's something." The fact that they were talking about two different things didn't matter.

Gracie ran her hand along the top of the car. "It's a
1955 model, just like the one Elvis bought for his
mother. The real one is on display at Graceland."

He smiled. "Have you been to Graceland?"

She shook her head. "I…haven't seen much of the
country."

"Did you grow up here?"

"Um…no. Do you know something about cars?"

He filed away the fact that she had sidestepped his
question, but let it pass. "A little."

Her eyes went round. "Do you think you could get
it running again?"

"I don't know—I can give it a try."

She grinned. "That would be wonderful—it would be

a boon to our business if we could offer couples a ride in a pink Caddy."

"Has anyone tried to fix it?"

She shook her head. "Just between us, Cordelia hasn't had the money."

He frowned. "Is business bad?"

"Well, the wedding chapel business isn't what it used to be—the competition is fierce, and taxes are astronomical. I think Cordelia would like to retire, but she doesn't want to put the rest of us out of a job." Then she wet her lips. "I'm sorry—I shouldn't be telling you Cordelia's business. I came out to get you—we need to prepare for the four o'clock wedding."

"Right," he said, lowering the hood and replacing the tarp. "The suit."

"Yes, the suit. And I have a favor to ask," she said, turning back toward the chapel.

When he lifted his head, he saw that she was wearing a thong, and all rational thought fled. "Anything," he murmured, hurrying to catch up with her.

"How do you feel about…singing?"

He blinked. "Singing?"

"It's just like karaoke," she said hurriedly. "The music will play, and the words will scroll across a screen."

"I don't sing," he said, shaking his head, his feet feeling heavier with every step. "I'll wear the suit, but I don't sing."

She bit into her pink lower lip. "I have to be honest with you, Steve. We really need the business, and we need a good Elvis to keep our customers happy."

"But I don't *sing*," he insisted.

She pshawed. "Everybody sings."

"Not me."

She crossed her arms under her breasts—an unfair and distracting maneuver, in his opinion. "Cordelia just told me that you said you'd do whatever we needed for you to do."

A sick feeling settled into his stomach. "I did say that, yes."

Her smile was brilliant, pushing her cheeks up, highlighting the little brown mole. "Good." She turned back toward the chapel, practically skipping. "We have just enough time for a practice run. Do you know the words to 'All Shook Up'?"

Steve closed his eyes and smothered a groan—what had he gotten himself into?

CHAPTER FOUR

GRACIE GLANCED at Lincoln, then back to the closed dressing room door. "We're waiting," she called pleasantly, although she was tapping her foot.

"Maybe I should go in and give him a hand," Lincoln offered with a grin.

Gracie gave him a withering look, then rapped on the door of the dressing room. "Come on out, Steve."

There was no response for several seconds, then, "I'd rather not."

Gracie rolled her eyes. "Steve, stop messing around—we're running out of time here."

Shuffling noises sounded, then the door swung open slowly. Gracie gasped.

"Oh…my…gawd," Lincoln murmured.

Excerpt for the surly look on his face and the bagginess of the oversize bejeweled white jumpsuit, Gracie would swear she was looking at the King of rock 'n' roll himself. From the lofty wig and long sideburns to the large gold-tone sunglasses with dark lenses, he looked every inch the beloved performer. Her heartbeat actually accelerated. "You look…*wow*."

His mouth tightened. "I look like an idiot."

"You look like a cash cow," Lincoln declared, then

clapped his hands. "Chop, chop—you've got twenty minutes to learn to moo."

Gracie could feel Steve's panic, and her heart went out to him. To keep him from losing his nerve completely, she put her hand on his arm. "Relax. It's like being in a play."

"More like a musical," Lincoln said over his shoulder, walking ahead.

"It'll be fun," she said quickly. "Everyone will love you." At his surprised glance, she swallowed hard. "The customers, I mean. The *customers* will love you." She smiled. "And I appreciate you being such a good sport."

She guided him toward the chapel, chattering to distract him. "You'll greet the customers in the lobby, then we'll reconvene in the chapel."

They walked into the smaller chapel and with a practiced eye, she glanced around to make sure the chairs, flowers and equipment were in the proper place. Gracie pointed to the tripod in the back. "You'll position the video camera and make sure it's on. At the front, Lincoln will start the ceremony and when the wedding march begins, you'll walk the bride down the aisle and give her away."

"Um, this is all new to me," Steve said.

"I know, but we'll get through it."

"No. I mean I've never seen a wedding before."

Her eyebrows went up. "Never?"

"Just on TV, and I try to avoid that whenever possible."

She pursed her lips—the guy was a bona fide wedding-phobe. Suddenly, the opening strains of the wedding march sounded over the speakers. Gracie jerked her head around to see Lincoln working the audio controls and wearing a mischievous grin.

"Show him," he said, moving his arm in a rolling motion. "Walk down the aisle together."

Gracie narrowed her eyes at him, but conceded the wisdom in a practice run. Suddenly nervous for no good reason, she smiled up at Steve. "Okay—pretend I'm the bride."

One of his dark eyebrows shot up, inadvertently making him look even more like the King. She walked to the back of the chapel and stared down the white cloth runner spread over the red carpet leading to the white arch at the front. It really was rather ominous what a simple trip down the aisle represented in Western culture—a journey to a new place. With her heart thumping, she tucked her hand into the crook of Steve's elbow.

"Walk slowly and let the bride set the pace," she murmured, then began walking, pausing with the completion of each step. His stride was longer and he stumbled a bit to stay abreast. She, meanwhile, was ultraconscious of the muscles in his arm beneath her fingers, and the occasional brushing of their hips until they found a rhythm.

"You've done this before," Steve said, breaking into her thoughts.

"Many times," she admitted.

"For real?" he asked.

A couple of seconds passed before she realized what he was asking, and she was the one who stumbled this time. "Oh—no, never for real. I mean…I've never been married."

He didn't respond and by that time, thank heavens, they were at the end of the aisle.

Lincoln shot her a triumphant smile before cutting

the music. "Then I'll begin the ceremony, talk about the sanctity of marriage, blah, bah, blah. Then I'll ask who gives this bride, and Steve, you'll say in your best Elvis voice, "It's now or never. I give this woman in marriage." Lincoln spoke in his own impersonator voice, which was bad.

Next to her, Steve shifted from foot to foot and looked up at the ceiling.

"Well, let's hear it," Lincoln prompted.

Gracie glanced sideways, holding her breath.

Steve cleared his throat and thrust his head forward like a rooster, and cleared his throat again. "It's now—" He stopped, then sighed and started again, ducking his head in an attempt to inject more bass into his voice. "It's now…or never."

Gracie winced inwardly. He was worse than Lincoln.

"You need to add a warble," Lincoln said flatly, then demonstrated. "It's n-o-o-o-w or n-e-e-ver. Try again."

She could feel the resistance rolling off Steve in waves—this exercise went against his every instinct, which she thought was odd for a creative person like a photographer. Maybe Lincoln was right—maybe Steve Mulcahy was on the skids and desperate for a job.

"Just try to have fun," she whispered.

"It's n-now or n-never," he murmured.

"That's not warbling," Lincoln said. "That's stuttering."

"It's fine," Gracie said quickly. "Just don't forget to add 'I give this bride in marriage.' At that point you can return to the camera."

"Then I'll finish the ceremony," Lincoln continued. "Yada, yada, yada, then I pronounce the couple man and wife, and you sing them out."

Gracie led him to the back of the chapel and pointed to a small television screen. "The words will scroll across. Lincoln, will you cue up the song?"

Steve wanted to fall through the floor. For the first time in his law enforcement career, he was tempted to blow his own cover—there were some things that a man simply should not have to endure. As "I'm All Shook Up" began to play, perspiration broke on his brow beneath the ridiculous wig. It was bad enough that he looked like a fool, but that he looked like a fool in front of Gracie Sergeant....

It shouldn't matter, he told himself. This was just a job, and singing karaoke was no different than assuming an accent to hide his identity, as he had many times. He would never see these people again—why should he care what they thought?

But inexplicably, he did. At least he cared what Gracie thought of him. Within a few hours of meeting her, she had gotten under his thick skin.

It was that darned kiss, he thought. And the transparent dress. And the tattoo. And the mole. The woman was a tight little package of sex appeal.

And he was dressed like Elvis.

He took the microphone she handed to him and held it to his dry mouth—he was all shook up, all right. He was shaking.

"Just follow the words on the screen," Gracie urged.

He did. Somehow. With his face flaming, he talked and hummed his way through the song, thinking the one saving grace was that his partner Karen wasn't there to watch the humiliating spectacle. Halfway through, howling reverberated through the room. H.D. sat in the doorway, his nose in the air, his eyes closed as he wailed at the offense to his ears.

Steve was in a sweat of degradation. "Forget it," he snapped, and extended the microphone back to Gracie. A man had his limits.

"Try again, Mr. Mulcahy."

He looked up and saw Cordelia Conroy crouching in the doorway with her hand clamped around H.D.'s muzzle. Her smile was part mocking, part challenging. "I suspect even Elvis didn't get it right in the first take." She walked away and the insolent hound, thank goodness, waddled after her.

Steve felt helpless—the woman had been clear that she expected him to hold up his end of the agreement.

To do whatever Gracie Sergeant told him to do.

He swung his gaze to the platinum-blond pixie and he nearly groaned in frustration—she must think he was a complete loser.

"Shall we try again?" she murmured.

He sighed and nodded, and Lincoln recued the song. Steve wiped the sweat from his forehead and, realizing that he had no pride left to salvage, sang the song again.

When it was over, there was dead silence in the chapel. Lincoln looked as if he'd just witnessed a human sacrifice. Gracie's eyes were rounded and she looked as if she were trying to think of something to say.

Finally, her mouth curved into a wide, forced smile. "All righty then." She turned to the front. "Lincoln, cue up the full track—we'll say he has laryngitis and let him lip-synch. Would you show Steve the break room in case he wants a drink of water before we get started?"

She flashed him another smile, but Steve could see

STEPHANIE BOND   47

the alarm in her eyes as she turned to leave. She was thinking that right now, a dwarf Korean Elvis was looking pretty darn good.

Lincoln walked up, his mouth pulled back in a wry frown. "Man, you're really bad."

Steve glared. "I *don't* sing. I've been trying to tell everyone."

Lincoln clapped him on the back. "Well, now we believe you."

Steve followed him into the hall. "Lincoln Nebraska can't be your real name."

Lincoln gave a dramatic sigh. "It is. My parents have a cruel streak."

Gracie's light floral scent lingered on the air. Involuntarily, Steve glanced toward the front of the building and caught sight of her silhouetted by the afternoon sun just before she disappeared around the corner.

"She's something, isn't she?" Lincoln asked.

Steve jerked his head back so quickly, he dislodged his wig. "Who?"

Lincoln laughed. "Yeah. Listen, man, you have six weddings to get through tonight. You can't afford to be distracted."

Steve frowned. Then someone should tell Gracie Sergeant to wear civilized underwear. He turned away, marveling over how he'd gotten himself into this bizarre situation. He, of all people, who was allergic to weddings. This had been the longest day of his life, and it wasn't even close to being over.

Lincoln led him into a room with a table, chairs and a small kitchen connected to the office he'd seen earlier. "Thirsty?"

Steve shrugged, past caring. "Sure."

Lincoln opened a cabinet and pulled out a bottle of vodka and two shot glasses.

Steve straightened. "Should we be doing this?"

"Absolutely," Lincoln said, pouring the shots, then handing one to Steve. "This should loosen you up a little. Unless you *want* to perform six weddings stone cold sober."

Steve hesitated a split second, then downed the fiery liquid. Surely the King would forgive him.

"So, Steve—what brings you to TCB?" Lincoln asked casually.

A warning flag went up in Steve's brain. He set down the glass and gave a little laugh. "I was under the obviously false impression that I was hired to take photographs. I wasn't aware of the full job description."

"So quit," the man said mildly.

FBI agents were taught to exhibit honor and dignity in their personal lives, but when put on the spot undercover, they were expected to be pathological liars. Steve decided the best way to get the man off his back was to enlist him as an ally. "I need this job, man. That's why I'm trying so hard." He scoffed and gestured to his costume. "Look at me—why would I do this unless I had to?"

Lincoln pursed his mouth, then made a rueful noise. "Good point." Then his eyes narrowed. "But if you're in some kind of trouble, don't drag Gracie into it. That girl is looking for happily ever after. Capiche?"

Steve nodded. "Don't worry—I'm not a happily ever after kind of guy."

"Good," Lincoln said. "Then we understand each other."

Steve bristled, but before he could respond, a chime sounded overhead.

Lincoln smiled. "That must be the happy couple. Let's go have a wedding."

Steve touched his hand to his roiling stomach. Just the words made him feel queasy…or was it the news that sexy Gracie Sergeant was off-limits?

CHAPTER FIVE

GRACIE RESISTED the urge to park her green Volkswagen Rabbit next to Steve Mulcahy's dark SUV and instead wheeled into a space a few feet away in the pay parking lot across from TCB and cut the engine. She hated being late, but that's what she got for staying up until 2:00 a.m. listening to "Are You Lonesome Tonight?" on continuous play on her phonograph and trying to pinpoint what exactly about Steve Mulcahy made her want to marinate in the music of old 45s?

It wasn't his impersonation skills, although she had to admit that he'd performed much better than she'd expected. What he lacked in lip-synching skills, he made up for in easygoing charm—the customers loved him, and he appeared eager to interact with them, asking questions and feigning interest, all in a southern bass that he seemed to have pulled out of thin air. Without prompting, he'd stayed "in character" until the clients left and he'd changed back into his regular clothes. Then it was as if a mask had been lowered back into place. He'd been cordial, had even walked Gracie to her car, but she could sense his distance—had he been afraid she was going to kiss him again?

The bad thing was that his fears would have been

well founded—their too-short kiss had dominated her thoughts for most of the day, reinforced each time the couples had kissed when pronounced husband and wife. There had been a few seconds last night standing next to her car when she'd thought he was remembering the kiss, too. But his cell phone had rung and he had said an abrupt good-night.

"Karen" had impeccable timing.

Gracie swung out of her car and jogged across the street. A rental car sat in the chapel drive-through, which meant Cordelia was busy at this early hour. A pang of guilt struck Gracie—Cordelia worked such long hours. It wasn't fair for her to arrive late, no matter what the excuse. Worse, she'd asked Steve to come in early today so she could pin the costumes for alterations—except she hadn't expected him to arrive *this* early.

Chastising herself, she opened the front door, enjoying the few minutes of humming quiet before the stereo and door chimes were activated. The scent of coffee called to her. Looking forward to a jolt of caffeine, she walked down the hall toward the kitchen, fighting a yawn. But at the sound of the photocopier running, she frowned. If Cordelia was working the drive-through, who was in the office?

When the office window came into view, she saw Steve standing with his back to the door, watching as the light of the photocopier flashed. He wore jeans and a baggy shirt, like yesterday. He craned his neck to look out the window where she knew he could see the drive-through. Frowning at his suspicious body language, she remained out of sight and watched incredulously as he removed her appointment book, turned the page and returned it facedown on the copier. Smothering a gasp, she flattened against the wall, her heart pounding. Why would he be interested in her appointment book? Was he some kind of saboteur from a competitor?

She stood, frozen. One part of her wanted to charge into the office and demand to know what he was doing, but another part of her railed against the idea that Steve could be involved in something illicit. True, she'd only just met him, but she'd gotten the feeling that he was an honest man.

She bit down on the inside of her cheek—she knew too many women who turned a blind eye to the obvious because they projected their own wants and desires onto a situation, and she wasn't going to be one of them. Taking a deep breath, she pushed open the door to the office, making as much noise as possible. "Good morning."

Steve jerked around, his eyes wide. "Good morning."

"What are you doing?" she asked cheerfully, nodding toward the edge of her appointment book that stuck out from under the lid of the photocopier.

A flash of guilt darkened his eyes, but he recovered quickly. "I thought I might be better able to prepare if I knew in advance what packages are booked…at least until I get the hang of things."

His story seemed plausible enough—maybe she had imagined his guilty reaction.

He gave her a little smile. "Cordelia said it would be okay to photocopy your appointment book—I hope you don't mind."

God, the man was so handsome—which only confused her further. Earlier she didn't want to think badly of him, but was she now looking for a reason to distrust him? If Cordelia had given him permission, then who was she to argue? "Sure, that's fine." But she studied him intently, and Lincoln's words from the previous day about why someone like Steve would be working at TCB came back to her.

He shifted uncomfortably. "I made some coffee," he said, jerking his head toward the kitchen.

"Thanks," she said, shaking her critical thoughts. Steve Mulcahy didn't deserve to be interrogated by her, not when her own life wasn't exactly on the fast track to success.

She went into the kitchen and poured a cup of coffee, spooked by her strong reactions to the man. Sure he was gorgeous, but there was something else…something about him made her feel as if her life were very small. Maybe because, for him, TCB was probably only a pit stop yet she had spent most of her adulthood within these walls. She frowned as she filled H.D.'s food bowl with kibble.

"Here you go," Steve said from the doorway, extending her appointment book.

Gracie straightened and took the book. Their hands brushed, and she had a fleeting thought that he held on longer than necessary. Her next thought was that she was reading too much into every little movement and she needed to keep the focus on business. "Thank you, Steve. Are you ready for the costume fitting?"

That uncomfortable look came over his face again. "I suppose."

She sipped from her cup, then winced when the liquid hit the back of her throat. "Oh, my."

"Did I make it too strong? Sorry."

"No, it's…fine," she squeaked. "Just what I need, actually."

"Late night?"

"You could say that," she mumbled as she began walking. *Fantasizing about you.*

He grinned. "Which casino?"

She frowned. "None. I don't gamble."

"No?"

She shook her head. "I don't have anything against gambling—I'm just not a very lucky person."

"I find that hard to believe. Especially since you have a four-leaf clover tattooed on your shoulder."

He'd noticed. She glanced down at the tiny image revealed by the thin strap of her yellow tank top. "That's precisely why I got the tattoo—I hoped it would change my luck."

"Did it?"

She shook her head wistfully. "Not yet."

He laughed. "But you're optimistic."

"Of course." She met his gaze and something electric passed between them. Her smile melted as the light in his eyes changed…to desire? A shiver skated over her shoulders as her body reacted to the thought. Her breasts hardened, her nipples beaded and the restlessness that had been plaguing her body seemed to coalesce in her midsection. Afraid that her lust was evident, she cast about for a safe topic. Recalling Lincoln's speculation that Steve was a gambler down on his luck, she asked, "What about you? Do you play the tables?"

"A little blackjack, a little craps."

The casual reply of a person with a problem? She couldn't tell. "Have you always been a photographer?"

"Um, no."

When he didn't expand, she pressed. "What then?"

Another laugh and shrug. "A little of everything, really. I guess you could say I'm a drifter."

Mostly physical work, she surmised from his athletic build, although his fingernails were clean and well kept. He had nice hands with long, tanned fingers.

She swallowed hard. "Where did you drift from?"

"Oh, all over," he said vaguely. "I was an army brat."

"Where is your family now?"

"Here and there. Yours?"

"Um, same," she lied, realizing he had turned the tables. Neither one of them wanted to divulge details of their lives. Fair enough. *Keep it light and breezy,* she told herself as she walked into the closet, trying not to remember it was there she had kissed him. She moved back to the clothing rack and removed the costumes, then handed them to him. "Why don't you take these into the dressing room and come out when you're ready?"

Steve drank in Gracie's luminous face and fought the overwhelming urge to take *her* into the dressing room. He had hoped that when he saw her this morning that his attraction to her would have diminished, but it hadn't. If anything, he was even hotter for her today in her little yellow tank top and swingy black skirt and black-and-white polka dot shoes. A black headband in her short spiky hair made her look even more kittenish and the violet dangling glass earrings perfectly mirrored her incredible eyes. He had a vision of those eyes slitted in passion, her creamy-skinned body beneath his.

"Steve?"

He blinked. "Hmm? Oh…right." He took the armful of colorful clothes and walked into the dressing room, telling himself he had to get a grip. This assignment was the result of Mitch Lundy eluding the FBI for years— he couldn't allow himself to be distracted by an inconvenient hard-on for this woman.

On the other hand, he had to stay on her good side. She was already suspicious of his motivation for being there.

He hung the costumes on hooks, growing more glum as he studied each one in turn—a gold lamé suit, a black vinyl suit, a loud Hawaiian shirt and white shiny pants, the perennial white jumpsuit and a black-and-white striped jail inmate outfit. He began to undress, frowning at the waist holster and revolver—what should he do with it? Knowing he was violating several policies about weapon handling while on duty, he tucked it under the jeans he'd discarded on a chair and, deciding to get the worst over with first, stepped into the gold suit that looked five sizes too big. His reflection made him wince.

"How's it going in there?" Gracie called.

Maybe it would at least dampen his libido, Steve thought as he opened the door and stepped out.

Gracie grinned. "Not bad."

He frowned. "Will this take long?"

"Not at all," she sang, holding up a pincushion. "Just let me mark a few adjustments." She pointed to a sewing machine in the corner. "It shouldn't take me too long to make the alterations. Hold up your arms, please."

Feeling guilty that she would no sooner get the alterations made than he would be gone, he said, "If this position has as much turnover as you say, I suppose you do this a lot."

She made a thoughtful noise while she reached inside the jacket and gave him what resembled a thorough pat down, running her hands over his chest and stomach. "It depends. We have some of the suits in different sizes, so sometimes we get lucky." Then she looked up suspiciously. "Are you already planning to leave?"

"No," he said quickly, then decided he could be realistic without blowing his cover. "Well...eventually, I suppose."

She nodded. "Right...that's what drifters do, I suppose—they drift."

The timbre of disappointment in her voice made his gut clench. "It's nothing personal. This just isn't the kind of job I see myself doing forever."

"Too bad," she murmured. "Everyone really likes you."

"Everyone?" The word spilled from his tongue before he could swallow it.

She glanced up sharply and wet her lips. "The customers, I mean. You're very good with them, getting them to talk about themselves."

Little did she know, he was simply quizzing everyone to make sure that Mitch Lundy wasn't sneaking in under his nose, disguised as Larry from Peoria. In fact, Gracie would freak out if she knew that her Elvis carried a .38 revolver on his waist, a .25 automatic in his boot and that his cell phone was equipped with a stun gun.

"But, if you're determined to leave," she said merrily, "I'll use Velcro."

Instead of pacifying him, her cheerful acceptance of his eventual absence rankled him further. And her hands all over his body were making him crazy—not to mention rock-hard. He dropped his arms in an effort to hide his raging erection.

"Stand still or I'll poke you."

Steve closed his eyes and gritted his teeth. He was thinking the same thing, although not quite in the same way. He tried to will away his reaction to her roaming touch, but it proved impossible when she bent over and he got a tantalizing view of her cleavage…and yet another lacy bra—this one black. Worse, he could guess that she wore a matching thong beneath her skirt.

"There," she said with a final pat to his chest. "Watch the pins when you take it off."

His relief in regaining control over his erection was short-lived when he had to repeat the process four more times. His cock hadn't gotten this kind of workout since high school.

By the time she finished pinning the black-and-white striped inmate outfit, he was sweating bullets—and his pride was in the gutter. "Thank God that prisoners don't have to dress like this anymore."

She, on the other hand, seemed unaffected as she giggled. "Our Jailhouse Wedding package is popular, although I don't quite understand why."

"Maybe they see marriage as a life sentence," he offered, then laughed at his own joke.

She narrowed her eyes at him. "That's not funny." But a smile played on her lips as she started to turn away.

Before he could think through the ramifications, he reached out and closed his hand around her wrist. "Gracie."

She turned back, seemingly startled by his touch, then inquisitive. "Yes?"

He pulled her close to him, slowly—in case she resisted...he almost hoped she would. But she didn't resist—only stared up at him with impossibly beautiful eyes, her mouth plump and inviting.

"We were interrupted yesterday," he said on an exhale as he lowered his mouth to hers. She opened to him, and her arms went around his neck. He sucked in a sharp breath as pins dug into his skin, but shoved aside the quick bite of pain. The floral scent she wore filled his lungs and the feel of her breasts pressed against his chest obliterated all other sensation. Their kiss went from exploratory to promising to preparatory as he slid his hands down her back and pulled her hips against his. Their moans mingled as he experienced a few seconds of blessed relief to connect with her body. Nearly out of his mind with wanting her, he pulled her toward the dressing room...and she went with him, devouring his mouth, her hands pushing at the costume. He grunted as more pins found their way home, but he didn't care.

The door to the dressing room closed behind them just as his shirt fell to the floor. He broke their kiss long enough to lift her tank top over her head and reveal the lacy bra. His sex jerked in anticipation of what lay beneath. "My God, you're beautiful." He pulled her close and lifted her skirt, sliding his hands down to her buttocks, finding them almost bare, spanned by a slip of a lacy thong. He groaned in pure ecstasy, and pushed the wisp of a garment over her hips and down her legs to her ankles. Heaven.

She stepped out of her shoes and the thong, standing

before him in the bra and flirty skirt. Her violet eyes sparkled like jewels—she was almost too beautiful, too perfect to touch. Desire pinkened her cheeks. She wanted him as much as he wanted her, and the realization made him slow down long enough for rational thought to work its way into his head.

He couldn't do this.

When she closed in for another kiss, he put out his hands and held her at arm's length in the tiny space. "Gracie, we have to stop."

She blinked, then glanced around, as if suddenly realizing where they were. "Oh." She crossed her hands over her bra. "Oh. Of course we do."

"Gracie, I'm sorry." He retrieved her yellow shirt and handed it to her.

She looked a little out of sorts and stumbled back, falling into the chair. From the sudden look of pain on her face, he realized she'd connected with something hard beneath his jeans—his gun.

"Ow!" She sprang back up. "What is that?"

Panic shot through his chest. "Sorry," he said quickly, moving to stop her from looking. "It's my cell phone."

She rubbed her hip. "It didn't feel like a cell phone."

"I think I left my camera there," he improvised, positioning himself between the chair and the door, forcing her to back up.

"Could I get dressed first?" she hissed, putting her arms through the sleeves of her shirt.

He felt like a cad…he *was* a cad. What was he thinking? If she'd found his gun…had been hurt… "I'm sorry, Gracie."

"You said that already."

"I can't get involved with you," he said.

"Does this have something to do with Karen, the woman who keeps calling?"

He looked surprised, then defeated. "Yes."

She nodded. "Well, for the record, I'm sorry, too." She yanked her shirt down and crossed her arms. "Okay—we both know there's an attraction here, so why don't we just agree to be adults about this and keep our hands off each other?"

He set his jaw and nodded.

A noise sounded outside the dressing room. "Gracie? Mr. Mulcahy?"

He winced—Cordelia was looking for them. Gracie closed her eyes briefly, then whispered. "I'll go out first. Stay here."

Before he could argue, she slipped her feet into her shoes, scooped up the pinned costumes within reach, opened the door just enough to slide out, and was gone. Steve pulled his hand down his face, thinking if he wasn't careful, he was going to botch this assignment. And if word got back that he was playing hanky-panky while on duty, his job would be on the line. He fisted his hands in frustration—he'd never let a woman get to him to the point of foolhardiness.

Somehow, some way, until this assignment was over, he was going to have to keep his distance from Gracie. He looked down at the floor and grimaced.

Right after he returned her thong.

CHAPTER SIX

WITH HER ARMS FULL OF COSTUMES and her heart clicking like mad, Gracie manufactured the best smile possible under the scrutiny of her boss. "Hi, Cordelia. Did you need something?"

Cordelia wore a bemused expression. "Just checking on you two."

Gracie walked over an air conditioner floor vent and realized with a frosty jolt that she wasn't wearing underwear. A hot flush began to make its way up her neck. "We were just having a fitting."

"Ah." Cordelia pursed her mouth. "And did everything...*fit?*"

"Not exactly," Gracie murmured.

"But you're getting there?" Cordelia prompted.

Gracie's skin tingled in embarrassment.

Cordelia sighed. "Gracie, you know I don't like to butt in to your life, but I don't like standing by and watching you get hurt, either. *Don't* fall for this guy."

Gracie's heart jerked sideways. Cordelia cared more about her happiness than anyone in the world. "Do you know something about him that I should know?"

A frustrated look came over her boss's face. "Only that Steve Mulcahy isn't the type who's going to stick around."

Gracie pressed her lips together. Hadn't Steve just reiterated that he didn't like staying in one place for long? Had he been warning her? *Don't fall for me—I'll leave.*

Cordelia's expression softened. "Gracie, you told me you were going to hold out for a guy who would be there for the long haul. Do you still feel that way?"

A lump formed in Gracie's throat and she nodded.

"Then stay away from Steve Mulcahy. Trust me—he will break your heart."

Moisture gathered in Gracie's eyes. Cordelia was right. She'd made a pact with herself to wait for love and a ring before she gave herself and her heart to another man. Yet she'd met Steve Mulcahy only yesterday and here she stood with her bare privates being subjected to an arctic blast. Shame rolled over her. "I understand what you're saying," she said carefully. "And I appreciate your concern, Cordelia. But you have nothing to worry about—Steve and I aren't involved."

"I'm glad to hear that," Cordelia said, although she didn't look completely convinced. Then she straightened, all business. "What time is our first wedding?"

Relieved at the subject change, Gracie inhaled deeply. "Four-thirty. Between answering the phones, I should have time to do these alterations by then."

Cordelia nodded. "And what will Mr. Mulcahy be doing?"

"I thought I'd take a few pictures of the chapel," he said, walking up behind Gracie. He was fully dressed and looked completely collected, the strap of his camera over his shoulder. But the memory of him without his shirt made her pulse skyrocket.

"Your shift doesn't start until four," Cordelia said to him. "You don't have to be here until the weddings begin if you'd like to leave and come back."

Guilt prodded Gracie because she knew the veiled antagonism Cordelia directed toward Steve was because of Cordelia's concern for her.

But he seemed to brush aside his new boss's slight. "I also brought a toolbox and thought I'd take a look at the Caddy, if that's all right, Ms. Conroy."

Cordelia hesitated, then nodded briefly. "If you wouldn't mind keeping an eye on H.D.—he needs to be outdoors more." On cue, the fat dog waddled into view, his tongue hanging almost to the floor.

Gracie smothered a smile at Steve's wry frown. "Okay," he said finally, then excused himself and walked out into the hall. He snapped his fingers at H.D. The hound turned as quickly as his thick body would allow and followed him, his collar jingling.

Cordelia went back to work and Gracie, after scouring the dressing room for her thong and coming up empty, was forced to look for Steve. She found him outside in front of the chapel with the camera to his eye. H.D. sat nearby, panting but with rapt attention focused on Steve.

She watched quietly as Steve shot the front of the chapel, then the road, even the parking lot across from them. To her untrained eye, he didn't seem to be taking time to frame interesting shots, yet the photos he'd taken after the ceremonies had shown a keen sense of composition. And the midday sun didn't strike her as the best light for taking photos, but for all she knew he could be using a lens filter.

It was a scorching hot day, rendered just short of miserable by the breeze. The wind ruffled Steve's dark, shiny hair and the sun silhouetted his broad shoulders and lean build. He moved more like an athlete than a photographer—his long muscular limbs sure and steady, with no movement wasted. How could a man who controlled his body with such unconscious resolve be a transient? Then she chided herself—there she went ignoring the obvious and projecting her needs onto the situation. Next, she'd be trying to convince herself that Karen wasn't his lover.

He slid the camera strap over his shoulder just as H.D. caught sight of her and barked hoarsely.

"Hi," she ventured casually, walking closer.

Steve raised the camera and pointed it at her. The whir of the shutter closing sounded several times.

She bristled self-consciously. "What are the pictures for?"

He shrugged. "Just practice."

"From what I saw of the photos you took yesterday, you don't need the practice."

"Thanks. I'm glad you're happy with my work." One side of his mouth slid back. "At least some of my work. I don't know that I'll ever get the hang of the lip-synching."

"You're doing fine. By the way, our other minister Roach will be performing this evening's ceremonies."

He pressed his lips together then asked, "Did Cordelia give you a hard time about...us?"

"Not really. She's just concerned about me, that's all."

"She seems very protective."

Gracie nodded, then cleared her throat. "Speaking of which, I'm, um, missing an article of clothing and I wondered if you'd seen it."

"Got it right here," he said, reaching into his jeans pockets and withdrawing a handful of black lace. His face reddened as he handed it to her. "I wasn't going to keep them or anything—I just didn't want someone else to find them."

"Right," she said, not sure whether she believed him, but wanting to. She palmed the filmy thong, feeling like a complete idiot. "Thanks."

She wheeled to go and the movement lifted the hem of her skirt slightly—just enough for a sudden gust to catch hold and send it straight up, baring her behind— and her befront—to the world. Gracie gasped in mortification and fought with her skirt while horns from passing cars honked in appreciation. In the process, she managed to let go of the thong, which promptly sailed airborne. She cried out and Steve, heretofore frozen, yelled, "I'll get it."

At last she got her skirt under control, holding the hem in her fist lest it get away from her again. Abject humiliation flooded her in waves as she imagined the spectacle she had presented. Worse, Steve had abandoned his camera and was chasing her underwear, which, being as light as a piece of paper, tumbled and rolled through the air and on the ground, always inches out of reach. H.D. lumbered behind, barking as if they were on the trail of wild game.

"This can't be happening," Gracie murmured to herself.

Oh, but it was.

Finally, the thong caught on a fence, allowing Steve to catch up. He plucked it like a flower and turned to hurry back to her, fighting an enormous grin and losing. By the time he reached her, he was struggling not to laugh. Between two fingers, he held out the thong, now dusty and peppered with bits of dry grass.

"Thank you," she said, snatching the underwear and wishing the ground would open up to swallow her whole.

"It was my pleasure," he said, then clamped down his jaw. His eyes, however, were dancing with laughter.

Gracie turned on her heel and, maintaining a firm grip on her skirt, marched back into the chapel with as much dignity as she could muster.

When H.D. started to follow Gracie, Steve snapped his fingers and called him back. "I know how you feel, buddy," he murmured as he stared after her receding figure. The belly laugh he wanted to release was tempered by the rigid erection pressing against his fly at having witnessed what was undoubtedly the most erotic vision he'd ever seen.

If he lived to be one hundred, he would never forget the sight of Gracie Sergeant fighting her wayward skirt, her long, slender legs and curvy rear end perfectly outlined in the sun. And, if he'd had any doubts, the lovely woman was *not* a natural blonde—another gut-clutching sight. He closed his eyes and groaned. If only he weren't on assignment. If only Gracie was willing to indulge in a quick fling, with no attachments. But he'd already been warned by Cordelia and by Lincoln that Gracie was looking for something he couldn't give: commitment, longevity, happily ever after.

A dull pain radiated out from his breastbone. If only—

The ring of his cell phone split the air. He unhooked it from his belt and glanced at the screen—Karen. He pushed the connect button. "Yeah?"

"Just checking in, partner. Any developments?"

"Uh, no." He rubbed stubbornly at the strange sensation in his chest. *At least no developments relating to the case.*

"Got those descriptions of everyone who works there?"

"I'm taking photographs. I'll have them to you in the morning."

"Great. I can't wait to see this woman with the amazing eyes."

He chose to ignore her. "Any more news from the informant?"

"No." Karen sighed. "She hasn't returned any of my calls—I'm starting to worry that maybe she's in trouble."

"What kind of trouble?"

"If someone close to Lundy found out that she's a snitch, she could be in danger. If she told them what she told us, Lundy could decide not to show."

"Or show up with firepower," Steve said, his adrenaline kicking in. A sudden pain in his foot distracted him momentarily—H.D. had once again decided to park his fat butt.

"That's not Lundy's M.O.," Karen said. "He's more likely just to lie low. The last thing he needs is civilian casualties at a Vegas wedding chapel—if he did something to scare off tourists, the city's business leaders would form their own posse."

"You're probably right," Steve said, yet he pivoted his head to look all around—up and down the street, in the parking lot across the road—searching for anything suspicious, anything out of the ordinary.

A wry frown worked his mouth. Such as a man and a hound running down the street chasing a woman's thong?

"Still, I wanted to let you know," Karen said. "Let's

not panic—our informant might simply be out of reach for a while. For now, we stick to the original plan. I'll keep you posted."

"Okay." He disconnected the call with disturbing what-if scenarios tumbling through his head—all of them involving Gracie getting hurt. He winced. The discomfort around his breastbone was back. With much effort, he dislodged his foot from underneath H.D.'s behind and limped toward the chapel, rubbing his chest.

CHAPTER SEVEN

GRACIE PASSED the next couple of hours working on the costumes in between answering the phone, although her preoccupation earned her several pricks with the needle. She relived the degrading Marilyn-Monroe-standing-over-a-grate-gone-wrong incident over and over, until she was sure her face would be permanently flushed. To prevent an encore, she'd sewn curtain weights into the hem of her skirt. And she'd washed the bothersome black thong in the bathroom and used a hairdryer to dry it enough to put it on.

From now on, she would wear nothing but tidy whities.

"Oh. My. *Gawd.*"

Gracie looked up to see Lincoln in the doorway. His arms were full of flowers and today his sunglasses were pink. She angled her head. "What?"

His jaw dropped. "Steve is outside working on the Caddy."

"I know."

"*Shirtless.*"

She smiled. "Oh."

"Gracie, the man is simply too gorgeous for words. You simply have to have sex with him."

She gave a choked little laugh. "I do not." Besides, she'd tried.

"You're killing me," he said. "If I were you, I'd wait to start looking for Mr. Right until after this guy *left*."

She laughed and helped him to arrange the flowers in the chapels and store the bouquets and boutonnieres in the refrigerator.

When they were finished, he said, "I'll see you tonight when I relieve Cordelia at the drive-through." He grinned. "Want to follow me out to take a looky-loo?"

She smirked. "No. And stop trying to get me into trouble. He has a girlfriend."

"Oh? You asked?"

"It…came up."

"Still—no ring, will fling."

"Goodbye, Lincoln."

He left shaking his head. For her part, Gracie tried to tamp down the image of Steve, bare-chested, and get back to work. After a particularly frustrating bout with the sewing machine, she sighed and held up the black-and-white striped shirt of the inmate costume—so many pins had been dislodged during their frantic groping episode that she wasn't sure she'd made the right adjustments. She checked her Betty Boop watch and stretched her arms overhead in a yawn.

A break sounded good, so why not check on Steve and ask him to try on the shirt? She had to face him sooner or later. Besides, she was dying to see if he'd made progress on the Caddy.

On the way, she stopped by the kitchen to grab two bottles of water in case he was thirsty. Her heart beat double time as she pushed open one of the doors leading to the back lot. Her breath caught in her chest.

Steve was indeed shirtless, leaning into the engine beneath the raised hood, working either to loosen or to tighten something, considering the way the muscles in his arms bulged with exertion. His back was slick with perspiration. He stood and wiped his hand across his brow.

If she lived to be one hundred, she would never forget the sight of Steve Mulcahy standing half-naked in the blistering sun, his developed pecs and six-pack abs glistening with sweat. He was simply the sexiest man she'd ever seen.

H.D., on the other hand, lay in the shade holding a wrench in his mouth, which he happily discarded when he saw Gracie, and lurched to his feet to greet her.

She smiled at Steve and lifted a bottle of water. "I thought you might be thirsty."

He nodded and reached for it. "Thanks." He opened the bottle, lifted it to his mouth, and proceeded to down it in one long drink, the column of his throat convulsing as he drained the bottle. She was mesmerized—more so when he grabbed a towel and wiped his chest and neck. "Wow, it's hot."

She couldn't have agreed more. To derail her wicked train of thought, she opened her water bottle and poured half of it into a bowl for H.D. She resisted the temptation to douse herself with the rest of it.

"Have you ever thought of getting a real watchdog around here?" Steve asked.

Gracie pouted. "H.D. is perfect just the way he is."

"Tell me something—what does 'H.D.' stand for?"

She grinned. "Hound dog, of course. What else?"

"Oh. I get it." He looked mildly amused. "Is he yours?"

"He belongs to Cordelia, really, although we've all adopted him."

"He needs to lose some weight. I'll bet this morning's run is the most exercise he's had in a while." His mouth twitched with humor.

She lifted her chin. "Let's forget this morning happened, shall we?"

He quirked an eyebrow. "Were they salvageable?"

"Yes," she chirped.

"Good." Laughter rumbled deep in his throat.

Flustered, Gracie gestured to the car. "How's it going?"

He sobered and shook his head. "Slow. I replaced the battery and all the hoses, but there's a lot more to do."

"But she's fixable?"

"Sure—eventually. But it's going to take a lot of time."

And he wouldn't be around that long. The unspoken words hung in the air between them.

"I need for you to try this on again," she said, holding up the striped shirt she had folded over her arm. "When you have time."

"Sure, give me a couple of minutes and I'll wipe my hands." He leaned back into the engine and applied a wrench to a thingamabob. "By the way, would you mind if I took a shower here instead of going home?"

"No, that's fine," Gracie said, then wet her lips. "Where's home?"

"Hmm?"

"Where do you live?"

He swung his head around, then looked back to his handiwork. "In an apartment a few miles from here. Nothing special. How about you?"

"Same," she said. "How did you learn to work on cars?"

"My dad," he said. "He always had a fixer-upper in the garage. There were five of us boys, so he said that the only way he was going to afford for all of us to have a car was if we all knew how to fix them ourselves."

Her eyes widened. "You have four brothers?"

"Yeah."

"Where are they?"

After a few seconds' hesitation, he said, "All over."

A sliver of disappointment sliced through her heart—secretly she had been hoping that Steve came from a big, boisterous, tight-knit family.

But there she went again—projecting.

Then a thought slid into her brain, one so shocking, she inhaled sharply: What if Steve Mulcahy was a criminal? An ex-con. That would explain why Cordelia was so worried about her getting involved with him, why she was so sure he would be moving on soon. Cordelia didn't talk about her past much, but Lincoln had said once that he'd heard that Cordelia had been on the wrong side of the law when she was young. Maybe she was trying to repay her debt by giving an ex-con a chance.

Which would explain some other things—like why he would be willing to take the low-prestige job in the first place. And him being in the office this morning, behaving suspiciously. And the fact that he wouldn't talk about his family or where he'd lived or what he'd done for a living. And that question he'd asked about the chapel having a guard dog—did he plan to rob them? That would explain why he'd been taking so many pictures!

Er, excluding the ones he'd taken of her.

"Gracie."

At the sound of her name, she jumped and looked at Steve suspiciously. "What?"

He lowered the hood of the car, sending the muscles in his back playing beneath smooth skin. "I said I can't do anything more here without a few parts. I think I'll take that shower now."

"Okay," she said vaguely, wondering if he planned to steal the Caddy, and if she should share her theories with Cordelia. "What about…clothes?"

"I have a change of clothes in the SUV."

Then again, Cordelia had hired Steve, so she would have performed a background check and would have known his past. If Cordelia had decided to hire him despite—or because of—a checkered past, then it was her business.

"Gracie, are you okay?" He was frowning at her.

"I'm fine," she murmured, backing away. "It's the heat. I need to get back to work."

"Hand me the shirt," he said, gesturing. "I'm dry enough to try it on."

She looked down at the striped inmate shirt and handed it to him, her heart in her throat.

He pushed his arms into the sleeves of the loose garment and made sure it met across the front. "Feels good to me. What do you think?"

What did she think? At the sight of the cartoonish prison garb, Gracie thought she should see a therapist about her projection problem. She smiled, feeling foolish for the thoughts she'd been entertaining. "It's great. When you finish cleaning up, come to the lobby and we'll go over tonight's bookings."

She called for H.D. and reentered the chapel, cursing herself for her active imagination. Her life wasn't nearly interesting enough to include a criminal—all the more reason why she needed to move on and expand her horizons. But as usual, when she thought about having that conversation with Cordelia, she balked. She owed the woman everything…how could she walk out on her, especially with business being so iffy?

Fighting a headache, Gracie put on her favorite Elvis CD—his 1968 comeback performance. Oh, sure it was nice to hear all the number one songs, but when she was feeling blue, she especially loved to hear the gospel medley featuring "Sometimes I Feel Like a Motherless Child."

Someday she would return to Oklahoma to visit her mother's grave and let the rest of her family know she was still alive…if they even cared. Going down that road of memories was torturous so she looked for something to keep her mind and hands busy.

Of course, Steve was just down the hall taking a hot, soapy shower.

She closed her eyes and sighed in frustration, wondering how one man could make her feel so many things at the same time—lust, annoyance, suspicion, hope. She laughed—Elvis had a song for each of those emotions: "All Shook Up," "Don't Be Cruel," "Suspicious Minds" and "The Wonder of You."

Elvis…now there was one romantic guy.

She laughed at her musings and threw herself into unpacking a box of souvenirs—Elvis Teddy Bears and T-shirts.

"Do you ever wonder what the King would think of all this?"

Gracie looked up when Steve entered the lobby. He wore jeans and his standard baggy button-up shirt. His hair wasn't completely dry, and his cheeks had the glow of a mild sunburn. His eyes…oh, those blue eyes. "Hmm?"

He gestured to the souvenir racks and picked up a deck of Elvis playing cards. "Do you ever wonder what the King would think of all this? Do you think he'd feel exploited?"

She squeezed a teddy bear to her chest. "I used to wonder. But honestly, very few people come here as a joke. Almost everyone comes because they love Elvis and his music, or because they're looking for a little magic touch for their wedding." She stood and gestured to the bulletin board. "All of these people can't be wrong."

He joined her and surveyed the photo collage. Some of the pictures were yellowed, some curled, some featuring people with hopelessly outdated clothing and hair. "But how many of these people do you think are still married?"

She shrugged. "I don't know. Most of them, I hope. Some couples send us a card on their anniversary. See this photo?" She pointed to a picture taken by the automatic cameras at the drive-through, this one of a young man with a military haircut and a dark-blond woman wearing a paper veil. "That's Redford and Denise DeMoss. They met in Vegas and were married here over three years ago when Redford was on leave from the Gulf." She sighed. "But they had the marriage annulled."

"I'm sure that happens a lot," he said dryly.

"Yes, but look at *this* picture." She pointed to a five-by-seven of a chapel ceremony, the dark-haired groom resplendent in his Marine dress blues, the bride radiant in a gorgeous halter gown.

Steve leaned closer. "It looks like the same couple."

She smiled. "It is. They came back a few months ago and got married again after reuniting. Isn't that the most romantic thing you've ever heard?"

He looked doubtful. "If you say so."

Disappointment shivered through her heart. "Well, think what you will, but I'm convinced that what we do here is fun and useful. We make people happy, and I think that's a noble pursuit."

"You're right," he said, nodding. "And is this what you want to do the rest of your life?"

She squeezed the teddy bear tighter. "It's all I know."

His gaze locked with hers and she felt a strong, un-explainable connection with this man that went beyond his amazing sex appeal, as if he were offering her some of his energy. She was overcome with the urge to tell him her entire, sordid life story. When her throat was on the verge of bursting, she averted her glance to regain her composure.

"Look at the time," she said, bustling over to the file cabinet. "We have to get ready for five weddings." She skimmed the appointment book. "The first two and the last one are the Aloha Las Vegas package. Think you can handle the 'Hawaiian Wedding Song'?"

He hesitated, then nodded sheepishly. "Lincoln gave me a tape of the ceremony songs to take home."

Gracie blinked. "That's…great." *And not the M.O. of someone who planned to leave.* Her stubborn heart took flight. "You'll need to wear the Hawaiian shirt and white pants, and the first couple asked for witnesses, so we'll have to do that as well."

He nodded, looking oddly intense. "When did you say the other minister was arriving?"

The roar of a motorcycle split the air as a black blur passed the window and zoomed down the side of the chapel. Gracie grinned. "Speak of the devil—there's Roach now. Let's go meet him—he'll be thrilled to know you're working on the Caddy."

Roach Hilton was a big, friendly bear of a man with a ZZ Top beard and a voice like thunder. He and Steve seemed to hit it off—Gracie was glad that Steve was beginning to relax. When Lincoln arrived to relieve Cordelia, Steve even took photographs of the group around the Caddy. Lincoln grabbed the camera and insisted that Steve be in some of them, which gave her the smallest amount of hope that he might stay long enough for something to develop other than film. At one point they were in a group shot standing next to each other and Gracie could feel his body speaking to hers. Their arms brushed, and they glanced at each other. Desire lurked in his gaze, but she looked away. They had an agreement, after all. And deep down, she was happy to know that he was being faithful to his girlfriend. It reinforced all the good things she thought about him…and the good things she wanted in *her* man.

Soon everyone scattered to their respective places. Steve got into his costume, wig and sunglasses in record time, looking fun and fit in the Hawaiian shirt and white shiny pants. When the first couple arrived, he took the lead in making them feel comfortable, drawing out details of their lives, all in his fake accent—already much improved over the previous day.

"Where did Cordelia find this guy?" Roach whispered. "He's a natural."

Gracie shrugged. "I don't know, but you're right."

Roach winked. "And he looks better in the suits than I did." He laughed and launched into the ceremony.

Gracie and Steve served as witnesses and everything went smoothly—Steve's lip-synching won rave reviews and later when Gracie witnessed how many pictures the couple wanted with Steve, she had the tingly feeling that business was poised to take an upward turn. Relief flooded every fiber of her being—if finances improved, she wouldn't feel so bad about leaving TCB.

But she frowned as a realization set in: Business would only continue to improve if Steve stayed on. She was officially in a conundrum.

When the last couple arrived—a May-December wedding, judging from the differences in their ages—Steve was even more attentive, joking around about how the couple had met and where they were going to take their honeymoon. He tried to get the man to trade sunglasses with him, but the man wasn't having it. It seemed apparent to Gracie that he was there because his young bride-to-be was an Elvis buff.

Gracie tried to signal Steve to back off this one, but Steve put his arm around the middle-aged man and poked him a couple of times in the chest, then in the stomach, apparently in jest. Gracie could see the man's demeanor change immediately—for the worse. Then inexplicably, Steve stumbled forward into him and knocked him down, sending the man's sunglasses flying. Gracie gasped.

He was blind.

"What is the meaning of this?" the man bellowed. "Give me back my glasses!"

Steve looked stricken and pulled him to his feet. "I'm sorry sir. I stumbled."

Mortified, Gracie moved in for damage control, bending to retrieve the man's sunglasses. "We're very sorry, sir. It was an accident."

"Let's get out of here, honey," the woman said, turning her back on hundreds of dollars worth of souvenirs she'd planned to buy.

"Maybe we can work something out," Gracie said, following them to the door.

"You're lucky I don't have you charged with assault!" the man shouted, and they left.

Roach and Lincoln appeared, both in black robes. "What's all the shouting about?"

Gracie glanced at Steve, then back to them. "It was just a rowdy customer. Changed his mind."

Roach glanced at his watch. "Is that all for tonight, then?"

She nodded. "That was the last one, so go home, Roach. Thanks. Good night, Lincoln."

When the men left, she turned to stare at Steve. "Maybe you'd like to explain what happened?"

"I tripped," Steve said. "It was an accident."

"An accident?" Gracie growled. "You practically mauled the man before knocking him down. Were you trying to pick his pocket?"

His eyes went wide. "What? No!"

She walked closer and narrowed her eyes. "Are you drunk?"

"I took one shot of vodka—"

"Stop right there." She was incredulous, shaking with disappointment. Was that his vice—the reason he was underemployed? "I know you don't consider what we do here to be important. I know this is just a filler job for you until you *drift* somewhere else. But TCB is important to me, and so is our reputation. I can't believe you were drinking on the job."

He pursed his mouth, then gave her a pointed look. "You were ready to fool around on the job."

Her head jerked back involuntarily. A direct hit. Worse, he was right. She bit down on the end of her tongue until she trusted her voice to speak. "Don't let it happen again. Go home, Steve."

Gracie turned her back to him and closed her eyes, wondering if the four-leaf clover she had tattooed on her shoulder was ever going to kick in.

CHAPTER EIGHT

STEVE DROPPED his film at a one-hour photo drive-through, then pulled away, antsy and wide-awake as he drove down the Vegas strip, bustling and so bright with neon, one could almost believe it was daytime.

He hated letting Gracie believe he was a drunk, but it was safer than admitting he had royally screwed up and nearly called for the takedown of the wrong man because the bride was so young and the groom wouldn't remove his glasses. He cursed his ineptness, but was thankful for the chance to see how difficult it could be to recognize Lundy if he did show up.

He dialed Karen's number, his apprehension over calling at such a late hour disappearing when she answered on the first ring.

"Baker here," she said.

"Hey, it's Steve."

"I must have been sending you vibes—I just got off the phone with our informant. Everything is still cool. You're a go."

He exhaled in relief. "Any more details? A day or time?"

"No, just 'soon' is all she'll say. Hang in there."

"I had a false alarm today. Identifying Lundy might

be harder than I thought. Will you check to see if there are any photos more current than the ones we have?"

"You still owe me some photos, too."

"Check your in-box tomorrow morning."

"Will do."

"Oh, and Karen—would you mind doing a general search on a Gracie Sergeant." He spelled the name. "Female, late twenties maybe."

"Do you have a middle name or initial?"

The monogram on her purse—he closed his eyes. "A."

"Any identifying marks other than violet-colored eyes?"

He'd asked for that. "A green four-leaf clover tattooed on her upper right shoulder."

"Am I looking for anything in particular?" she asked, her voice bursting with innuendo.

"No," he said. "It's just a hunch."

"If she's in the system, I'll have the printout tomorrow. Anything else?"

"Are you at your computer?"

"Always."

He swallowed. "I need her home address."

Silence hummed over the line, then, "O-kaay."

He heard computer keys tapping in the background.

"Here it is." She rattled off the address. "Hmm—not the best part of town."

He was thinking the same thing, and hated the protective feelings rousing in his chest. "Thanks, Karen. Take care of yourself."

She laughed. "Excuse me? Was that a pleasantry you just dispensed? Wow, this woman must be under your skin *bad*."

He frowned. "I'm hanging up." He disconnected the call and drove toward Gracie's neighborhood. His stomach was growling, so he picked up a pizza along the way. He didn't know what kind of reception he might get, or even for sure why he was going, but he knew his chances improved if he arrived bearing gifts.

He found her apartment building and parked around the corner. After a few seconds' hesitation, he locked his weapon in the glove compartment. When he reached her building, he followed another resident through the security door into the lobby—the place was a real Fort Knox. He found her apartment number by searching for initials on a wall of mailboxes.

He climbed two sets of stairs, telling himself with every step that he was probably making a mistake. But something indefinable compelled him forward. He located the correct door, took a deep breath, and knocked.

AT THE TAP on her door, Gracie pivoted her head, then uncurled herself from the comfy velvet couch with a resigned sigh. It was probably Mrs. Wingate from down the hall, unable to sleep and wanting to chat under the pretense of borrowing something obscure.

She glanced through the peephole, and her heart skipped a beat. Steve? How did he know where she lived and what was he doing here holding a pizza? She looked down at her clothes—holey exercise pants and faded T-shirt—and frowned. Her makeup was long gone. Her apartment was clean, but not exactly tidy. Then she chastised herself—if the man was going to show up unannounced, what did he expect? Besides, he might not want to come in—maybe he was just bringing her dinner.

And even if he did want to come in, she didn't have to let him.

She opened the door the few inches the chain would allow and peered out.

He straightened. "Hello."

"Hello," she said. "What are you doing here?"

He held up the pizza box. "I noticed you didn't have time to eat tonight—I thought you might be hungry."

She pursed her lips. "How did you know where I live?"

"Directory assistance."

"My number is unlisted."

His smile was sheepish. "Okay, a computer friend found it for me." He shifted from foot to foot. "I came to apologize for my behavior at work this evening, and since I couldn't find an olive branch, I was hoping an olive pizza would do."

Gracie smiled—tentatively. Lincoln had confessed that he'd encouraged Steve to take a shot of vodka to loosen up. "I like olives."

He brightened. "Great."

"Thanks very much. Just set it on the floor and I'll get it when you leave."

His face fell. "Oh. Okay, sure." He crouched and placed the pizza on the floor in front of her door, then stood and pulled his keys from his jeans pocket, his expression quiet and unreadable. "Gracie, I...like you. And I'm sorry that I did something to make your job harder. I truly am. Good night."

Gracie heard his words, but was captivated by his hands—his keys actually. He had a four-leaf-clover key ring. She swallowed—that had to mean something, didn't it? A sign of some kind? As he walked away, she closed the door and unhooked the chain, then opened it again.

"Steve?"

He turned around.

She gave a little shrug. "I'm hungry, but I don't think I can eat an entire pizza by myself."

A smile curved his sexy mouth.

Gracie's neighbor Billy, a slim, bespectacled college student, walked by. "Hi, Gracie."

"Hi, Billy." She pointed to Steve. "This man's name is Steve Mulcahy—he's a co-worker of mine and I'm letting him in to share a pizza. If anything bad happens to me, he did it."

Billy held up his cell phone in front of Steve and hit a button. "I got your picture, dude, so no funny stuff."

Gracie grinned. "Thanks, Billy."

"No problem."

Steve retrieved the pizza with a little laugh. "I guess I'd better be on my best behavior."

Gracie's pulse raced as she held open the door. "I guess so." He walked in and she closed the door behind him. "Welcome to my home."

He looked around and she tried to see her apartment as he might—low, ambient lighting, eclectic, retro furniture with feminine touches. Her sitting area was compact, the kitchen hidden from view by a rice-paper screen. A café table and two chairs sat tucked into a corner, although the stack of magazines on one chair, she realized, was a telltale sign that she usually ate alone.

"Nice place," he said, and sounded as if he meant it.

She smiled and moved toward the kitchen to get plates and utensils. "It's small, but I like it."

"I guess I thought it would be crammed with Elvis memorabilia."

"Oh, I have a good Elvis music collection." She gestured to the wall. "And an autographed photo that I bought at a swap meet."

He lifted the lid on the pizza box and leaned closer to the picture. "How do you know it's real?"

She shrugged. "How do we know that anything is real? I just go on gut instinct."

He had been transferring pizza slices to their plates, but stopped so abruptly, she was afraid she'd said something wrong. Then he smiled. "I guess you're right."

A warm, tingly sensation spread through her chest—she had a feeling that something was happening here. "M-my couch is more comfortable than my table and chairs—want to sit there and eat?"

"Sure."

"How about some music?"

"Surprise me," he said.

She put a stack of albums on the phonograph. They settled down with a chaste amount of space between them and dug in. Gracie moaned in appreciation when the salty olives and spicy sauce burst over her taste buds. "This is awesome—thank you."

"Thank you for not slamming the door in my face."

She studied him while she chewed, his powerful profile cast in low shadows. He seemed so relaxed and confident, as if he could fit in anywhere—no doubt a product of being an army brat. "You're a mystery," she said suddenly.

His dark eyebrows went up. "What do you mean?"

"I mean, I don't know what to make of you."

In that instant, something changed in his expression. His eyes darkened, his mouth softened. "I could say the same thing, but like you said, sometimes, you just have to go on gut instinct."

She swallowed hard. "What…what is your gut instinct telling you right now?"

His gaze locked with hers. "To kiss you."

She moistened her lips and met him halfway, reveling in the salty taste of his mouth on hers. He parted her lips with his tongue and delved deeper, slanting his mouth over hers. His moan of desire reverberated in her mouth and seemed to reach down inside her soul. Impossibly, she was already half in love with this man— the connection was too fast, too natural to be wrong.

He deepened the kiss and pulled her onto his lap, sliding his hand down to her breast. She moaned as he caressed her beaded nipple through her thin T-shirt. Liquid fire pooled between her thighs…she wanted this man so badly. When he tugged on the hem of her shirt, she lifted her arms to allow him to pull it over her head. He stared at her breasts, his eyes hooded with desire. "Gracie, my God, you're…amazing."

She arched with pleasure and pulled his head down. He devoured her, licking and kissing one breast, then the other, drawing deep on her nipples, sending moisture to her thighs, readying her. Slowly they undressed each other. He kissed every inch of skin as it was revealed. She thrilled in running her hands over his smooth, muscular chest and back. He slipped off his boots and jeans and then only their underwear separated their bodies—her black thong and his briefs, which did not quite contain his erection. She slid her hand inside to stroke the head of his rigid shaft, gratified when he groaned in her ear as she wrapped her hand around the length of him.

"These look familiar," he teased as he fingered the lacy thong.

She started to respond, but when he slipped a finger into her folds, she couldn't speak, only cling to him as he began to massage her core in rapid little circles. "Does this feel good?"

"Oh, yes," she moaned against his shoulder. His sex pulsed in her hand and she stroked him slowly while moving her hips in rhythm with his massaging hand. A vibration began deep inside, building, seeking liberation. She was powerless to do anything but yield to the intensity of the sensation as it climbed higher and rippled in wider circles through her midsection. She strained against him, whimpering, groaning, pleading for a quick release. But he maintained a steady pace that tantalized to a slow, agonizing build until she thought she might scream…and when she suddenly climaxed in a burst of molten bliss, she did scream.

He covered her mouth with a deep kiss until the spasms slowed. "Shh," he murmured, laughing. "Or that neighbor of yours will call the police."

"That was…otherworldly."

He lifted his hand and inserted the magic finger into his mouth, moaning his agreement. Gracie was mesmerized, watching him lap up her juices and scent. She moved her hips against his, and pushed at his briefs. In a matter of seconds, they were gone, as well as the beleaguered thong. Steve reached for his jeans and withdrew a condom. Gracie helped him to roll it onto his slick shaft, then pulled him down on top of her. He nuzzled her neck and ear. "You smell great. God, you're so sexy."

Gracie closed her eyes, engorged with desire, and the fact that he wanted her as much as she wanted him. His sex probed hers and she opened her knees to give him full access. He thrust deep, taking her breath, then he tensed and remained still, allowing them both to adjust. Slowly, he began to slide his fullness in and out of her. He twined his hands with hers and buried his face in her neck. Another orgasm started its humming song in her womb, and she felt overwhelmed with lush awareness of her body and his.

By unspoken consent, their rhythm intensified. She climaxed in a great, crashing wave of emotion, and took him over the edge with her. He tensed, shuddered, and pumped himself into her, groaning his release. "Gracie…ohhhh…Gracie."

She recovered slowly, her body pulsing, her heart full—this was what it was supposed to be like between a man and a woman: thrilling, passionate, satisfying. How easily she could fall in love with this man….

She didn't remember falling asleep, but she must have because when she awoke, the phonograph had switched off…and Steve was gone.

CHAPTER NINE

"THE PHOTO that you have of Lundy is the most recent available," Karen said. "And I got your photos this morning. I take it the blonde is Gracie Sergeant?"

"Right," Steve said into the phone. He sat in the parking lot across from TCB, loath to go inside.

"Did you find her apartment last night?" Karen's voice was bursting with curiosity.

"Yeah—thanks for the info."

She made a humming noise. "And Steve—I got that printout you asked for."

His chest tightened. A printout meant a hit. "What did you find?"

"It might not be the same person, but I got a Gracie Alice Sergeant reported as a runaway from Marion, Oklahoma, ten years ago. No mention of a tattoo, but could this be your girl?"

He thought he had detected a Texan flavor in her accent, but Oklahoma was close enough. "It could be." And it would explain why she didn't want to discuss her family or background, and why she was so close to Cordelia Conroy—the woman must have taken her in.

"Someone even took the time to file missing person's reports in the surrounding states, but she was never found," Karen continued. "I got images of the flyers that were distributed. The picture is degraded, but I think it's the same woman. She didn't have a social security number, and since she was seventeen at the time, I doubt if any of the agencies put much energy into it."

No social security number at seventeen meant that she hadn't had a driver's license, which meant she probably had escaped a poor and/or sheltered upbringing. He winced—no wonder Gracie Sergeant was looking for a happy ending. And he was the last person in the world who could give it to her. Last night had been great— mind-blowing, even—but he was not a marrying kind of guy.

So you should have kept your pants zipped, his conscience whispered.

"Are you still there?" Karen asked.

"Yeah, I'm here. Anything else on the printout?"

"Nope—if your girl is this runaway, she's led a squeaky clean life."

"Thanks. Put the file on my desk. I'll call you later." He ended the call and rubbed his face. Now what?

He opened the envelope of extra pictures that he'd taken and flipped to the ones he'd taken of Gracie yesterday, when she'd walked outside. She was stunning, like a movie star from the sixties, compact, graceful, sexy. Especially considering that she hadn't been wearing panties.

Gracie was a beauty, but he'd resisted plenty of beautiful women in his lifetime—what about her had hit him between the eyes and made him want to break the rules?

He pulled out the close-up photo of her and tucked it in his shirt pocket, then heaved a frustrated sigh—he'd have to face her sooner or later. He grabbed the envelope with the extra photos and swung down from the SUV. He rubbed the four-leaf-clover key chain. If luck were with him, Lundy would show up today and the takedown would be textbook smooth. Then he could leave before things got more complicated.

GRACIE LOOKED at her watch—with less than an hour until the first wedding, she was growing more and more nervous that Steve wasn't going to show. Unemployment was one way to avoid morning-after awkwardness.

She'd spent the day alternating between reliving their incredible lovemaking and kicking herself for letting him in her apartment. If he quit because he didn't want to face her, what was she going to tell Cordelia, especially since her boss had specifically warned her to steer clear of Steve?

And worse, if he didn't come back to TCB, what did that say for how he felt about her? That their encounter was just a one-night stand? That he hadn't felt the powerful connection between them that she had?

The door opened, triggering a "Love Me Tender" chime. Steve walked in and gave her a flat smile, his expression unreadable. Her initial relief to see him quickly plummeted when she saw the lines of tension on his forehead.

"Hi," she ventured.

"Hi," he said, nodding curtly, as if they were strangers.

"I was starting to think you weren't going to show," she said with a little laugh.

"Because of last night?" he asked. "I still have a job to do."

Her heart sank at his matter-of-factness. "Right. Of course."

"I had a great time," he said. "Really great."

"Good," she said stupidly. "Great."

He handed her an envelope. "I had the photos from yesterday developed. I thought you might like them."

"Thank you," she said woodenly.

"Guess I'd better get ready," he said, and disappeared down the hall.

She closed her eyes, pulsing with shame. How awkward was this working relationship going to be? And had she really, truly, deep down, expected anything less than rejection?

"What's up with Steve?" Lincoln asked, coming through the door.

She straightened. "What do you mean?"

"His face is longer than H.D.'s."

Gracie averted her gaze.

"Wait a minute—did you two hook up?"

She inhaled and exhaled.

"You did! You did hook up!" Lincoln tucked his arm in hers. "Was it divine?"

She gave him a sad smile. "Yes."

"I knew it!"

"And now he wants nothing to do with me," she said.

He frowned. "Really? What a jerk."

"And if you tell anyone else, I'll spread the rumor that you use carnations in your bouquets."

"I do not!"

She smirked and made a zipping motion with her hand, glad to joke about it with someone.

"What are those?" he asked, pointing to the envelope.

"Pictures that Steve took yesterday."

Lincoln flipped through them. "Wow, these are really good. Oh, wait—I took this one."

She peeked over his shoulder to see Cordelia, Roach, H.D., her and Steve in front of the pink Caddy. She and Steve were looking at each other, her head tilted up, his head tilted down. They seemed separate from everyone else—it was if there was no one else in the world. Her heart swelled.

"Want to keep it?" he asked her quietly.

She hesitated, then shook her head. "No thanks." She looked at her watch. "I'm going to check the chapels."

"What's on the agenda for tonight?" Lincoln asked, glancing at the appointment book. "Wow, only three ceremonies?" Concern crossed his face. "That's not good."

"I know," she said with a sigh. "Something's got to give."

He made a rueful noise. "Anything exciting in the lineup?"

"Not really. One Aloha Las Vegas package with a hula girl."

Lincoln laughed. "Oh, that's always fun—you're good at that."

She smirked. "Thanks. And one Love Me Tender package and one Teddy Bear package."

"Got it," he said. "See you in a few."

Gracie went through the motions of donning a grass skirt and lei in preparation for the first wedding, but her heart wasn't in it—she wanted to go home and put on old 45s and wallow in her misery for a few hours, to cry Steve Mulcahy out of her system. She finally shook her malaise when the couple arrived, reminding herself that

this was their wedding day, and they deserved everything to be just right.

Even if they were a strange-looking couple.

Michelle Paddington and Thomas McDonald arrived
fully dressed—the stocky bride stuffed into a high-
necked, long-sleeve satin gown, her face obliterated by
a veil, the slender mustached man was half her size and
quite effeminate. But who was she to judge? They had
found love and she hadn't.

Still, she made a mental note not to make eye contact with Lincoln during the ceremony, else he would
laugh. Pathetically, she'd probably be looking at Steve
the entire time, anyway.

WHEN STEVE came out to the lobby in his Hawaiian
garb, he almost swallowed his tongue—Gracie was hard
to resist in holey sweatpants and a ragbag T-shirt, but
in a grass skirt, she was spellbinding. Her long slender
legs peeked through the grass all the way up to her…
was she wearing underwear? He blinked to refocus.
Probably a thong, which meant when she turned
around…

She turned her back and he caught the flash of the
curve of her behind. Yep—a thong. He closed his eyes
briefly. How he'd ever get through this wedding, he
didn't know. If she started dancing, he was liable to hit
his knees and beg her to let him mow her.

He greeted the couple, keeping one eye on Gracie.
They were a pitiful pair from Tacoma, Washington. Michelle Paddington was either practicing a religion that
required her to shield her face, or she was one ugly
woman. Meanwhile, Thomas McDonald was as gay as

the nineties, Steve was sure of it. Oh, well—there was someone for everyone.

Himself excluded.

The ceremony began and Steve walked the hefty woman down the aisle. Within a few steps, warning bells started going off—something wasn't right. Women, he had learned, walked straight ahead. Men, on the other hand, moved side to side when they walked.

Michelle Paddington was walking side to side— maybe she was a transsexual. In fact, looking at Thomas McDonald, maybe they both were—that would explain a lot. He deposited the bride next to the groom and gave her away on cue, then returned to the back of the chapel to check the camera. The more he watched the two of them through the lens, the more he was convinced that he was watching one of those couples on TV who wake up one day and decide to swap sexes.

It took all kinds, he supposed.

He straightened from the camera to have the best view possible of Gracie when she began her hula dance. His sex hardened instantly, remembering every detail of what lay beneath that grass skirt. He couldn't remember wanting a woman so badly...and wanting her again so soon. The strange chest pain that had been plaguing him struck again.

That olive pizza had been repeating on him all day.

When the ceremony concluded, Steve prepared to lip-synch "Hawaiian Wedding Song." When he was halfway through the song, something that had been niggling the back of his mind slid to the forefront—*Paddington.* He'd heard that name before, but it wasn't the name of a person...what was it?

He struggled to keep up with the song, trying to listen, read lyrics, and think at the same time—field agent training hadn't included karaoke under pressure.

Paddington was a *bank,* he remembered suddenly. A bank in Reno…

Owned by Mitch Lundy.

He continued performing, but took another look at the couple at the end of the aisle—the effeminate man, the masculine woman.

No…Lundy wouldn't dress up as a woman… would he?

You dressed up as Elvis, his mind whispered.

And wouldn't Lundy love boasting that he had gotten married right under the nose of an undercover agent? Fear bolted through Steve's chest—if Lundy had gone to such lengths to disguise himself and try to pull one over on the feds, then he knew who Steve was.

And everyone in the room was in danger, including Gracie.

Everyone was looking at him—he had stopped lip-synching. They knew something was wrong. Lincoln was rolling his hands frantically, trying to get him to continue.

Steve saw the "bride" lean over and whisper something to the "groom" and they started walking toward the door. He had no time to call for an arrest team to meet Lundy. The best he could do was call for backup. "Gracie, Lincoln, get down! Stop Lundy, FBI, you're under arrest!" He pulled his gun with one hand, radioed for backup with the other.

Lundy's "groom" bolted for the door. But Lundy ripped off his veil and grabbed Gracie, positioning her in front of him, jabbing a handgun under her chin. He glared at Steve, then laughed. "Almost had you fooled, didn't I, Berringer? I was really looking forward to telling all the boys about it over poker."

Steve's heart thudded in his chest—Lundy wouldn't think twice about killing Gracie, or Lincoln. Although since Lincoln had fainted and lay prostrate in front of the altar, he was no longer a concern.

"Let her go, Lundy!" Steve shouted. "The place is surrounded—you have nowhere to go."

Lundy laughed. "All the more reason to take a hostage with me, wouldn't you say?"

"Don't make me shoot you, Lundy."

"If you shoot me, I'll still be able to fire a round." He began to back up, working his way toward the door. Gracie's eyes were wide with terror.

Perspiration beaded on Steve's upper lip as helplessness raged in his chest. He held up his gun. "I won't shoot, Lundy, let her go." He hoped he didn't sound as desperate as he felt.

"I don't think so, Berringer. Like you said, I still have to get out of here."

Steve's mind raced—if the backup arrived, Gracie could be killed in the crossfire. He couldn't let that happen. Just as he started to lower his gun to shooting position, he spotted H.D.—lying on the floor directly in Lundy's path.

Good boy, he thought.

Lundy took a step back, tripped and fell hard, dragging Gracie with him, but the gun fell from his hand and spun away. Steve charged forward, "Roll, Gracie, roll!"

She did, rolling away from Lundy's grasp.

Steve stopped a few feet from the criminal he'd been chasing for years, a bead on the man's forehead. "Don't move, Lundy, or I'll shoot."

Unarmed and tangled in the ridiculous bridal gown, Lundy was powerless. He cursed a blue streak. "Man to man, you can't let me be taken into custody like this."

Steve smiled. "Oh, but I can." He lifted the radio to his mouth. "Karen, Lundy is secure."

"Glad to hear it," she said. "Your backup is outside, holding Lundy's girlfriend."

"Good," Steve said. "Call the TV stations. I'll be bringing Lundy out in ten minutes, and I think everyone will want to see this."

"Roger that," Karen said. "Civilians accounted for?"

Steve glanced at Gracie, cowering wide-eyed with Lincoln, who appeared to have come around. "Civilians accounted for," he said, breathing a colossal sigh of gratitude.

GRACIE SAT on the front steps of the chapel, dazed, watching FBI agents and reporters swarm the property. She didn't want to talk to reporters, but Lincoln had been happy to spill his guts—conveniently omitting the part about passing out, she presumed. H.D. lay next to her, snoring.

She watched Steve—minus the wig and sunglasses—as he talked to other agents and systemically cleared the area. One very pregnant female agent handed him a folder that he seemed interested in. Everything made sense now—why he had come, his covert behavior, the calls from "Karen," the mixed sexual signals.

He walked in her direction. Her pulse spiked, but she

remained seated to try and appear calm. He stopped in front of her, his expression apologetic. "I'm sorry… about everything. The half-truths and outright lies I had to tell, and especially for getting you in the middle of things. It wasn't supposed to happen like that."

She smiled. "That's the way life is, I suppose. Did I hear Lundy call you 'Berringer'?"

He nodded. "Agent Steve Berringer, at your service."

Not true, she thought. "So, Agent Berringer, where are you off to next?"

He shrugged. "Wherever the next assignment takes me."

"So you were just passing through?"

He nodded. "I'm afraid so."

Her heart squeezed. And she was just someone to pass the time with. He would move on to another assignment, find another diversion.

"I'm sorry about a lot of things, Gracie." He wet his lips. "But I'm not sorry about last night." Regret pinched his face. "I wish I had more to offer, Gracie, but I don't. You're looking for someone to settle down with, and marriage just isn't for me." He looked down at the folder in his hands, then extended it to her. "This is one small thing I can give you. I hope it helps you to find all that good luck you're looking for."

Gracie frowned in confusion, but took the folder. When she looked up, Steve had disappeared into the shadows.

CHAPTER TEN

"WE'RE GOING TO HAVE to hire a full-time receptionist," Cordelia said, her face all smiles, "so that you can concentrate on the ceremonies. Between the publicity the chapel got over the Lundy arrest, the restored Caddy and the new ad campaign you designed, business is booming!"

Gracie heaved a sigh, then sat down in the chair opposite Cordelia's desk. "Cordelia…while you're at it, you should advertise for a new wedding director, too."

"What do you mean? Are you leaving?"

Gracie summoned her strength, then nodded. "Yes."

Cordelia grinned. "Thank heavens!"

Gracie laughed. "That wasn't exactly the response I was expecting."

Cordelia came around to give her a hug. "Gracie, sweetheart, you know I love you, but it's time for you to spread your wings and fly. You're beautiful, you're talented and you're educated—you can't waste away here at TCB." She squeezed Gracie's hands. "Where will you go?"

"I'm not sure," Gracie said, thinking of the missing person's file that Steve had given her before he left. "I need to go to Oklahoma first and make peace with my family there, and visit my mother's grave. Then who knows? Maybe I'll just throw a dart at the map and see where it lands."

"Good for you," Cordelia said, and brushed Gracie's hair back. "I know you still miss him, sweetheart, but it's time to move on."

"Miss who?" Gracie asked lightly.

"You know who. But if Steve Berringer didn't recognize a good thing when he had it, then you don't need him."

"I know," Gracie said, her throat thick. "But I do love him."

"And you'll find love again," Cordelia promised.

Gracie took a cleansing breath and nodded. "I need to get ready for a wedding."

"Okay, we'll talk again before you leave."

Gracie returned to the lobby which was freshly refurbished with paint and new carpet that someone else would have to wear thin, she noted happily. She looked at the pictures on the bulletin board and thought how much she would miss seeing people starting new lives together, but was looking forward to this new and necessary chapter in her own life. One picture in particular caught her eye—the picture of her and Steve looking at each other that Lincoln had cropped from the original photo. She removed the pin holding the photo and ran her finger over his face.

She had met so many people at TCB over the years, now blurred faces and names. A few months from now, Steve Berringer's face would be just as fuzzy.

She could hope.

The new intercom beeped and Lincoln's voice sounded. "Gracie to the drive-through, please. Gracie to the drive-through."

She smiled—the world didn't stop for heartache.

She put the picture in her pocket and made her way back to the booth where Lincoln was working today, surprised to see Cordelia there as well.

"What's up?" she asked.

Cordelia nodded to the booth window. "We have a special guest I thought you might like to see."

Curious, Gracie looked through the window to the SUV waiting outside. Steve sat in the driver's seat, his expression anxious. Her heart thumped against her breastbone as she fumbled for the intercom button. Her brain raced with possible reasons for his return, but remembering her penchant for projecting what she wanted onto a situation, she reined in her galloping emotions. "What…what are you doing here?"

He hesitated. "I'm…proposing."

She squinted and crossed her arms. "Proposing what?"

He looked startled, then said, "Proposing marriage."

Joy leaped in her heart, but she wasn't about to let him off the hook that quickly. "What if I've found someone else in the three months you've been gone?"

His brow furrowed. "Have you?"

"No. But you don't call, you don't e-mail, you don't send a telegram all this time and now you just show up and propose?"

"I've been undercover," he said quickly. "I came here as soon as I wrapped up the case. I decided it was time for me to take care of business and get my life in order. I love you, Gracie. I can't stop thinking about you. Please…marry me."

Her toes curled, but she pursed her mouth. "And what if I say no?"

"I'll come back after every assignment and ask again until you say yes." He looked stricken. "Is that a 'no'?"

"No," she said.

His shoulders fell. "No?"

"No," she said with a grin, "that's not a 'no.'"

He looked confused. "So that's a 'yes'?"

She opened the sliding glass window. "That's a 'yes.'"

Steve leaned out, capturing her mouth in a hungry, happy kiss. "I've missed you."

"I've missed you." Her heart swelled with emotion and her eyes grew moist. This man was her home...they would start their own family. "My four-leaf clover finally kicked in," she murmured.

"So did mine," he said, his eyes shining with love. Then he looked up. "And somewhere, I think the King is smiling down on us."

In the background, someone put "Can't Help Falling in Love" over the speaker.

Gracie pressed her forehead to Steve's. "I love you," she whispered.

"I love you, too, Gracie."

Some things, she thought happily, really were meant to be.

PLAY IT AGAIN, ELVIS
Jo Leigh

CHAPTER ONE

THREE ELVISES—or was that Elvi?—came into the Five
and Diner and sat at the table directly across from Charlie Webster's. They had all chosen the white suit, the one
with the sequins and the big belt. Not bad on the hair.
The boyish wave over the forehead, even though none
of them was exactly a boy, and the sideburns, which
weren't just mutton chops but entire sheep, were all
disturbingly black. He watched, fascinated, as they chat-
ted. Even here, off the Strip, with no audience except
himself, a couple of other early birds and the waitress,
they kept up the Elvis-speak. Thankyouverymuch.

He tried the move himself. The insouciant curl of the
upper lip, the left brow arch, the southern drawl. He
sounded like a dork.

He shouldn't be watching them, he should be working. Molly needed some new material, especially since
the whole talk show thing was picking up steam.

She'd be great as a talk show host. Charming, hysterical, personable. She listened in a way most people—especially entertainers—didn't. It was exceptional
for a comic. Comics, in his humble opinion, were su-
premely self-obsessed, and he should know, he'd been
a comedy writer for almost ten years. Which didn't
seem possible.

How was it that he'd managed to get to the ripe old

age of thirty-one when he was still so incredibly immature? It was an enigma, but it was also a good concept
to pursue for Molly's routine.

He sipped some more coffee, wincing at how cold it
had become, and stared at his yellow legal pad. He'd
managed to do a fair amount of doodling—mostly eyes,
one palm tree, something faintly pornographic, but
when it came to actually writing comedy, he'd drunk a
lot of coffee.

The ugly truth was that his output had been lousy
lately. Not funny. Which wasn't good because being
funny was his thing. The reason he got paid. Not gener-
ically funny, but Molly Canada funny.

Her show at the Hilton had been running for two
years. In addition, there were her television appear-
ances, her voice-over work, her charity benefits and her
occasional trip to New York comedy clubs to try out routines. Which kept them all damn busy. Her manager Estelle, her director Bobby Tripp, Marley, who did her
makeup and hair and of course, him. A fine group of as-
sorted nuts who normally got along ridiculously well.
But since he'd fallen completely, deliriously, stupidly in
love with Molly, things had been a bit…dicey.

Since he'd never been in love before, he hadn't realized the ugly side effects. That his sappiness level would
rise to untold heights while his sense of humor would
be reduced to knock-knock jokes.

The Elvi laughed. He'd never realized there was an
Elvis laugh. His gaze went to their table, wondering if
they'd all ordered fried banana and peanut butter sandwiches. If there was an Elvis convention in town, which
would mean a person couldn't spit without hitting an
Elvis, and if Molly's audiences would be filled with lots
of dark-haired, white-suited impersonators. What did

one call a group of Elvises? A gaggle? A flock? Perhaps an entourage of Elvises. He liked that.

Okay, enough. To work. He put pen to pad and wrote down "Age, immaturity??? Molly's personal Elvis obsession? Why love sucks the big one?"

He sighed, disgusted with his own ineptitude. Where was the waitress? Turning, he saw the door open, and he nearly choked when he saw Molly Canada walk into the diner. Oh, crap, she looked great.

She wasn't the kind of beautiful that made men walk into light poles (well, he had that one time, but that was different). Her beauty was more subtle. Her hair color changed with her moods, her wardrobe was, okay, weird yet somehow chic and the woman couldn't stop biting her nails for the life of her. And her smile lit him up like a lightbulb.

"Yo, Charlie," she said, slipping into the booth across from him. She flipped her hair behind her shoulder as she took his coffee cup from the saucer and sipped. She winced. "Ugh, cold."

"What are you doing here?" He looked again for the waitress, caught her attention and waved her over. Molly wasn't an early riser. Perhaps she hadn't been to bed yet.

"Looking for you." Molly spread out on the plastic seat. She had on a tank top, purple, that sort of clashed with the vivid red of her hair, and low-riding jeans. Low enough to show off the tattoo at the small of her back. He loved that tattoo. He wanted to lick that tattoo.

"Why?"

She narrowed her eyes at him. Such a look. As if she could see right through him. Only, she couldn't because she had no idea. Not one. She saw him as good old Charlie. Buddy. Nerd. Eunuch.

"I'm obsessing," she said. "What if someone comes

on the show and I hate them. Or they're morons. Or I forget how to be funny."

"First, the show's not a done deal. Second, when it does happen, you're going to be brilliant. You've never had a difficult time talking to anyone in your whole life. I've seen you with morons, remember? Every time we go to L.A. You're still funny, you're still charming, and besides, no one's going to be looking at your guests. They're going to be looking at you. So stop it."

"Stop it?" She gasped dramatically. "Oh, okay. I will. Gee, thanks. If only I'd thought of that."

The waitress came over to the table with coffee and a menu. Molly turned over the second cup on the table but didn't look at the menu. "I'll have a waffle. And bacon. And two eggs, scrambled."

The waitress, who either didn't recognize Molly or didn't care, turned to him. "You want something to eat?"

"No thanks." He'd have plenty. Molly ordered like a football player and ate like a ballerina. He pretty much subsisted on her leftovers.

Once they were alone again, she leaned over the table. "What's with the Elvis contingent?"

He shrugged. "Even Elvi have to eat."

She nodded. "So, I see from the enormous blank space on your yellow pad that this hasn't been a morning filled with inspiration."

"I think my doodling has improved."

"Great. I'll do a slide show on stage. Charlie's Doodles, we'll call it."

"Hey. I'm trying."

"I know. So what gives? You've never had trouble. You're the rock. The man. The dude."

He doctored his fresh coffee, not knowing what the hell to say. "Writer's block?"

"Oh, no. You're not allowed to have any neuroses. I've got that covered for the both of us."

"Sorry, kiddo. I'm trying to get it in gear, but…"

"Okay, I've been thinking," she said, sitting up straighter, getting that fabulous determined look on her face. The one that made him want to slay dragons. "Let's do something on talk shows. What makes them weird. Why people watch them. Like that."

"Good. That's good. We can do that. There's everything from *Charlie Rose* to *Montel* to *Oprah* to *Springer.* Lots to mine."

"Exactly." She grinned.

It made his heart hurt. And yet, he said nothing. He sat there, smiling lamely, wanting desperately to tell her. To declare himself, to make her see that they were supposed to be more than co-workers. That they were, in fact, destined to be lovers. World-famous lovers. Bogie and Bacall. Napoleon and Josephine. Yeah, like that.

Which would, of course, elicit gales of hysterical laughter and perhaps a look of disgust that frankly, he wouldn't survive. So he remained quiet. Dying inside, but quiet.

"Let's eat, then put our heads together. That always works."

He nodded. Drank coffee. Wished he was someone else. Anyone else.

MOLLY SAT in her dressing room, staring at her reflection in the mirror. She should be getting ready. Her show started in forty minutes, and she needed some time after she was dressed to get herself into the groove. She had to shake this…

Charlie.

Something weird was going on with him. She couldn't exactly put her finger on it. He simply wasn't Charlie. Adorable, dopey, odd Charlie. Her best friend. The most wonderful partner ever. Actually, she'd only had one other, but eek, that had been a nightmare.

Rand had been a terrific comedy writer. Not as good as Charlie, no, but he'd had his moments. And he was sexy as hell. Tall, gorgeous, with a body to salivate over. They'd gotten together in Wichita, and at first it had been incredible. Slowly, things had gone south. She should have gotten a clue when she caught him with one of the other comics in a Podunk town outside of Michigan, but it was a guy, and they were both dressed, and well, she was pretty stupid. The really bad part was that it had almost destroyed her. Not that he'd been with a guy. What killed her was that he'd been with so many guys. Always promising to stop. Declaring his love. Claiming she was the most important thing in his life.

Ha.

She'd lost her timing. Almost lost her sanity. Until she'd had enough.

She couldn't lose Charlie. God, what would she do without him? He was the one thing in her life that totally worked.

She'd always been able to depend on him. To write the goods, to make her laugh, to keep her grounded. He was the big brother she'd never had. He was Charlie.

But lately he'd been distracted and nervous. The work wasn't up to par. No, something was going on with him. A woman? Hmm. Maybe. She hoped so. He should have someone. Of course, that someone would have to be special, because underneath his sad wardrobe and his lame haircut, he was a gem. He deserved the best.

She sighed as she opened her makeup bag and

started plastering it on. It really wasn't good for her complexion, but the lights were so severe they made her look dead if she didn't slather it generously. Heavy on the eyeliner and mascara. Dark lipstick. And then forget about the face, forget about wardrobe, just do the gig. Connect with the audience. Listen. Let it be the first time, the only time. And stop worrying about Charlie.

TWO O'CLOCK in the morning and he was still at the Hilton. In the showroom, sitting way the hell back in the sound booth, staring at his yellow pad. The rest of the room was dark and quiet. It was hours after the last show and he was alone.

Outside the doors were the tourists and the gamblers. Pushing the buttons, throwing the dice, cursing Lady Luck. He didn't indulge. It was too seductive for his simple tastes. There was this guy he knew who'd come to Vegas on a business trip, won eighty grand at the craps tables. Called his wife to pack up the house and move, 'cause he was a winner! Of course, a year later they were living in a trailer park on Sahara. It was just so easy.

People got crazy in Vegas. At least in that respect he fit right in.

He kept staring at his notes. He'd gotten it together enough to do a little riff. It needed some finesse, but there was something there. Probably all he was going to get for tonight. So why was he still here? Sitting with his watered-down soda, in the dark of the Hilton showroom, with all the empty seats and the big, blank stage.

He'd tried it, years ago. Getting up there... Well, not there. He'd done some comedy clubs in L.A. God, he'd stunk. Flop sweat, stammering, forgetting everything. He could write it but he couldn't do it. Which was fine with him. Watching Molly was enough. Knowing it was his material. Their material. They blended like milk and Ovaltine. A perfect pair.

His head dropped to his hands. This was not good. He'd go to the gym. Open twenty-four hours a day, it was a blessing to all the shift workers in town. Of course the whole town was open night and day. Supermarkets, dry cleaners, restaurants. There wasn't a thing around here that couldn't be had whenever the mood struck.

So he'd go. Work out. Run. Punch things. Yeah. Hitting was always good, especially when no one punched back.

He sat up, reached for his pen and that's when the lights went on. Not lights. Light. One light. On the stage. In the middle. A spotlight. On Elvis.

Yeah. That Elvis.

CHAPTER TWO

CHARLIE LOOKED at his soda. It hadn't tasted funky, but someone must have spiked it. At least he hoped someone had because if not, he'd just dived headfirst into the crazy pool.

"Hello, little brother."

It spoke. His hallucination spoke. And sounded like the best Elvis impersonation Charlie'd ever heard. "A joke. This is—" He spun around, expecting the camera crew. "Is this *Punk'd?* Or *Candid* whatsit? Ha ha. Very amusing. Now cut it out."

Only, there was no camera crew. Nothing he could see at least. But it was a big theater, and there had to be plenty of room to set stuff up. So he'd go along with it. Never let it be said Charlie Webster wasn't a good sport. "Hey there, Elvis," he said as he turned back to the stage. He sounded casual. As if this was just your usual wee hour of the morning visitation from a deceased celebrity.

Elvis laughed. Charlie realized that there was an Elvis laugh but the boys at the diner had it wrong. This felt completely genuine. A laugh that matched his memories of all those movies he'd seen. *Blue Hawaii. Girls! Girls! Girls! Kissin' Cousins.* Yep, this guy sounded like the real thing.

"It's me, little brother. Cross my heart and hope to die."

"Too late. You look damn good. Considering."

"Thank you."

"Come here often?"

Again, the laugh. And the voice was spot on, too. Now that he looked carefully, there wasn't a mistake anywhere. Not the hair, the outfit, the posture, the smile. Not that Charlie was an aficionado. Not like Molly. Man, if she could see this, she'd flip. She loved the King. Had every record and every film. If he wasn't absolutely sure she'd have him committed, he'd call her right now and have her come down.

"I hear tell Good Time Charlie's got the blues," Elvis said, stepping a little closer to the mike.

"Huh?" And that mike hadn't been there earlier. Had it?

"I can help."

"Help? With what? And why am I asking a hallucination?"

Elvis brought his hand to the stand mike, which is when Charlie saw that the mike itself wasn't what the Hilton used. It was older, boxier. Weird that he'd come up with a suitable mike for his dead friend.

"Well, son, you've got a burnin' love for that gal of yours, but you've got some work to do."

"Huh?" he said again, glad that he was a writer and could so readily come up with such witty bons mots.

"She's not gettin' the picture. You need to make some changes."

Blinking, Charlie wondered if his health plan would cover his therapy. He'd recognized a few song titles in that little speech, which was fine, except that he'd also found himself listening intently, hoping that Elvis, who was incontrovertibly dead, was going to help him with Molly. Uh-huh.

He leaned over the desk, starting to get a little annoyed at whatever the hell was going on. "Fine. Okay. All righty then. Tell me, Elvis. What kind of changes?"

The man on stage smiled. And if it wasn't Elvis, it was his clone, because, damn, that was friggin' Elvis Presley. No impersonator could be that good. That accurate. Right down to the dimples. Not the Elvis in the last years of his life, but in his prime. Jeez, he got it now. No wonder the ladies threw him their panties. Which was beside the point. "Well?"

"First things first. That hair. It looks like a raccoon up and died on top of your head."

Charlie blinked. "There's nothing wrong with my hair." Only, Elvis wasn't there anymore. The spotlight was still on and the mike was there—

"Son, you can listen to me and get your hard-headed woman to see you're her true love, or you can keep on bein' so square, baby, she won't care."

Charlie gasped. Elvis hadn't left the building. He was standing next to him. Right there. Close enough to touch.

Someone was doing this. Yanking his chain, big time. Who knew about Molly? He hadn't told a living soul. And how could…? Who could…? "Who are you?"

Elvis smiled. "You just follow my lead, son. Follow my lead."

Everything went dark. Totally black. Charlie was pretty sure he must be dead, but why would his last thoughts be of Elvis? John Lennon, maybe, but Elvis Presley?

The lights came back on. Not all of them, and there was no spotlight on the stage. That was dark. No mike, no guitar. No Elvis. It was just empty and big and Elvis-free.

"Oh, crap," he whispered as he fell back in his chair. "Seriously weird. *Twilight Zone* weird. I've been in Vegas too long."

He took in a deep, slow breath, and let it out in a sigh that didn't make him feel one bit better. "Least you could have said something helpful," he called out. "And there's nothing wrong with my hair!"

"I'M NOT KIDDING," Molly said, walking back to the lone tall stool in the middle of the stage. The audience was behind her, but she felt them. So good. They were digging her, ready for more, wanting to laugh, and it didn't get any better than this.

She turned, accustomed to the lights in her eyes, to not seeing the folks, but hearing them just fine. "So I was at this club in L.A. and it was crowded and there were all these studs spreading their tail feathers. This guy, and he wasn't exactly George Clooney, hell he wasn't even George "Goober" Lindsey, comes right up to me. Plants his boots, puts his hands on his hips, puffs up the chest. He looks me right in the eyes, then looks down. Yeah, there. He knows, see, that I'm gonna look, too. And, boys and girls, he's sporting the wood. We're talking major tenting. The pants. Did I mention the pants? Leather. Honest to God. Leather. Brown and so tight I could tell his religion. So we're both staring at it. It was impossible to turn away. It was, well, big. Mesmerizing. I couldn't move, not a muscle.

"I don't know how long we just stood there. Both of us looking at his crotch. But it was a while. Songs ended and new songs began. Finally, he says, 'Well? It's not gonna suck itself.'"

Waves of laughter poured over her and made her shiver she adored it so much. This was the biggest high known to man. Or woman. When it clicked, when they got it, when they loved her and loved her and loved her…

This was what she lived for. This was where it all happened, the rest was just a dress rehearsal. She didn't need a man. She needed a hundred men. And women. All of them right out there, watching, laughing. Loving her.

CHARLIE WAS still clapping when she met him backstage. She gave him an enormous hug before she turned around to take a curtain call. Damn, it had been a good night. Molly'd been on fire, and the crowd had been in the palm of her hand. He loved nights like this. They'd go out, celebrate. Get something good to eat, talk and talk. And she was her most creative when it was a great show. Some of their best routines had come from late-night sessions after a hot show. Not that he was going to be much help.

After a really good night's sleep, well, day's sleep, he'd come to the conclusion that seeing Elvis was a manifestation of his subconscious. That his subconscious was trying to tell him he was wacko sort of bothered him, but hey, at least there was an explanation.

He'd tried not to think about it, which hadn't worked at all. But now that he was going out with Molly, he could focus on his other unhealthy obsession, so okay.

Here she came again, practically bouncing with energy. She glowed. He always thought she was beautiful but tonight she was magic. She thumped into him, wrapped her arms around his neck and kissed him.

On the nose.

"Charlie, you are the man. The main man. The only man. You are…"

"A warm puppy?"

"A genius."

He wanted to be pleased. Really. But that nose thing…

"Where are you taking me? How about the Voodoo Lounge? No, too crowded. I don't want crowds. I know, let's go to Henderson, to PTs. I'll kick your ass at pool while you get me drunk."

Charlie laughed, hard and fake. "Anything you say."

She looked him in the eye, and he knew he'd been busted. Leave it to Molly to know him so well. Only she could have picked up the insincerity—

"Charlie?"

He rolled his eyes, trying not to look too embarrassed. "Yeah."

"Did you get a haircut?"

He blinked. "Uh, yeah."

"It looks really good. Let me go change. I'll be ten minutes. See if anyone wants to come. Not Gary though because he's been pissy all day, but if any of the other guys want to tag along…"

"Sure," he said, as she headed for her dressing room. "No problem. Wouldn't want us to be alone," he called after her, but she couldn't hear him. She was already gone.

He walked over to the mirror in the hallway that led to the dressing rooms. She'd noticed his hair. He checked himself out again, still shocked that he'd spent a hundred and forty dollars in a beauty salon. He'd asked for something cool. And he'd ended up with this kind of slick deal that required gel. He didn't get it. But the consensus amongst the hairdressers was that it was hot. Hot.

Twenty minutes later he and Molly were in the parking lot of the Hilton, making their way to his car. Just the two of them. The others would follow. He wasn't sure how many would show up, but for them, one o'clock in the morning was the shank of the evening. They did their sleeping during the day. Like vampires.

Molly had calmed down some, but her high wouldn't end until much, much later. It was like recharging a battery. The reverse was just as intense. If it went wrong, she crashed and burned, and it took a hell of a lot of coaching to get her back to level. No matter what the cause. It could have been her own timing, or a crappy audience. Either way, she let it get to her.

All the good ones did. The comics who weren't so jaded they phoned in their routines. Molly wasn't like that. She needed the folks in the crowd. Needed the immediate feedback. Her ability to make things fresh constantly amazed him. How she played off the audience and made each night's show her own was a wonder to behold.

They reached his convertible and Charlie opened the passenger door for Molly. The top was down and the night was beautiful, warm and clear. He'd have preferred a long drive to Red Rock or maybe Hoover Dam, but Molly loved to shoot pool, so they'd go to PTs where the music was loud, the drinks were strong, and at least he'd be with her. Which was better than not. Although if she ever kissed him on the nose again, he'd have to shoot himself.

She squirmed on the leather seat, watching him as he walked around the car. The moment he turned on the ignition she pounced on the radio. Groaning at his choice of NPR, she switched it to head-banging rock and turned the volume up so high it grounded air traffic from McCarran.

It took a while to get to the freeway, but not much longer to reach Henderson. Molly sang the whole way. Loudly. With fervor. Hitting him several times in the shoulder for emphasis. But finally, they were inside, and while Molly grabbed them an open pool table, he got drinks.

By the time he reached the table, she'd racked up for eight ball.

"Ready to take me on, Charlie?"

Just as he was about to respond, the music changed. Got Louder. It was him. Elvis. *Hound Dog,* baby.

Oh, yeah.

CHAPTER THREE

MOLLY HELD her cue loosely in her left hand as she reached for her drink with her right. She paused mid-grope because she couldn't stop staring at Charlie.

It wasn't just the hair, although, damn, it sure made a difference. She'd never thought about him with good hair. His had always been kind of long and dark and shaggy, with no real style at all. He didn't pay attention to that kind of stuff. Not his hair, not his clothes. He always smelled good, though. Mostly, he wore jeans and T-shirts, and when he had to dress up he wore plain slacks that didn't fit all that well, and nondescript shirts, ties, jackets. Never anything embarrassing. Just Charlie stuff.

This haircut… It looked good. She'd never noticed his cheekbones before.

She swallowed her shot of tequila and shivered as it slipped down her throat. Pool. They were going to play pool. "Wanna shoot for break?"

He shook his head. "Go ahead."

"Don't be so nice, Kemo Sabe. You'll curse me before the night is through."

"Only if I lose."

She blinked. "I'm sorry. Did you infer that you would beat me at this game?"

He smiled enigmatically.

"Oh, please. I'm going to kick your ass."

"You're going to try."

"Oooooh, you are so dead."

He walked toward the rack of cues on the wall, and she watched him, puzzling over this mystery. He never beat her at eight ball unless she did something stupid, like sinking the eight before the end of the game. And that didn't happen very often. So what was with this cocky attitude? No, not cocky. Confident. Which she expected when he was working, when he knew he'd hit on something good, but not here. Not in PTs, and certainly not at the pool table.

Maybe it was the hair? A sort of reverse Samson thing? Oh, please.

She got the white ball, put it in position and broke. The sound of the balls clacking together was balm to her soul. She loved shooting pool. Her own cue was being fixed at the moment, and she missed it deeply. But it wasn't the cue that made the game, it was the player.

She got stripes. And something was definitely up with Charlie. Usually, he sat at the closest table, nursed one beer all evening, and accepted defeat with grace. But there he was, standing, watching, rubbing the tip of his cue with blue chalk.

Molly focused on her shot. Stood up, pushed her hair back and this time she really concentrated. The ball missed the hole by a hair. Her gaze went right to Charlie. He hadn't moved, except he wasn't chalking anymore. His expression was different. A slight smile. Calm. As if he already knew the outcome of the game.

He turned a little to his left, and she sighed. Okay, there was her Charlie. He'd gotten chalk on his cheek. A rather large blue smudge. "Go for it, babe."

He came to the table, studied his options, and made

his first shot as smooth as silk. After a wink, a *wink!* in her direction, he got the four ball in the side.

On his way to his next shot, she stopped him with her hand on his arm. He looked at her questioningly. "Uh, you have some…" She wiped his cheek with the side of her thumb.

His whole posture changed. Sort of deflated. Weird. Very, very weird.

"It's still your shot."

He nodded. Lined up. And missed by a mile.

"Charlie, are you all right?"

"Fine," he said. "Just fine. Swell. Never better."

"Yeah. Right." She would have pursued it, but he turned, found a seat at the closest table, then signaled the waitress.

As promised, she kicked his butt. But it wasn't quite the victory she'd expected.

CHARLIE STOOD in his bathroom, staring at himself in the full-length mirror behind the door. He was naked. And very, very depressed.

He'd screwed the pooch. Come to think of it, that expression was deeply disturbing, but that was neither here nor there. The fact was, he'd messed up. It was the hair. The hair, thank you very much, Mr. Presley, had given him false hope, delusions of grandeur. For about half an hour, he'd been James Friggin' Bond. Cool. Calm. In control.

And then she'd wiped his face with her thumb. Much like his mother would have, if she'd been in PTs and not Ohio. First a kiss on the nose, then the fatal face wipe. And she'd won every game.

Yeah, that's what women want. Losers. He might as well have a big *L* tattooed on his forehead. Because there was no way Molly would ever see him as anything else.

"It was only your first night, little brother."

Charlie shrieked, covering his crotch with both hands. Elvis Presley was behind him. In his bathroom. His *bathroom*.

He spun around. His mouth opened, but no words came out. He would have rubbed his eyes but that would mean moving his hands.

"Calm down, son."

A sound came from Charlie's throat, but it wasn't really a word. More like a girly whine.

"You did good, son, with the hair." Elvis looked past him to the mirror and checked his own do. "And she noticed, now, didn't she?"

Charlie tried to get his breathing under control. He really couldn't hyperventilate, because, again, there was the hand issue. "You're not real."

Elvis smiled. "I'm real, little brother. But that's not the point. I told you before, you have to make some changes."

After another deep breath, Charlie, with as much dignity as he could manage, said, "Can one of these changes be putting on some pants?"

Another of those crooked smiles. "Sure thing." And then he was gone. Just…gone.

Charlie leaned back, yelping as his naked butt touched the cold mirror. This was getting seriously weird. Psychotic break weird. But he didn't want the men in the white coats to take him away while he was naked. Even crazy people need some dignity.

He opened the bathroom door, checked his bedroom for dead superstars, then hurried to his closet to grab some jeans and a T-shirt. Once he was dressed, he felt a little more in control. There must be an explanation for this. Something logical that wouldn't mean he was completely whacked.

"Clothes."

Charlie spun around. His personal ghost sat on the edge of his bed. He didn't imagine it was very comfortable. That big red belt had to cut into him. But Elvis seemed more concerned with Charlie's wardrobe than his own. "What about clothes?"

"Son, you're in a sad, sad way."

He looked down. The T-shirt was one of his favorites. Lenny Bruce on black. And these were his favorite jeans. "There's nothing sad about my way. I'm fine."

"Do you have her? Is she yours?"

"No."

"Then there are things to be done."

"Is this some kind of Faustian deal? I get the girl then spend eternity in hell?"

Elvis didn't answer for a minute. It gave Charlie time to really look at him. He sure seemed real. Much better-looking than Charlie'd ever imagined. That's what was so nuts. He'd never been all that big a fan. So why would his Harvey be Elvis? A six-foot invisible rabbit would actually have made more sense than Elvis Presley.

On the other hand, this was Vegas.

"I don't think so."

"Huh?" Charlie cringed. He had to stop saying that.

"I don't think you'll end up in hell."

"Wow, what a relief."

Elvis stood. He was tall, too. Jeez, if anyone needed wardrobe counseling... "This was from another time, son."

"So, you can hear my thoughts?"

"Seems so." He walked to Charlie's closet and flipped through the clothes.

"Great."

"It also seems I know quite a bit about your time. And, little brother, you're not dressin' like you should."

"Okay. So you hate my hair, and my clothes. Is there anything else?"

Elvis turned. "A whole lot."

Charlie sighed. "Oh, boy."

"Don't worry. I'll be there."

"That makes me feel so much better."

MOLLY DUG INTO her chicken chow mein as she listened to Estelle go over the latest in the negotiations for the talk show. There was so much to consider. Time to sleep, for example. If she taped the shows during the day, and did her thing at the Hilton at night, that would leave twenty minutes for all the other things in her life. Like eating, sleeping and, dare she even think it, dating.

Dating. Ha. The last time she'd been out with a guy, she'd fallen asleep before he'd gotten to first base. So humiliating. He'd been a total babe, too. Tall, blond, surfer-dude tan, pale blue eyes. So pretty. And so appalled. He'd shaken her awake. She'd tried to explain it wasn't him, but then he'd pointed out that she'd drooled on his satin pillowcase.

And that was one of her better dates.

"Are you listening to any of this?"

Molly put down her chopsticks. "Sorry. Sorry. I'm all ears."

"Good. Now, where's Charlie? He should be listening to this, too."

"I don't know. I thought he'd be here already."

"You'll catch him up. We have to decide what to do about the Hilton."

"So you don't think I can do both?"

"Molly, honey, how many shows do you do a week?"

"Eight."

"Right. And you'd have to tape five chat shows a week. There's no way you can handle both."

"I love doing the Hilton."

"And you'll love doing TV." Estelle dabbed her mouth with her napkin. She looked tired. She'd been working like a demon on this deal, and she had a lot of other clients. Big name comics. Of all the managers Molly could have hooked up with, Estelle was the best. She'd done everything right. Even during the whole Rand period, Estelle had been behind her. In fact, she was the one who'd hooked her up with Charlie. Bless her heart.

"What about a compromise? I cut back on the Hilton shows? Tape three days a week, do the Hilton three nights a week."

Estelle touched the side of her glasses. "I don't think they'll go for that, honey. That real estate is prime."

"Don't you have someone in the stable who'd like to do the other shows? Couldn't that be a solution?"

"I'll see what I can—"

"Estelle?"

"Oh, my God. That is nice."

Molly watched Estelle's mouth open as she stared at someone or something behind them. She turned, and it was perfectly clear what had changed her New York manager into Cletus the slack-jawed yokel. The man standing by the front entrance of the restaurant was seriously cute. But he needed to turn around. Not that the view of his ass wasn't worthy of concentrated focus, but she needed more. A face to go with.

"The shoulders. The butt. Must be a dancer," Estelle said. "Therefore, must be gay."

"Now come on. They're not all gay."

"Right. Wait, he's turning."

Molly watched, not even trying to be discrete. She simply stared. And nearly choked on her bamboo shoot.

Estelle gasped. "It can't be."

Molly blinked. Held her breath.

"It is. Oh my God that's…"

"Charlie."

CHAPTER FOUR

CHARLIE SPOTTED Molly's table. He closed his eyes for a moment, listening to "King of the Whole Wide World" in his head, the beat infusing him with a confidence he hadn't felt since, well, last night.

He'd spent a damn fortune on the new clothes. At The Forum Shops, no less. Everything from the ground up, so to speak, and nothing he would have picked out on his own. The salesmen seemed to think Charlie's poltergeist had taste. Which begged the question how had Elvis gotten said taste? Television in the great beyond? Fashion magazines? How would they get delivered?

He'd ask later.

He headed over to the table. Molly and Estelle had clearly noticed something different about him, but their expressions seemed more shocked than awed.

"Estelle, Molly." He sat between them and picked up his menu.

"What's this?" Estelle, who been his manager for seven years, looked at him as if she'd never seen him before. "I can't believe it." She leaned over and kissed him on the cheek. "You, my dear Charlie, look hot."

He felt himself blush, so he hid behind the menu. But he didn't look at it. Instead, he peeked over the top to see if Molly agreed with Estelle.

She didn't look like she was going to kiss him. Basically, she just looked confused. Really confused.

"What brought this on?"

He turned to Estelle. "Time for a change."

"It's fabulous. I had no idea. All these years and you were hiding behind those shlumpy clothes. Amazing. And that hair. Ms. Jones, you're beautiful without your glasses."

"Estelle…"

"I'm just saying. It's quite a difference."

"Thank you. I think."

"No, definitely a good thing. I mean, that ass. Molly, did you know about his ass?"

Back behind the menu, he actually tried to see the printed words, but gave it up. This blushing business had to stop. He peeked once more, wondering if Molly had an opinion about his ass, but nothing had changed. Perplexed? Weirded out? He couldn't be sure. But he didn't think it was good.

Estelle left the subject of his rear end to fill him in on the latest discussions with the network. He listened as well as he could with Molly staring at him so hard. The song came back. Only it wasn't so loud anymore. In fact, it was fading fast. What was she thinking? Why didn't she say something? What the hell was Estelle talking about?

"The exposure is going to be invaluable. I mean, look what's happened to Ellen. She's doing amazingly well. Right, Charlie?"

"Whatever Molly wants," he said, still watching Molly watching him. "I support her."

"You're seeing someone."

Charlie blinked. Finally, Molly had spoken. She hadn't made a lick of sense, but words had come out of her mouth. "Huh?" he asked, in what was quickly becoming his motto.

"The hair. The clothes. You've got a girlfriend."

Again, the blushing.

"Is that true, Charlie?" Estelle asked. "Who's the lucky girl?"

"I, uh—"

"It's that dancer, isn't it?" Molly leaned forward. "From the Rio. Laurel. That was her name. No, wait. It's Jana. Oh, my God, you're going out with Jana."

Estelle looked from Molly to Charlie. "Who's Jana?"

"She's a blackjack dealer," Molly said. She leaned back in her chair, looking mighty pleased with herself. "Damn, Charlie. Why all the secrecy? Jana's cool. We should do lunch or something. Invite her backstage. Jana. Wow. Does Bob know?"

"No."

"Seriously, Estelle. Jana's great. She could be a model, she's so pretty."

"Molly, wait."

"Wait? Too soon, huh? Just getting to know each other? She's funny, right? I mean, she gets your sense of humor?" Molly took a big drink of her iced tea. "You wouldn't go out with someone who didn't get you, that would be nuts."

"Uh, Moll…"

The waitress came to the table. Charlie ordered Crab Rangoon and a beer, welcoming the interruption. He needed to get it together here. Molly seemed awfully glad he was dating someone. Else.

"Charlie?" She looked at him expectantly.

God, she was amazing. She'd pushed her hair back with one of the bands that he associated with grade school girls, but on Molly, it worked. Everything worked. From her green T-shirt to the tiny little mole on her cheek, she was…

"Charlie?"

"I'm not dating Jana."

"No?"

He shook his head.

Molly's hand came up. "Don't tell me. I want to figure it out myself."

"But—"

"Listen, kids, I have to go." Estelle stood up, kissed him on the cheek, kissed Molly on the lips, which made him wonder about a lot of things, but then it was just him and Molly.

For about five hot seconds.

"I've got pilates," she said, as she pulled out her wallet. "Sorry, but you were late."

"Uh—"

She threw down a twenty, ruffled his hair with her hand, then walked out of the restaurant.

Ruffled his hair. Kind of like what he did to his five-year-old nephew. What he'd never do again, that's for damn sure. "Thanks a lot, Elvis."

"Uh, it's Eileen," the waitress said from behind his right shoulder. She put his appetizer and beer down, and walked away, shaking her head.

Charlie sighed.

"YOU'D BETTER tell me, Bobby. I swear, if you don't, I'll…"

"What'll you do, Molly? Take away my lunch money?"

Molly crossed her arms over her chest and frowned. They were in her dressing room at the Hilton, and damn Bobby Tripp, he wasn't giving her anything. If anyone

knew who the new woman in Charlie's life was, it had
to be her director, even though Bobby wasn't around so
much these days. He was working a new show at Star-
dust with a bright young comedy team. But he talked to
Charlie all the time. Aside from her, Bobby was Charlie's best friend. "Come on, Bobby, this is important."

"What do you care who he's seeing?"

She got up and grabbed a soda for herself and one
for Bobby from the small fridge in the corner. "I don't.
He can see whoever the hell he wants as long as it
doesn't interfere."

"With what?"

She sat again. Looked at the pictures that lined her
big makeup mirror. Charlie was in a lot of them. Most
of them. "We're on the brink, here. All of us. It's the
most important time in our careers."

"And?"

She looked at Bobby. He wasn't dense. In fact, he
was one of the brightest men she'd ever met. He was
also a weird little guy, short, skinny, with a pixie nose
and an ear for comedy that couldn't be beat. "Have you
seen the new, improved Charlie?"

"It doesn't matter. Even if he'd gotten a damn Mo-
hawk, who cares? He's not going anywhere."

"It's not just his hair. He was wearing Hugo Boss."

Bobby sat back. He pulled a cigarette from the pocket
of his denim shirt and slowly lit up. "Hugo Boss," he
said finally. "That changes everything."

"Smart-ass. The point is, he's…different."

"So what? You think he's fallen for someone? Well,
good for Charlie. Although why I haven't heard anything about it…"

"That's right," she said, jabbing her soda his way.
"Distraction. He's been acting weird for months now,

and why is that? Huh? Because he's fallen for someone who's…"

"Who's what?"

"Bad."

Bobby laughed. "Bad?"

"If it was someone, you know, cool, then we'd have met her by now. Am I right?"

"Charlie's a funny guy. He's private. For all we know she's a kindergarten teacher from Henderson."

"You have to find out."

"I'm not gonna pry. If he wants to talk to me about it, then I'll listen, but I won't press him. And you, young lady, better not, either. Charlie's the most sensible guy I know. If he hasn't told us about her, I'm sure he's got his reasons. So let it go."

"We have some really important decisions to make, and soon. How can we do that if he's hiding this woman? It stinks, Mr. Tripp. And I think Charlie's in trouble."

"You do your own dirty work." He stood up. "I've gotta go. And you need to chill."

"I'll chill when I know what's going on."

Bobby came up to her and kissed her on the cheek. "Careful, honey. Charlie's a keeper. Don't do anything to screw it up."

"Yeah, yeah. Get out of here. Who needs ya?"

"You do, my love. We all need each other."

She stood up, gave him a huge hug, then let him go, although she didn't let go of her worry.

Something was going on with Charlie. She did not have a good feeling about it. Even though, she had to admit, he had looked damn good. Who'da thunk it? Charlie looking sharp, like a movie star. Hell, she'd been around when they'd shot *Ocean's Eleven* at the

Bellagio and he would have fit right in with Brad and George. Which made no sense.

Charlie was the most humble man in show business. He never made a fuss, never needed the spotlight. He would have been perfectly content to be the silent partner. She'd insisted he get credit. Everyone on the Strip, in the whole comedy world, understood Charlie's talent. Everyone but Charlie.

He could be such a dope sometimes. In the years she'd known him, he'd dated. Not a lot, but enough. And not one of the women was good enough for him. They either took advantage of his kindness or they didn't appreciate the weird way his mind worked. But one thing was for sure, he'd never gone to this much trouble for any woman before.

He just didn't care about that stuff. The clothes, the do. He was unassuming and sweet. One of the last of the true nice guys.

And she wasn't about to let him get hurt. Not on her watch.

She looked at the time. It was still early, and if she was smart, she'd get some rest before the first show. Yeah. Rest.

CHARLIE SAT at the farthest end of the little bar. He'd been nursing a scotch and soda which was pretty much just melted ice by now, but he couldn't be bothered to get another one. The bartender had gotten the message after the fourth attempt to freshen his drink.

There were others at the bar, but they were mostly on the other, better-lit side of the room. Playing video poker. Laughing, drinking, having a swell old time.

He'd bet good money that not one of them had seen Elvis in their bathrooms. Lucky bastards.

Elvis Presley. It made no sense. Well, duh. Elvis was dead. For real. Maybe, instead of listening to the stiff, he should just call the *Enquirer.* Make some of the money back that he'd spent on clothes.

No, he'd be too embarrassed to tell anyone, even a reporter, that he was being visited. Visited. What a joke. Tormented. That was more like it. Being driven to the brink of insanity.

And for what? Molly didn't see him as anything but Good Old Charlie. She was thrilled that he was dating. Anyone but her.

The jukebox changed songs. Guess who.

"Bartender? I'll take another. Make it a double."

CHAPTER FIVE

MOLLY STRIPPED. Everything except her panties. She threw the clothes on her bed on top of the five other outfits she'd rejected and opened her closet again.

There was no time to go shopping. In fact, she was already fashionably late for the party, and at the rate she was going she'd get there ten minutes after the booze ran out.

Damn party. She didn't want to go. But she had to because the network people were going to be there, and she had to be sparkling and charming and funny and sexy and yeah, right. What she wanted was a few choice pints of Ben & Jerry's and a tablespoon.

At least Charlie would be there. At least, she thought he would be there. They hadn't talked all day. She'd left messages, but he hadn't returned her calls, which, now that she thought about it, was damn weird, and who was this woman he was dating, anyway?

Oh, God, he was going to bring her.

"So what?" she said aloud. She was probably someone Molly knew, so no biggie, right? Or maybe it was someone from his gym. If it was, she was probably hot. Of course she was hot. Charlie wouldn't go out with someone icky. Although she might not be sizzling, more quietly seductive.

It didn't matter. Whoever she was, as long as she wasn't… As long as she was…

She'd better be nice, that's all. Nice and sweet and she'd better treat him like the wonderful guy he was, and she'd better not even think of interfering with their partnership, because oh, baby, if that bitch tried one thing to screw up this deal…

"Get a grip," she said. Out loud. "And get dressed."

She flipped through clothes, most of them picked up at secondhand stores, but some of them given to her by big name designers for awards shows and premiers. Her hands stopped on a silver dress. "Ah-ha."

She gave it a once-over. It was small. Not tight so much as not much there. Short, spaghetti straps, low cut. Sex on legs. She slipped it on, went to the mirror, and smiled. "Hell, I'd do me," she said.

But, she still needed makeup. And to fix the hair. So get your ass in gear, Molly.

HER CHEEKS HURT from smiling. She'd talked to the executive in charge of programming, the executive in charge of daytime, the executive in charge of production and if there were any more executives in charge of anything, she didn't want to know about it.

Estelle was flying, helped along on the wings of Johnnie Walker Red, but it was okay, because it looked an awful lot like this thing was going to happen. That *The Molly Canada Show* was going to be on the air, five days a week. With guest stars and everything. She'd already started her list, topped by Jude Law. Well, she wasn't stupid.

And while she'd been funny, etc., etc., she'd also been acutely aware that one Charlie Webster was missing in action. She'd been late almost two hours ago. All the shrimp cocktail was gone, the ice sculpture had melted into something vaguely scary, and her feet hurt.

Dammit, where was he? He never missed stuff like this. See, this is why she was suspicious, and Bobby Tripp could just take all his "calm downs," and shove them where the sun don't shine. Whoever this babe was, she was definitely trouble, and something must be done.

Molly got herself another drink, a killer apple martini, and set out to find Mr. Tripp. She air-kissed far too many people, including some of the hottest acts on the Strip, all of whom congratulated her on the show, and pitched for a guest spot for themselves, which actually felt pretty freakin' good, but Bobby was nowhere to be found.

The music, which had been piped into the penthouse suite all evening, changed from Top 40 to something that calmed her immediately. Elvis. Always good for what ailed her. Appropriately, the song was "Suspicion." She took another sip of her drink, and that's when Charlie walked in.

Charlie and a woman.

A strange woman. Not odd, but someone she didn't know. A total hottie, which made sense because, holy crap, Charlie looked amazing. His hair was all uh-huh, and he had on a suit that was so cool it refroze the ice sculpture.

She wore a Band-Aid masquerading as a blue dress, with heels that had to be causing serious damage, and the look she gave Charlie was such a blatant invitation, Molly blushed.

To make matters worse, the chick, bottle-blond and a piss-poor job of it, touched his sleeve. It was one of *those* touches, the kind that pretend to be all casual and innocent, but are really the keys to the bedroom door. Molly knew all about those touches. She and Charlie had done a whole routine about them. She still used it from time to time. The routine and the touch.

She headed toward the door, but she was stopped by a hand on her arm. It was Kelly, one of the dancers from Splash.

"Is that Charlie?"

"Yeah."

"What the hell happened to him?"

"He was on *Extreme Makeover.*"

"Well, damn, it sure looks good on him."

"Excuse me." Molly continued through the big living room, converted by the hotel staff into party central, watching the reaction of the womenfolk to the new Charlie. It was ridiculous. For heaven's sake, it was still just Charlie. But everyone who knew him looked stunned. As if he'd been transformed into… someone else.

"Molly."

"Charlie."

His smile looked so innocent. As if he didn't know. "Who's your friend?"

His brows came down and his smile faded. "Friend?"

She let her eyes move to her right, but only her eyes. Charlie's face didn't change. And then it did. "Oh."

"Yeah. Oh."

He turned to the blonde. "Felicity, this is Molly Canada. My partner."

Felicity giggled. "Oh, I've been to your show. You're so funny."

"Yeah, I'm a scream."

Fluttering eyelashes this time, in addition to the giggle.

"I'm sorry I'm late."

She looked at Charlie again. "No biggie. Just our future."

"Did something happen?"

"I spoke to them."

He put one hand in his slacks pocket. Only it was sexy. Smooth. Like he was, well, debonair. "Them?"

"The executives."

"Oh."

She raised a scathing eyebrow.

"And?" he asked.

"They wondered where you were."

"Really?"

She sipped her drink. "Well, they didn't actually say the words, but I could tell they were thinking it."

"I see."

"So, uh, why where you late?"

Charlie smiled. It was far too knowing. "You want another drink?"

"Yes."

"Good." Then he walked away, toward the bar. Leaving her and Felicity in his wake.

"He's really cute," Felicity said.

"Bite me." Molly walked away, not feeling the least bit repentant. She followed Charlie, determined to get to the bottom of this whole thing.

Before she reached the bar, Kenny Burrell, one of the choreographers from *O,* sidled up to Charlie. They'd been friends for a while, and Kenny would understand when she shooed him away.

Except, why was Kenny's hand on Charlie's ass?

Charlie seemed as surprised as she was, but Kenny just laughed and wandered away.

This was worse than she expected.

"Aha," he said. "I just put your order in."

"Kenny put his in, too, I see."

Charlie looked a little panicked. "Uh—"

"It's okay, Charlie. I understand. If you want to go…"

His face got all red.

"I'm kidding. I know if you were gay you'd have much better taste."

He smiled, turned to find Kenny standing with his crew. "I don't know. He's pretty cute."

"Which is what Felicity said about you."

"Really?"

"Charlie, what the hell's going on?"

"What do you mean?"

She sighed. "Come on. The hair. The clothes. The new 'tude. If it's not Felicity, it's someone."

"You're right."

"I knew it. Tell me she doesn't want you to quit. Please tell me."

"She doesn't."

"Thank God." Molly picked up her drink. "So who is she?"

Charlie got his own drink and took a sip. "What's that song they're playing?"

She didn't even have to think about it. "'Devil in Disguise.'"

"Elvis, right?"

"Yeah, it is, and stop avoiding the question."

He looked at her through narrowed eyes. "Molly, you don't look like you're having a very good time. This party is for you."

"It's for us."

"No, babe. It's *The Molly Canada Show*. It's gonna change a lot of things."

"You're starting to scare me."

"Don't be scared. Be excited. You deserve this."

"We do. We. Not just me. We're partners, remember?"

He gave her a crooked smile. It disconcerted, that smile. Because it wasn't really Charlie. Not her favorite buddy. Not the guy that she'd call at three o'clock in the morning when she couldn't sleep. The guy who knew just when to buy her something shiny, how to lift her moods, who didn't care when she was a first-class bitch, but loved her all the same. This was Charlie's hot brother. A doppelgänger. And she didn't know what to do with him.

"We're partners," he said. "But it's your show all the way."

"I wouldn't be here if it wasn't for you."

"Yes you would. You'd have found someone else to write with."

"No."

"Yeah."

"I don't want someone else."

"Good."

"So, does this mean you're not leaving?"

"Why would I leave?"

She stepped back, looked him over from top to toe. "Who the hell are you, and what have you done with Charlie?"

He laughed. "It's me, kiddo. Just new wrapping."

"Nope. That's not all. It's this woman. I know she's doing something. And Charlie, please believe me, I want you to be happy. But I also want you to be careful."

"I'm a big boy."

She touched his wrist. Held on a little. "I'm not kidding."

"Neither am I. Now, where are those executives we're supposed to schmooze?"

She didn't want to end the conversation, but this wasn't the time. He'd admitted all this was over a woman, but clearly it wasn't Felicity. It wasn't anyone here.

Why wouldn't he tell her? It was going to drive her

insane, that's all. Insane. But for now, they had another
hour at least of pressing the palm. She led him toward
the gaggle of execs huddled together halfway between
the bar and the door. "I don't remember any of their
names, so introduce yourself first."

"Got it."

"And say good things about me."

"What else is there?"

"I'm not kidding."

He stopped, which stopped her. She looked at him.

Charlie looked right back. And once again, she was
off center, not at all sure who she was with. "I'm not kidding either," he said.

Before she could ask what he meant, one of the suits
came right up to them, and Charlie handled him like a
pro. All she could do was stand back and watch the
magic. He'd never been good with the business side.
That's why they had Estelle. But he had all of them
cracking up. Smiling. Patting him on the arm.

Weird. So incredibly weird.

FINALLY, they were able to leave. Half the crowd had already gone, including Felicity who left with one of the
suits when Charlie didn't heel, but they'd waited until
the network folks left. Then they beat feet to the elevator.

Molly listened to Charlie chatter about the night,
about the show, about everything but what she wanted
to talk about. It would kill her to go home without knowing. She'd never get to sleep, and dammit, she needed
to sleep.

When they got to the casino floor, there was no use
trying to talk. Not over the sounds of the slots and all
those tourists. So she waited. But the second they were

outside, well, after they gave their tickets to the valet, she pulled him over to a quiet corner.

"What?" he asked.

"Charlie. Tell me."

"Tell you what?"

"Don't make me get snippy. Tell me who this woman is."

He laughed. Laughed! "Molly, you are too much."

"Screw that. Just give it up. I can't stand this another minute."

"Did I tell you tonight that you look gorgeous?"

She lifted her hands to wring his neck. "Charlie."

"You do. You were the most beautiful woman there."

"Flattery will only get you killed."

He laughed again. Looked behind her. "My car."

"I don't care about your car. I want to know who this woman is that's turned you into Brad Pitt."

He looked at her for a long moment, and just as she was going to whack him a good one, he grabbed her upper arms, pulled her close and kissed her.

It definitely wasn't a Charlie kiss.

Not the old Charlie, that is.

She parted her lips as her stomach did flip-flops, and then it wasn't just a kiss but a *kiss* and holy crap, her whole world turned upside down and sideways.

When he let her go, she had to remember how to breathe. How to think.

He walked past her. She turned, knowing her mouth was open and that she must look as shaken as she felt. But he just smiled again. And got in his car.

CHAPTER SIX

CHARLIE RODE down Las Vegas Boulevard with the radio pumping out rock and roll. Molly's station. Loud. And he sang.

The wind whipped his hair, the moon shone down on his smiling face, and he didn't even care when the driver of a Toyota nearly ran him off the road.

He'd kissed her.

Boy, he was flying. The look on her face! And damn if it wasn't the best exit known to man. He'd been cool as a cucumber, which was also an expression he should include in Molly's routine, but that wasn't important right now. What was important was that he was *the man*.

He howled. Then coughed for awhile, but that didn't matter. It had to be the clothes. The clothes and the hair. Both. That Elvis thing. Yeah. Elvis.

He'd just been, you know, going through a phase. He hadn't really... I mean, that would be nuts. Elvis was dead, and besides, he hadn't been around even once today. Nope, Charlie had dressed himself.

Which, now that he thought about it wasn't something to necessarily brag about, but screw it. He'd picked out the clothes. After only half a dozen tries.

They'd been a hit. Molly had thought he was with Felicity. Ha. A couple of days ago he could have saved

Felicity from a gang of marauding bikers, and she wouldn't have given him a second look, but tonight? She'd given him the touch.

He knew about the touch. And the hair flip. And the fluttering laugh accompanied by the giggle. He knew about women. Oh, yeah.

He put his right arm over the passenger seat back. Slicked his hair with his left hand. If it wasn't completely dark out, he'd have put on his sunglasses, because that's just how cool he was.

"So you think you got it made, do ya, little brother?"

The car swerved to the left and he had to grab the wheel with both hands to avoid the bus. "Shit!" He looked at Elvis, sitting right there, the white suit glittering in the moonlight. "What the hell are you doing? We could have been killed."

"We?"

Charlie stared at him. Elvis *was* dead. A dead man was in his passenger seat. Nope, it didn't make any more sense now than it had in the Hilton showroom. Or his bathroom. Or The Forum Shops.

"What's the matter, Charlie? You did good tonight, son."

"Damn straight I did good. Did you see her face?"

"Uh, son?"

"Yeah?"

"You'd best look at the road."

Charlie's head snapped front and he jerked the wheel. He smiled as the nice man in the Porsche gave him the finger. Once his heart calmed down to mere panic, he glanced, briefly, at Elvis. "What now?"

"Why don't we get home, then we'll talk."

"Home? What, you're moving in?"

"Until it's over."

"My life?"

Elvis laughed. "No, son. Until you get the girl."

Charlie thought about that for a minute. "Why?"

"Because you need help."

"So you're here because I'm pathetic?"

"Yep."

"Great." He turned off the radio. Eased up on the accelerator. He'd been the man. The dude. And now?

"You're on the right road, so don't you fret."

"Why not? It's something I do so well."

"You looked fine out there tonight. Miss Molly was impressed."

"Miss Molly's worried about the act."

"That's true. She just doesn't know yet, that's all."

"Know what?"

"That you're the man she's supposed to be with."

Charlie gaped. Then looked back at the road. "Okay, you were right. Let's get home, then we'll talk."

It didn't take that long to pull into his driveway, but in the interim he'd come up with about a zillion questions. Why he hadn't asked them before perplexed him, but he sure as hell was going to ask them now.

He got out of the car and nearly had heart failure when Elvis popped up in front of him. "Don't do that."

"Maybe I should drop by another time."

Charlie reached for his arm, and grabbed a bunch of nothing. He recovered quickly, though. "No. Tonight. I need some answers."

Elvis took off his big old sunglasses just to arch his right brow.

"First of all, why me?"

"Why you?"

"Don't be doing that repeating thing. We'll be here all night."

A sigh, a shift of those legendary hips. "All right."

"So?"

"I don't know."

"Huh?"

"I said, I don't know why it's you. I never know why."

"You don't?"

Elvis shook his head, dislodging a thick strand of hair so it flopped over his forehead.

"But you've done this a lot, right?"

"A few times."

"Does it always work?"

"I wish it did."

Charlie sighed and leaned against his car. "So all this could be for nothing?"

"I hope not."

"You can come back from the dead, but you can't see the future? What kind of bull is that?"

"It's the way it works."

"What else haven't you told me?"

"I don't follow."

"Come on, *big brother*. What else?"

"Just this. It's up to you."

"Huh?"

The left corner of his mouth lifted. Just like in the movies. "In the end, it's up to you."

Charlie opened his mouth, but the word turned into a yelp as Elvis disappeared. "Oh, crap."

He turned in a complete circle, looked in the front seat, the backseat, across the street, but Elvis had left the building.

"You bastard!" He looked up to the heavens, then realized that was the wrong direction. "Don't leave me like this. I don't know what to do."

MOLLY CRAWLED into bed, turned off the light, and stared at the dark ceiling. She'd been home for over an hour, and she still couldn't stop thinking about Charlie.

She was the woman he'd changed for? Her? No. That was just crazy. Because Charlie was…Charlie. Her buddy. Her pal. Her partner.

And the best kisser on the planet.

She turned over. Punched her pillow. No. This was not good. Not even a tiny bit good. It was the opposite of good. Which would be, uh, bad. Well, okay. It was bad. Bad that Charlie thought about kissing. Her.

"Shit, shit, shit."

Of course, his timing was impeccable. Now, after all the years they'd been working side by side with not a sign, not a whisper that he wanted anything else, bang, just as she was being given the biggest opportunity and challenge of her life, he has to pull this? Nice, Webster, real damn nice.

"Idiot," she said, fighting the urge to call him and say it again. "Moron. We're getting a nationally syndicated show, and you want to play footsie? Not a chance."

The pillow got a few more punches, but at least she had a focus now. Anger. She was *angry*. What was he thinking? They couldn't kiss. Or, heaven forbid, sleep together.

The thought made her stomach clench. Not in the way she expected.

Oh, crap.

She took a deep breath. And remembered.

It had seemed so perfect. Loving Rand. They'd worked together like a dream, and when they first made love it was magic. None of that hearts and flowers junk, just hard and nasty in the best possible way. They'd been animals. She had to touch him all the time. Couldn't get enough. She'd been delirious with happiness, never better on stage, and together they'd written some of the funniest stuff ever.

And then it had all gone to hell. Not just their relationship, but everything. The writing. The comedy. Her self-worth. Her sanity. Rand had nearly sent her back to Ohio, and she'd sworn she'd never go back there. Not to her dismal hometown, or her alcoholic mother. Not to working dead-end jobs that made her want to scream. She'd hated it there, and yet, it had seemed a viable alternative to being in the same room as Rand. Being in the same state.

She would not do that again. Charlie was as different from Rand as pickles were from whipped cream, but it didn't matter. They were writing partners. She'd stretched it into friends, and even that had been scary. So his kiss had given her goose bumps. So her whole body had melted despite the fact that she'd never been so shocked in her life.

Honestly, she loved him. But she wasn't in love with him, and never could be. Absolutely not. Charlie needed to find a nice girl, someone who wasn't insane, who didn't live her kind of life, who knew how to treat a guy. How to keep a guy.

She was the absolute worst thing he could do to himself. Bonehead. Why did he have to go and fall in love with *her?*

Love? That was probably jumping the gun. Lust. Yeah, okay. It happened. They spent a hell of a lot of time together, and he didn't get out much. But still. Dumb. Stupid.

He had to know she was lousy with guys. That her preferred M.O. was hit-and-run. Bobby kidded her all the time that she was more of a guy than he was. She didn't mind. It worked for her. She'd get her ya-yas out, no harm, no foul, nobody got hurt.

Is that what Charlie wanted? A night of no-holds-barred rumbling?

She thought about it for a moment. Okay, ten moments, and the idea had its own warped appeal, especially now that Charlie had gone *GQ*, but no. Not smart. She could see all kinds of complications, the biggest being that Charlie was a sweetie. A true-blue romantic. He's the only guy she knew who never failed to send her tulips on her birthday. His presents… Jeez, he remembered everything, and when it came to gifts, he was spot on.

Last year, on her birthday, he'd gotten her a really rare collector's edition of *Elvis Live* on vinyl, no less. She knew for a fact he'd had to do some serious searching and that it wasn't cheap. But she'd mentioned in a casual conversation shortly after her birthday the year before that she'd love to have it.

He was amazing. Some woman would be incredibly lucky to have him. ·

Damn, but he'd looked fine. It was quite the transformation, worthy of *The Swan,* but the truth was, Charlie hadn't changed anything but the outside.

When she told him there was no way, would that change his insides?

He was such a sensitive guy. And how he'd looked at her the moment before he'd kissed her. She'd probably remember that look long after she'd forgotten the feel of his lips. The way he'd tasted. The heat in his hands, in his body.

She moaned. Turned over.

Oh, yeah. She was gonna get a real good night's sleep. Uh-huh.

CHAPTER SEVEN

"HEY, CHARLIE."

At the whispered voice behind him, Charlie turned although he didn't want to. Molly was onstage, and it was another incredible night. There was nothing like watching her hold an audience in the palm of her hand. Almost nothing.

It was Sam Masters, an up-and-coming comic he'd known slightly for a couple of years. "How you doin'?"

"I'm good." Sam nodded past the curtains. "She's on fire."

Charlie smiled. "You got that right."

"Which is kinda why I'm here," Sam said. He moved a little closer, right into Charlie's space.

"You trying to steal her material? Have you given any thought to being a little more discreet?"

Sam laughed. "Funny you should say that."

Now Charlie was worried. He didn't know Sam well, but he did know the man was something of a hound dog, to quote Charlie's favorite dead friend.

Sam gave him a look. A really uncomfortable long look. "I see you've been making some changes."

"Uh-huh."

"And word is, it might be more than just, you know, the Armani."

"Oh?"

"Yeah, so" he glanced at Molly again, a little nervously. "I just wanted to let you know that I'm, uh, looking."

"For?"

"A writer, man."

Charlie laughed. "Thanks, Sam, but I'm not—"

"Well, think about it, okay? Whatever you're making, I can match it. More than match it."

"I'm not looking to make a change," Charlie said. "Not that kind, at least."

Sam's gaze darted back to Molly. "Okay, sure. No sweat. But do me a couple of favors, okay?"

"That depends."

"Don't dismiss the offer out of hand. And don't tell Molly."

"Yeah, yeah. Get out of here, ya mook."

Sam punched him in the shoulder. Hard. "You're a good man. I could use your talents."

"They're taken."

Sam raised his bushy eyebrows, then headed to the stage door while Charlie wondered, for maybe the zillionth time what the hell was going on. Everything had been screwy since his nocturnal visit from you-know-who. He still didn't understand why Dead Elvis wanted him to succeed with Molly. Okay, maybe the question should still be why Dead Elvis at all?

On the other hand, why not? Why not Elvis, and why not miracles and why not Charlie as a hottie, and why the hell not Molly and Charlie making it? Going the whole nine yards? Stranger things had happened. Not that he knew of personally, but hey. Stuff like this probably went on all the time, and no one talked about it because, well, Dead Elvis.

He listened to the rhythm of Molly's routine, waiting for the laugh. Not yet, not yet…

There. Damn. Killer material. Together they'd made that. Sitting in diners, in the empty showroom, on her ugly couch. The best times of his whole life. Everything was better when it was Molly. Her laugh. Her smile.

She turned, making her way to her water glass, and he grinned at her. Gave her the old thumbs-up.

Usually, at this point, she'd wink, get the water, then move right into the bit about her mom. Only, she didn't. She just stared at him. Mouth slightly open, eyes unblinking. The laughter from the audience had faded, and if she stood like that for another minute, they were going to get mighty itchy.

"Go," he said, waving at her frantically.

She got her water, turned with flare and fell apart.

Charlie's breath caught, and he watched her flail on stage, trying to pick up the bit, searching for her groove, but it was like watching a car accident. Her cheeks turned pink, she gripped the mike like a lifeline, and he was already halfway to yanking the curtain.

Then she stopped. Laughed. Took a deep breath, and started again.

Okay, she was back. But not with that same fire. She'd stumbled on the high wire, and it wasn't easy to recover. Molly was a pro, she'd find it again, he was sure of that. What he was also sure of was that he was the cause. She'd blown it because of him. Because of the kiss. Because he was screwing with something sacred: the work.

He couldn't get out of the Hilton fast enough. Cursing his own stupidity the whole damn way to the parking lot, he dropped the keys twice. When he got in the car, he slammed his head into the steering wheel, but all that did was hurt. Moaning, he rubbed the blossoming lump and went back to swearing.

That didn't help either.

MOLLY TOOK her final bow and walked off stage with as much dignity as she could muster. The moment she was behind the blue curtains, she grabbed on to the wall so she wouldn't fall down.

She breathed, filling her lungs with air, fighting the urge to throw up. It had been years since she'd blown it like this. Lost her footing, nearly tumbled down the mountain. The last time was when she'd been with Rand.

He'd been offstage, too. Of course the room hadn't been this large, the stakes not nearly so high. But being with Rand, letting her personal life mix with her profession had nearly ended everything.

If she'd needed proof that she and Charlie could never get together, she'd gotten it tonight.

"Hey, Molly, you okay?"

She smiled at Gwen, the stage manager. "Sure, no sweat."

"Good show."

Molly's stomach clenched again. "Yeah, right."

"Hey, it happens. But you came right back, girl. They left happy."

"Thanks."

Gwen squeezed her arm and headed toward the dressing rooms. Molly waited a few seconds, then followed. She didn't think Charlie was here. He'd seen it. Seen her crash. And he must have figured it had everything to do with last night.

By the time she got to her dressing room, she was shaking. Funny, she hadn't onstage, but now that she was out of the spotlight, she was a complete mess.

Bobby had given her a fifth of Chivas when she'd opened at the Hilton, and there was still more than half a bottle left. Now seemed like a real good time to finish it.

She only spilled a little when she poured, and damn, but it burned all the way down her throat. On the other hand, she did feel a bit better.

She sat down on her ugly wooden chair and put her head in her hands. "Oh, Charlie. Why?"

Why did he have to kiss her? And why did it have to feel so amazing?

The bitch of it was, she could see them together. God, he was right for her in so many ways. She'd never had a friend like him before, let alone a partner. She'd tried to go solo, after Rand, but while she could deliver the goods, she needed a catalyst to write the material. If it hadn't been for Charlie, she'd have given it all up. And missed the best ride anyone could ever dream of.

And now, it was all going supernova. The TV show was way outside her wildest dreams. The money, the fame. It was all right there, just within reach. She couldn't risk it. Not now.

She stood, ran her hand through her hair, hating the red. Maybe she'd go blond again. Yeah, she'd felt good as a blonde.

She felt good with Charlie.

The thing is, it would end. There was no doubt in her mind. She tried to think of one couple she knew that had made it more than five years, and you know what? There wasn't one.

Yeah, she knew it happened, but not in her world. There was too much in her universe. Too much money, booze, excitement, notoriety. It was hard enough to keep her sanity, let alone a lover.

So even if they did get together, and it was great for a while, the inevitable would happen. Something would go wrong. He'd find someone else. He'd get tired of her hours. Jealous of her always being the one to get the applause.

She'd seen it before. Lived it. And it would kill her if it happened with him.

She sat again and opened the jar of cold cream. Once she had her makeup off, she'd go to Charlie's. They'd talk. He had to see that they weren't meant to be. He had to.

CHARLIE SAT in his living room staring into the dark. He hadn't turned on the light. The drapes were open and the moon was bright through the sliding glass doors. He listened to the hum of his air conditioner as his thoughts tumbled.

He remembered the first night he'd seen Molly on stage. It had been at a horrible comedy club in New York, a real dive. Most of the customers were drunk off their butts. Molly hadn't let it phase her, not even the heckling, which had been downright brutal. He'd been enchanted. Laughed until he had to wipe his eyes, and when she was through he'd gone backstage, excited to meet her. Estelle had sent him, hoping they would click, and click they had.

They'd found an all-night coffee shop and talked until breakfast. Two days later, they were an official team. The next two weeks were some of the most exciting he'd ever had. Individually, they were good; together, they were extraordinary.

It was as if they'd been born to work together. From that time on, they'd had success after success.

Jeez, that first time on *The Tonight Show*. She'd been so nervous she'd thrown up for two days. But once she went on, she'd been brilliant. Leno had cracked up, and after, he'd given her a standing invitation, which was something quite rare. She'd gotten better and better gigs, and even hosted an HBO special.

He wondered if he'd been in love with her all that time. It felt like it, but was it true?

He'd only admitted his feelings a few months ago. Maybe the saner part of him understood it couldn't really happen. That he had as much of her as he could hope to have.

It was the crazy part of him that wanted more. The part that saw Elvis. Which, for the first time, made sense.

He knew he wasn't Madame LaFarge, drooling on the bedsheets crazy, but he also had ample evidence that he was slightly left of center, and seeing Elvis was just the most obvious sign. Loving Molly was a lot more subtle but crazier still.

Unfortunately, knowing it was hopeless didn't make it hurt less. He wanted her as he'd never wanted anything before. She was his soul mate. Not that he'd ever say those words to another human being, but it was true. She was his destiny. His reason.

And working together had to be enough. Now, the thing he had to focus on was not his stupid dreams, but Molly. He needed to convince her that the kiss was nothing. A joke. No reason for her to see him and lose it. No reason to run for the hills.

He was just her buddy Charlie. Different haircut, different clothes, but the same guy she could always depend on.

And he had to promise her, with complete and utter seriousness, that he'd never, no matter what, kiss her again.

CHAPTER EIGHT

MOLLY STOOD at his door, wanting to knock but she couldn't lift her hand. And then when she did get her hand up, she just stood there.

She sighed as she turned to face the suburban street awash in moonlight.

All these people, wives and husbands and little kids, they were all sleeping at this ridiculous hour, peaceful in their ordinary lives. None of them were going to host a nationally broadcast talk show. They didn't know what it was like to be on stage in front of hundreds, all expecting to get their money's worth of laughter. None of them had writing partners who wanted more than they could give.

It was the life she'd chosen and she loved it. But there were trade-offs. She slept during the day, she saw the world through the lens of comedy, which wasn't always the healthiest perspective but it beat watching the world through tears, and she couldn't have Charlie as anything but a writing partner.

She turned back, knocked on the door, knowing he would still be awake. She rang the doorbell, too. This had to end. Now.

The door opened, and Charlie's expression spoke volumes. "Hey," he said, and she hated the resignation, the sadness in the one brief word.

"Hey yourself."

He stepped back and she walked in. She liked his place, and wondered why they never worked here. It was so much cozier than her house. Not that she didn't like her house, she'd just never invested much of herself in the decor. Here, on the other hand, you'd have to be a complete stranger not to see Charlie in every piece of furniture, every tchotchke on every shelf.

Moving straight to the dark living room, her gaze went to the mantel where he had his American Comedy award, his prized picture of him standing with George Carlin and Robin Williams. Behind the couch there were more photos, his wall of fame, as he called it. So many of her.

She stopped by the old coffee table, the one he'd found at a secondhand store in Tucson.

"I'm sorry," he said.

She turned, still not used to seeing him look so sophisticated, so handsome. No, that wasn't true. She'd always thought he was good-looking. Shlumpy, but hunky. "Talk to me, Charlie."

He shook his head. "Can't we just forget it? It's over."

"What's over? What happened? Aren't you happy?" She walked closer to him, and he took a step back. "Charlie, please. We need to talk about this."

He nodded. "You want a drink? I'm thinking tequila and lots of it."

"Orange juice?"

He nodded, then left her in the living room. She wondered if she should turn on the lights, but figured it might be easier for both of them if they didn't see too much.

Instead, she sat down on the couch and ran her hand over the soft Italian leather. Her sofa was an exercise in ugly, and she kept meaning to get a new one, but she wasn't a good shopper. Charlie would go with her. He'd offered a hundred times, and the last time, she'd just told him to go pick one out, but he wanted to do it together.

Closing her eyes, she chased away visions of them as a couple. Shopping for couches, buying groceries, climbing into bed together.

He came back into the room holding two screwdrivers.

"Speak to me," she said.

He handed her a drink, then sat down across from her in the big recliner he liked so much. "What do you want me to say?"

"Why don't you start with the clothes."

He shrugged, and although she couldn't see it, she knew he was blushing. "I don't know. It seemed like a good idea at the time."

"Don't get me wrong, you look great. It's just…"

"Not me?"

She nodded.

"I know. I guess I got tired of being the same old Charlie." He sipped his drink. "I'm a little old for college grunge."

"It's a good change," she said. "Honest. You look fabulous."

"When it's all said and done, I'm still just me."

"Thank God."

His head dipped. "It's okay, Molly. I swear. Nothing else is going to change. I got a little nuts. It was a momentary whim. Nothing to fret about."

She could let it go now. Crack a joke. But a joke wouldn't resolve a thing. "That's not what it felt like from this side."

He looked up again. "I don't know what to tell you."

"The truth?"

"I don't think so."

"That's what I thought. How long?"

"What?"

"Charlie."

He drank more. Held his glass with both hands. "I thought there could be, I don't know, more."

"You're not happy with what we have?"

"Yeah, I'm happy. It's the best."

"But?"

"I like being with you, okay? More than I've ever liked being with anyone else."

"How long were you with Kim?"

"Kim's ancient history."

"But didn't you tell me she was *the one?* That you figured you would be with her for the rest of your life?"

"It didn't work out that way."

"I know. You were together for two years, and then she left. She fell in love with that drummer. And you were knocked on your ass for how long?"

"What difference does it make?"

She leaned forward, putting her elbows on her knees, wishing now that she had turned on the lights. "Because they end, Charlie. All of them. And when they do, it's a bloody mess. You know that. I told you what happened with me and Rand. I won't let that happen to us."

"Okay, fine. It won't happen to us."

"Having unresolved feelings will be just as bad."

"I can't simply turn it off, Molly. It doesn't work that way."

"So what can we do?"

"We? *We* can't do anything. I will do lots of things. Starting with not talking about this ever again."

Molly drank some and stared at her feet. "What do you like?" she asked, finally.

"About?"

She looked up. "Me."

"Oh." He smiled at her. Not one of the big jolly smiles. Just a quirk of the lips that was everything sweet. "What's not to like?"

"I'm serious."

"So am I. But if it's details you want…"

She nodded.

"The way you think."

"Well, that's just perverse. We both know I'm incredibly twisted and that a normal thought hasn't passed through this brain in years."

"Exactly," he said.

"Okay. Go on."

"The look on your face when you're about to kick my ass at pool. The way you talk to your cats. How you shine on stage and how everything in you is about connecting with the people, about making them see how absurd it all is, and how great it can be. I love how you don't give up, ever, and how you keep on going even when you're scared to death. And most of all, I love the way I am with you. The way you think I'm a riot. How you make me believe it, too."

Molly closed her eyes. Tried to swallow the lump in her throat, but it wouldn't go away. What he'd said was beautiful, wonderful, but how he'd said it made her ache.

"Molly? You okay?"

She shook her head. "No."

"Shit. I'm sorry. I don't seem to be doing much right, do I?"

"It's not…" She looked at him, seeing beyond the hair, the new look. "When you kissed me—"

He stood up so quickly she jerked back on the couch. "Stop it. It happened. It was a mistake. It didn't mean anything."

"That's the problem. It did."

He looked at her and even in the dark she could see his confusion. It matched her own. "What?"

She stood, too. Moved closer. "I keep trying to convince myself that I didn't feel anything. That it was just, you know, lips and stuff."

He didn't say anything. He swallowed though. And blinked.

"But things did occur."

"Things?" he asked, his voice so low she had to move closer still.

She nodded. "We can't do this, you know. It's a total mistake, and we're minutes away from the biggest break of our lives, and this would complicate things beyond belief, and God, the worst possible outcome is that we lose what we have because of all the crap that comes along with relationships, and Charlie, that would kill me because I can't lose you, you're the best thing that's ever—"

He kissed her. Again.

It wasn't at all like the last one. There were no bruising hands on her arms, no stunning timing to make her gasp. No blinding shock that stopped the night.

This was warm breath, softness. She could feel him caring, feel him wanting. Just lips, but oh, how the touch of those lips infused her with a kind of wild peace that made no sense at all.

His hand cupped her jaw. Fingers, cool and tender.

She let herself fall. Only for a minute, and then she would stop. It would stop, and they would go back to what they were supposed to be. Friends who worked together. Friends without benefits. Just pals.

But first, she parted her lips and his tongue slipped inside. How could it possibly be so different to touch this part of him? They'd held hands, hugged, been through a million moments, and none of them had been close to this.

Jeez, it was good. So very good. Good like a perfect show, like winning the big stuffed bear, like a sunset on Maui.

And when he moaned and his hand went to the small of her back to pull her close, the way his body pressed into hers it didn't stop the night. It started her heart.

CHAPTER NINE

CHARLIE WAS in heaven. He felt her body pressed against his own, which was more than he'd ever hoped for, but then her sweet fingers inched along his neck until she held him steady, kissing him more deeply.

Kissing him.

He caressed her back, the curve of her hip as he learned her taste, how he could make her whimper with a thrust of his tongue.

It would all have been perfect except for the voice at the back of his mind asking him what the hell he thought he was doing. She'd said no, she'd given him very clear, rational reasons for the aforementioned no, and he'd agreed with her. And yet, there was kissing. Touching. A surprisingly insistent erection.

Her other hand came to his chest, and he thought she was going to push him away, but she didn't. She just rested it there, close to his heart, and he felt sure she could feel the steady, rapid beat.

He had to leave her lips, just for a breath, and to open his eyes. He needed to see her expression. She didn't seem upset. Just kind of zoned, which was a good thing. He bent to kiss her again when something behind her made him look.

"Oh, God."

It was him. Elvis. Standing right there.

"I know," she whispered, taking his mouth again.

He turned his head, moving her to the side so he could see. Shit, he was still there. White suit, big belt, dark sideburns. He glared at the ghost, who didn't seem very intimidated if his broad smile was any indication.

"This is what I was talkin' about," Elvis said.

Charlie gasped, pulled back. Looked at Molly to see her reaction, ready to explain. But Molly wasn't looking at Elvis. She was blinking. At him.

"Oh, no," she said.

"What? What's wrong?"

She stepped back, out of his grasp. "I shouldn't have—"

"It's okay. It's fine. We're fine. Everything's fine."

Her head went to the left, which gave Charlie an excellent view of Mr. Presley. "Charlie?"

"Yes?" He smiled. Tried to keep his gaze on Molly.

"What's going on?"

"Nothing. Not a thing. Uh, that was, uh… But it's really late, and uh…"

"Dammit, Charlie, I'm sorry. See? It's already doing things to us. Mostly to you, but still. Not good."

He forgot about Elvis, his focus totally on Molly. "Not good? Are you kidding? It was amazing."

She looked down. Sighed. "Yeah, dammit. It was."

He touched her cheek. "I don't regret it. Not for a second."

"I don't either, I suppose. But it makes the next part more difficult."

His chest constricted, knowing what she was going to say. He couldn't think of a thing to counter her objections. She was right. It was a huge risk and they had so much to lose.

"Son," Elvis said, "Don't let this moment go. You've got to tell her."

"What?"

"What's in your heart," Elvis said. At the exact same moment Molly said, "You know it can't work."

This was hard enough without invisible Elvis. "But what if it could?" he asked.

Molly winced. "Please don't, Charlie. You've already seen I'm not good at this."

"I'd say you were really good at leaving. What I'm asking you to do is stay."

Elvis nodded, and Charlie nearly had a heart attack when he got a load of the guitar, which hadn't been there seconds ago. Elvis started playing. Surely, Molly had to hear it, right?

If she did, it didn't show. She just kept looking at him as if she'd never seen him before. As if what he wanted was unthinkable.

"I want you, I need you, I love you…"

He was singing. The ghost of Elvis was singing songs in his dark living room. Great. Just swell.

Charlie opened his mouth as the end of the lyric reverberated in his brain.

Elvis rolled his eyes, strummed and sang it again.

Charlie got it. He took hold of Molly's upper arms. "I want you," he said, knowing it wasn't just a lyric, but the truth. "I need you. I love you."

Molly shook her head. "No, you don't. You think you do because we spend so much time together. Trust me on this. It can't work."

A new chord. Another song. "Any Way You Want Me."

"It can," Charlie said. "Any way you want it to."

She winced. "I want it the way it's always been."

"Don't say that. Please. At least think about it. Think what we could have."

"I have," she said. She moved, dislodging his hands. Before he could stop her, she turned.

He gasped, expecting a scream. Or something.

Elvis shook his head. Molly walked toward him. Walked through him. Like a hologram. Like a ghost.

"I just hope it's already not too late," she said.

Charlie reached out to throttle Presley, but he really couldn't worry about it while he was so busy losing the woman of his dreams. He ignored the apparition. "It's not. No matter what, we're partners. I just think we'd be as good at this other thing."

She turned once more, and Charlie had to step to the left to see her. "I can't risk it. Not with you. I won't."

He heard her. Despite what had happened moments ago, he got it. Even if she had feelings for him, she wasn't going to give it a chance. It was over before it had begun.

Everything in him hurt. A physical ache in his chest, in his stomach, in his veins. How in hell was he supposed to go on from here? At least before, his pain contained a ray of hope. This was a hurt of a whole different kind. Longing was better. Wishing didn't steal his very breath away.

"I'm sorry," she said. "I think I'd better go."

He nodded, not trusting his voice.

"Let's take a couple of days, okay? I think we both need a little time." She headed for the door.

Charlie watched her walk away, and he knew that no matter what he said, no matter how he wanted to go back to the before, he couldn't. He loved her. It wasn't negotiable. And it wouldn't matter how many days they took, when he saw her next he would die inside. He would want her and know he couldn't have her.

She put her hand on the doorknob, but she didn't leave. Instead, she turned. "Charlie?"

"Yeah?"

"It's gonna be all right."

"No, I don't think it is."

"What?"

He closed his eyes. "I got an offer."

She didn't say anything, and he didn't open his eyes.

"Sam Masters wants me to work with him."

"I see," she said. "So what you said about us being partners no matter what, that was a complete lie?"

"I don't want to go," Charlie said, forcing himself to look at her. "But I don't know if I'm strong enough to pretend."

"Whatever you need to do," she said, her voice filled with hurt. "I hope you'll reconsider."

"Me, too," he said.

She looked at him for a long, long moment. Then she walked out his door.

Charlie didn't move. Hardly breathed. It had all gone to hell. Every plan, every dream. Gone because he'd been a fool. He'd crossed the line and blown the best thing in his life.

"Well, son—"

"Get out," he said, not even glancing back. "Get out and stay out."

"But—"

"You've done enough. Just go."

When Charlie finally turned, he was alone. Completely, utterly alone.

MOLLY DIDN'T drive home. Instead, she went to Horizon Ridge and parked on the mountainside. The sky had turned pale; the sun would come up soon.

She got out of her car and walked to the edge. It wasn't a far drop, but that wasn't why she was there. It was the view. From here, she could see across the valley. The Strip was lit up, as it always was, as it always would be. It didn't matter what was going on in the real world, Las Vegas was the ultimate playground. Nothing counted in Vegas. Not the money, not the parties, not the people.

She sat down, not caring about the dirt. Her legs just wouldn't hold her anymore.

How had things gotten so screwed up so fast? And what the hell was she supposed to do now?

Her gaze shifted from the casino lights to the first glimmer of sun. Another day. She should have been in bed. Sleeping the sleep of the just. Instead, she was out here, wondering if she would be able to salvage her life.

"Goddamn you, Charlie," she said.

She swiped the tears off her cheek. Why, why, why? Why had she kissed him? There was that one moment, that tiny little window of opportunity when she could have made it right. He'd apologized. She'd believed the sincerity in his voice, his honest desire to take it back.

And then she'd kissed him, and for the life of her she couldn't understand why. Was his first kiss so amazing that she had to repeat it? Or was she trying to prove to herself that it wasn't amazing at all?

Unfortunately, she knew the answer. It had been…

She sniffed. Watched as the sky infused with a pink so vivid it made her sigh. Kissing Charlie had changed everything. Changed the way she saw the world. The way she felt about every kiss she'd ever had in her whole life. Changed the very nature of the universe.

And it didn't matter.

He might turn her inside out with his touch, but he was still her writing partner, and that was sacred. It was the cornerstone of her career, and no matter what, she couldn't mess with that. Not that.

Not now.

They wanted her for the talk show. Estelle was working with them to make sure she could still do her gig at the Hilton, but on a limited basis. The important thing was TV, the exposure. It was everything she'd ever dreamed of, and it was right here.

Dammit, it was everything Charlie had dreamed of, too.

Maybe he was afraid. This was unprecedented success, and Charlie wasn't used to that. He was a rare commodity. Most comics worked alone. Others had writers, but they were anonymous, and they certainly didn't work they way she and Charlie did.

It didn't surprise her that Sam had tried to steal him. Others would, too. He was a brilliant writer who didn't need the spotlight. There weren't many like him.

But he was also her friend. Her best friend. A few days ago, she would have said he was like her brother, but now she knew that there was nothing brotherly in how he felt about her.

To be honest, she would never feel like his sister again, either.

Maybe he should take that job with Sam. How was she supposed to go on as if nothing had happened? To show up for work every day and know that he loved her? That she felt…something.

God, she didn't even know. Did she love Charlie?

Of course, she loved him, but was it more than that? Could he be the one? The forever-dreamed-of perfect guy? Her soul mate?

It was in the realm of possibility.

So, what? Let him go off with Sam, and then they could date? How insane was that?

All she knew for sure, for absolute, rock-solid, spit-in-your-hand truth, was that she couldn't have it both ways. Because even if it was great, even if they were perfect partners in bed and at work, she'd be waiting, every single day, for the other shoe to drop.

It wasn't fair. None of it. And her heart ached at the choices she faced. One way or another, they were both going to lose. Big time.

CHAPTER TEN

CHARLIE PARKED in the Hilton lot, but he didn't get out
of the car immediately. He wasn't ready to walk into the
showroom. No one would be there but him, and the silence scared him. He couldn't stop thinking about her.

But it was hot, and sitting in the convertible wasn't
exactly making him feel great. He stepped out, locked
the car, put the keys in the pocket of his ratty old jeans.
Screw the new look. What had it gotten him? He was
who he was, and a flashy wardrobe wouldn't change
that. It wouldn't change a thing.

Instead of heading to the showroom, he started walking. Not on the Strip, but a side street. Away from the
crowds and most of the traffic.

The scent of beer and hot dogs made him look up.
An old casino, faded in the brilliant sun enticed the pas-
sersby with cheap foot-longs and cold draft. It might
have been three in the afternoon, but Charlie had only
gotten out of bed an hour ago. He needed coffee, that's
all. Coffee and a heart transplant.

His gaze moved to the far end of the street. In one of
life's cruel ironies, there were wedding chapels on all
four corners. Very Vegas. Get your vows here! No waiting! All major credit cards accepted!

He picked up the pace, anxious to get past the chapels to the coffee shops beyond. He'd hardly ever noticed

them, actually. The chapels, not the coffee shops. They were just there, ubiquitous, all vaguely alike. But like a broken toe that kept knocking into chairs, he couldn't escape.

Hurrying, his eyes downcast, he didn't notice the man standing in front of the Taking Care of Business chapel. He bumped into him, hard, and looked right into the eyes of Elvis Presley.

Charlie's adrenaline shot through the roof, and his hand curled into a fist, but before he did anything stupid, well, stupider, he saw that it wasn't Elvis at all. This guy's hair wasn't the right black, the sideburns were too fuzzy and well, this guy was alive.

"Hey, little brother. Watch where you're going."

Charlie fought the urge to tell the wannabe that his voice inflection was off. Nothing the impersonator could wear or say would change the fundamental error. It wouldn't have made a difference. Elvis, even as a ghost, had an undeniable charisma. Style. Grace. And absolutely no idea how to help two people fall in love.

MOLLY LOOKED at her bedside clock. Three-thirty. Thank God she didn't have to go to the Hilton until six o'clock. She felt as if she'd been run over by a bus. Her dreams had been awful. One after another, they'd all been about Rand. About the pain. The betrayals.

She threw back the covers and as she climbed out of bed she thought about Charlie. Not about last night, or even the first kiss, but about little moments. Like the first time they'd stayed up all night talking and laughing their asses off.

As she got into the shower, memories of the comedy club in Atlanta came to mind, and how she'd gotten so sick between the first and second show. Charlie had taken such good care of her, even though she'd been a disgusting mess. He'd been amazingly sweet. He'd brought her soup, medicine, taken her temperature, changed the pillowcases when they got too hot from her fever.

She dried herself, pulled on a pair of shorts and a T-shirt and headed for the kitchen. First, coffee, then she might be able to face the day. She leaned against the counter as the coffee dripped. A flash from her dreams last night made her chest ache, and she retreated to Charlie.

For every rotten thing Rand had pulled, Charlie had provided five wonderful moments that warmed her from the inside out. Charlie was the anti-Rand. Even his humor was kinder, gentler, although God knows, his satire was as sharp as a blade. But Charlie was never mean. Never cruel.

Time to stop thinking like this. Yeah, Charlie was a peach, but that offered no guarantees. People changed when they got into relationships. Had to happen. Inevitable.

She walked over to her counter radio and turned it on. Music would chase her thoughts away. Ah, Elvis. Excellent. Only the song, and she knew all the words, wasn't going to help at all. "Are You Lonesome Tonight?" Yeah, she was lonesome. She turned to her second favorite station.

Elvis, again. But the song wasn't any better. "Could I Fall In Love?" "Yeah, okay? I could. But I won't."

She tried her luck on station three. Whoa. Elvis again. "I'm Falling In Love Tonight."

Molly turned off the radio, wondering what the deal was. It wasn't Elvis's birthday. Not the anniversary of his death. Anyway, the coffee was done. She got her cup, put in too much of everything and sighed as she took her first sip.

Okay. She didn't want to sit here and think. She didn't want to go to the Hilton just yet. Maybe there was a matinee she could catch. A thriller or a comedy. Something scary, perhaps. She loved those.

She turned. Gasped. And barely heard the sound of her mug shattering on the hardwood floor.

CHARLIE FINISHED his coffee and put the cup down on the desk. He'd had to come back here eventually, and better to do it now, before anyone else showed up for work.

The Hilton showroom hadn't changed since his first Elvis sighting. Still dark, still cavernous, still comforting in an odd yet familiar way.

He glanced down at his yellow pad. Nothing had changed there, either. He'd not had one idea. Not even a germ of a thought. He hadn't even been able to doodle.

His walk had done him some good, at least. He'd come to a decision. He wasn't going to take that other job. For better or worse, he was going to stick it out with Molly.

Even though it would hurt like hell. Even though his heart would ache every time he looked at her. He was still her partner. And frankly, being with her, despite everything, was better than being apart.

Time would help. Eventually, the ache would dull. His humor would reemerge. At least he hoped so. And the show would go on.

The new TV program would be a welcome distraction. A lot of stress, but he figured it would be a lot of fun, too. Certainly exciting.

No, he'd carry on. Satisfied enough that they were friends. That she loved him, in her own way.

He reached for his pen, but froze as he heard a noise

behind him. There was no doubt who it was. Damn ghost couldn't take a hint. "I thought I told you to get out and stay out."

"Oh, well, I uh—"

Charlie spun around the second he recognized Molly's voice. "No, no I thought you were someone else."

She seemed confused. "Who?"

"Not important." God, his heart was beating so fast. Not from the surprise either. Just from seeing her. She'd pulled her red hair back in a loose ponytail. Her T-shirt was one of her favorites, Hello Kitty, of all the damn things. And her shorts showed off her long, slender legs. He wanted her with an intensity that overshadowed his need to breathe.

"Charlie, can we talk?"

He nodded.

She came closer, down the carpeted aisle until she joined him in the booth. She perched against the railing and crossed her arms over her chest. Then she stared at him. Not saying a word.

"I'm not gonna take that job," he said finally.

She nodded. "That's good."

He didn't know what to follow it with. He could tell her he loved her again, but she knew that. He could say he'd never bring the subject up again, but he wasn't sure if that would be a lie. So he waited.

Her hands dropped as the slow seconds ticked by. And then she smiled. "I've done some thinking."

"Oh?" He didn't want to feel this hope.

"You're nothing like Rand."

"I know."

"Really nothing like him. He was a total schmuck, you know?"

"Yeah."

"In fact," she said, her smile a little wistful, but still there, "you're the best person I know."

"Well, I wouldn't go that—"

"Shush. Let me do this, okay?"

"Sure, Molly. Whatever you say."

She stood up, walked slowly toward him. "The thing is," she said, "well, I love you."

"Huh?"

"I'm scared to death, I won't lie about it, but you…"

"I…?" His heart was now hammering. His hands shook. The next words out of her mouth could change everything.

"You're amazing. Everything sweet and wonderful and good. And I can't lose you."

Charlie closed his eyes. Nothing had changed. Not a damn thing except for his hopes and dreams being dashed to bits. "Don't worry, kid. As I said, I'm not going anywhere. I'll still be your partner."

"Will you?" She moved closer still. Cupped his jaw in her hand.

He nodded, trying hard not to let his disappointment show. "Sure. Can't miss out on the opportunity of a lifetime, can I?"

She shook her head slowly, studied his eyes so carefully. "Me neither."

"Okay, then." He turned away, breaking the contact. "We're all set. Wanna grab some dinner before the show?"

"Charlie."

"Yeah?"

"You're not getting it."

He didn't face her. He couldn't. "Getting what?"

"I'm in love with you. I want it all."

He cleared his throat, not daring to believe… "What was that?"

"Turn around."

He obeyed, although he wasn't sure how, as his brain was stuck and he couldn't feel anything below the neck.

She smiled at him, and what he saw there in her beautiful face kick-started the whole business again. His heart, his pulse, the shaking hands, everything.

"Oh," he said.

"Oh, indeed." Then she leaned forward and kissed him, very gently, on the lips.

His eyes closed as he let the truth sink in. She was in love with him. In love. Not platonically, not like a pal, a buddy. *In love.* And yet... He looked at her, at her beautiful eyes. "Not that I want to jinx this. In fact, I'd rather go naked bungee jumping, but what about all the things you said? What about you and me repeating your not so swell history?"

She sighed. "I still have some reservations," she said, but they're about me, not us. I had something of a...revelation...about us. About all of it. That I was letting fear run my life." She leaned back against the rail, her hands bracing her on either side. "The thing is, if we're both committed to making this work, then we can. Yeah, people change, but I know you. I know that when it comes to the big stuff, you're a rock. You don't cheat, you don't lie, even when it would make your life easier. Rand had no moral center, and that relationship was doomed from the start."

"You think I've got a moral center, huh?"

She shook her head. "Not think. Know."

"Cool."

"Of course, I still think you're nuts for wanting me. I'm nothing if not certifiable."

Charlie laughed. "I've heard it said that the best you can hope for is to find someone whose insanity is compatible with your own. I'm pretty sure we've already met that criteria."

"In every way but one."

He opened his mouth. Then shut it again. "Oh, shit."

"Don't freak now, Webster. I'm pretty damn certain that's not gonna be an issue."

He quirked his left brow. "There's one way to find out."

She nodded. "Only one."

"My place?"

She stood up, walked close. "Nope. See, I'm a headliner at this here hotel. Which means that when I call the GM and ask for a room, they pretty much have to say yes."

"You got us a room?"

"A suite," she whispered, and then she kissed him.

He parted his lips and felt her hand slip behind his neck. He pulled her close, body to body, heart to heart, and the kiss wasn't so gentle anymore. It was everything perfect. All the happy endings in the world.

It was Molly. And she was his.

MOLLY HADN'T meant to cry, but she felt the tears trickle down her cheeks. She'd done it. Thrown caution to the wind, put the ugly past behind her and stepped out on a very thin limb. But she had Charlie to hold her if she started to fall.

She kissed him harder, free now to let go. To show him everything, to show herself that the truth was bigger than the both of them. That she'd probably been in love with him for ages.

It all made wonderful sense. She was in the right place at the right time with the right man. How she got here was another story, and not one she was going to share any time soon, but it didn't matter, because, damn, it was Charlie. And he was hers.

She pulled back, just a little, and noticed a light on the stage. Without letting go, she stared at the man who was suddenly there. In the spotlight. His black hair glistening, his white suit flashing. His smile filled with a contentment she knew all about.

He didn't say a word. He just lifted his hand and waved.

Molly waved back and watched him slowly fade, disappear to wherever he'd come from. "Thanks," she whispered.

Charlie laughed. "Thanks for what? Loving you? Easiest thing I've ever done."

She looked at him again. "And yet," she said, "you do it so well."

His lips quirked in that funny way of his. "Yeah, well, I had something of a revelation of my own. Now, what were you saying about a suite?"

CHAPTER ELEVEN

One Year Later...

THE AUDIENCE was on its feet, the applause, the whoops, the hollers filling the sound stage. Molly stood by her comfy chair, her smile as bright as the lights above her. She nodded at her fans, overwhelmed at their acceptance, as always. She turned her gaze to the left, past the edge of the set. To Charlie.

He was there cheering her on. Loving her. It was something she never got used to, never took for granted.

The show had been an amazing success, especially since, after six months of phone tag, she'd finally gotten her interview with the delectable Jude Law. Only now that she and Charlie were together, it didn't give her quite the same thrill. Almost, but not quite.

She bowed once more, then motioned the crowd to simmer down, to go back to the casinos and the magic of Vegas. The house lights went on, and the back doors opened. It was over, at least for today. Tomorrow, she'd tape three more shows. The following night, she'd be at the Hilton. And Charlie would be with her through it all.

She took off her microphone, leaving it on the chair, and headed right for him. They'd debrief the show with the producers, and then apparently Charlie had a surprise for her.

He wrapped her in his arms. "Wow," he said. "You did it again. Amazing."

"Thanks."

"You ready?"

"Give me ten to get the makeup off, then I'll meet you."

"Okay." He kissed her. "See you then."

Molly watched him walk away. He had on one of his Hugo Boss suits which had something to do with the surprise, although other than that, he'd given her no clues. But damn, he looked fine.

How things had turned out so well was still a mystery, but one she no longer questioned. She'd never told him about her strange encounter with the ghost of Elvis, and she never would. Not that he wouldn't believe it. He trusted her implicitly. But she didn't want him to think she was crazier than he already guessed.

Anyway, she needed to get her act together. It took her a few minutes to get to her dressing room. Unlike the Hilton, this was a pleasure palace, with her every whim accommodated. A fabulous sound system, furniture to die for, a stocked fridge, a huge closet and, in the back, she even had a bed. Which, thank you very much, she and Charlie had inaugurated on the first day of taping.

Then it was smearing and wiping, and when her face was clean as a whistle, she put on her street makeup. Then she slipped into a pale blue Prada dress, her favorite. Whatever the mystery was, she wanted to look good for it.

Once she was satisfied, she headed out to the conference room. Charlie was already waiting, and the way his eyes lit up when he saw her gave her goose bumps. This was going to be the fastest debrief ever.

CHARLIE HAD NEVER been more nervous in his life. He'd planned everything to the last detail. Had dreams, and nightmares, about her reaction. But somehow, he knew that this was it. This was what they both wanted. What was meant to be.

It was zero hour, and he could tell Molly was getting antsy to know what was going on. No more games.

"Walk with me," he said.

She nodded, although he could see the questions in her eyes.

They were on the street at the back of the Hilton, heading east. He remembered another time he'd walked this path alone. A year had passed since those crazy days, and his life had changed in ways he could never have predicted.

They lived together now. Not in his place or in hers, but in theirs. A great house in Henderson, with a pool and a big old outdoor kitchen and a bedroom that was roomier than most apartments. The show had done amazingly well in the ratings, and Molly's star had never shone more brightly. She was a celebrity. Her fan mail was so plentiful they had two full-time employees to handle it all. And Molly still loved him. A whole lot.

"Charlie? I can't take this anymore. You have to tell me where we're going."

"It won't be long. Just trust me."

"I do. You crazy bastard."

He laughed. This was either going to be the best surprise known to man, or things were going to get real… interesting. There it was, halfway down the block. In a few minutes he'd know. She'd know.

He squeezed her hand as they walked to the entrance of the Tender Loving Care wedding chapel. Then he stopped. Held his breath.

Molly blinked as she finally understood his surprise. "Oh my God," she whispered.

"Uh, is that a good 'Oh my God'?"

She didn't answer him right away. She was too busy processing this monumental step. It wasn't that she didn't love him to pieces, it was that marriage was so…formal. It was forever. No more escape clauses, no more safety nets. This was it. The real deal. Did she want that?

"Molly?"

She turned to Charlie. Smiled at the panic in his eyes. Poor baby, he was terrified she'd say no. "It's a very, very good 'Oh my God.'"

He laughed, his relief written all over his face. "Okay then. Shall we do this thing?"

She nodded, struggling not to cry. "I'm in."

He led her forward into the reception room, his gaze hardly leaving her face. Watching her as if she might bolt. But then she got it. He wanted to see her expression when she saw all the people she loved already waiting for her. Bobby Tripp, Estelle, Mike, the producers of the show, the gang from the Hilton. They were all of them there, dressed up pretty, grinning like fools.

She kissed and hugged each one, and then, in a daze she couldn't quite shift, she signed papers, accepted a beautiful tulip bouquet, tried to stop her hands from shaking.

Charlie took her hand, and led her into the chapel proper. There were pews and a red aisle and tons of flowers. At the end of the carpet there was an Elvis impersonator, and she had to laugh. If Charlie only knew.

Music started. Piped in. Elvis, of course. "Love Me Tender." Perfect.

Charlie held her hand as they walked to the tune, and squeezed it as they stood before the man in the white suit. He actually wasn't a very good Elvis. But she didn't mind. This was perfect. Just perfect.

"Thank you," Charlie whispered. "I love you."

She turned. Looked deeply into his eyes. Eyes she knew so well. Loved so well. "Me, too."

Elvis cleared his throat, and she turned to face him. To say her vows.

Only, it wasn't the impersonator. It was *him*.

Charlie gasped. She turned to look at his face. "You, too?"

Charlie hesitated for a second, then nodded.

She laughed out loud, turned back to their ghostly Cupid. "Just tell me one thing, Elvis. Is this going to be legal? Are we really going to be married?"

Elvis smiled. "Oh, yeah, little lady. In this life and the next."

GOOD LUCK CHARM
Joanne Rock

CHAPTER ONE

RULE NUMBER ONE for successful séances—never allow
yourself to get distracted by thoughts of a man. Especially if the man in question wasn't the one you wanted
to conjure.

Disappointed with another failed attempt to summon
her icon—Elvis Aron Presley, undisputed King of rock
'n' roll—Alyssa Renato blew out the candles on her
makeshift séance table in the back room of her Las
Vegas memorabilia shop, The Good Luck Charm. Hot
wax had dribbled down the side of her white tapers,
sealing her only good linen tablecloth to the round slab
of cypress wood beneath.

Blast Brett Neale for foiling the latest "Meet the
Presleys" séance and ruining perfectly good linen. She
had no business thinking about him tonight when she
needed answers only Elvis could provide.

"We'll reach him next time," a soft voice assured her
from behind.

Turning, Alyssa found her séance medium packing
up her black velvet invocation bag with a Ouija board
and enough incense to cause smog in Vegas for the rest
of the year. Laura "Stargazer" Grimaldi was five years

younger than Alyssa's thirty-two years, but she possessed enough personal dignity to carry off her medium role with class and style. No easy feat while wearing a crystal-adorned turban.

"I hope so." Alyssa scooped up a few scattered plates from the appetizers they'd eaten earlier, then followed her five guests through the back room toward her storefront. "After tonight's contact with Sonny Bono, I don't know how many more dead singing celebrities we can possibly encounter. I loved *Sonny & Cher* as much as the next girl, but the heavens must be hard-up for singers willing to talk to us if he's the best we can summon."

They wound their way through the store, passing stacks of velvet paintings, a rack of vintage leather jackets and movie posters for everything from *Love Me Tender* to *Viva Las Vegas*. Alyssa surrounded herself with all kinds of music industry memorabilia, especially anything Elvis-related. The King had been a family icon since she and her sister were apparently singing "Heartbreak Hotel" in a Tijuana orphanage when they'd been chosen by their adoptive parents. The Renato sisters had been taken in by great people, and although neither of the siblings had any real memory of the orphanage, they'd embraced Elvis as their personal patron saint.

They'd even carried that bond with their idol into adulthood. Alyssa had become a talent manager while Rosa, the younger sister by two years, had parlayed her love of music into a singing career. Together they had made it to number one on the pop charts, until a bout with anorexia nearly killed Rosa and forced Alyssa— who'd always felt light years older even though only twenty-four months separated them—to call an abrupt end to her sister's career.

"Oh come on, Alyssa. Sonny was as charming as ever. Much nicer than cranky Kurt Cobain who couldn't be bothered to give us more than a grunt last time." Laura lifted her velvet bag over the stacks of old LPs that had slowly infiltrated the aisles in the two years Alyssa had been running the Good Luck Charm. The quirky Vegas shop seemed a long way from the top of the *Billboard* charts, but at least it gave her a small connection to the music business she'd always loved.

A connection that sexy rock musician Brett Neale wanted her to reopen. Why couldn't he understand that she could never go back into the industry that had nearly stolen her sister from her?

"You're right," she admitted, setting the snack plates beside the register while she said her goodbyes. "I'm just eager to conjure the right man."

From a few feet ahead of them, a silky feminine voice called back. "Maybe next time we should play dress-up in the store before we do the séance. We can all wear capes and sunglasses and see if that helps."

The suggestion came from Alyssa's ever-helpful sister, Rosa. Every one of the "Meet the Presleys" séance group members loved the King, but Rosa was the biggest zealot of them all.

In fact, Alyssa's biggest reason for wanting to conjure the legendary singer was so she could ask him if they'd done the right thing quitting the music business. Alyssa had carried tons of guilt over the whole incident for the past two years, and by now her relationship with

Rosa was so strained they could barely carry on a real conversation without one of them losing her temper. But if Elvis agreed they'd made the right choice, surely Rosa would forgive her.

And, perhaps more to the point, maybe Alyssa would finally forgive herself.

"Nice try, sis, but you're not getting your mitts on my new merchandise." A red, floor-length cape had been specially made by a designer who had spelled out "Elvis Lives" in rhinestones on the back. The garment was pure poetry and had to be kept in a glass case—mostly to keep Rosa from stealing it when Alyssa wasn't looking.

At least they had a relationship now. Things were slowly healing after the first year of mostly silent recovery from Rosa, but neither of them ever brought up the old days. Too painful. Too many unresolved hurts.

After making plans to meet again the following week, Alyssa unlocked the front door and said goodnight to her guests. Rosa blew a kiss over her shoulder, her raven-dark hair streaked with skunky white highlights this week. She looked happy and had mentioned things might be getting serious with the new man in her life, but Alyssa could only think about the fact that her sister hadn't eaten anything despite the wealth of snacks she'd served. Rosa might have gained weight over the past two years, but she remained rail-thin. Couldn't she have made an effort to munch a few carrot sticks? A scoop of warm Brie and apples?

Maybe Alyssa should have offered fried peanut butter and banana sandwiches.

Peering out at the street, she watched to make sure

everyone made it safely to their cars and that Madame Stargazer managed her obscenely large bag of séance paraphernalia without incident. Alyssa was about to go back inside when a shadow caught her eye on the other side of the door she still held wide.

Hurrying to shut the door just in case that shadow meant trouble, she paused when a man's voice called her by name.

"Alyssa. It's me." The rich baritone with its smoky note halted her. Which was stupid, considering any brand of street thief or doped-up murderer could easily possess a beautiful voice. But before she could scuttle back into the safety of the store, the man stepped into full view.

Brett Neale.

The very recent cause of her séance distraction.

Her breath caught for a moment, hitching in her throat as she took in his shaggy dark hair half-covering one eye, although even that didn't dim the mesmerizing blue of his gaze. Tall and lanky, he possessed muscles of the understated variety, the kind that didn't draw your eye until they flexed right in front of you. The way Brett's did now as he reached up to grab the door for her.

She glanced at the tattoo of Graceland on his right bicep. She'd noticed it before when they'd met in a music shop downtown six months ago as they both reached for a copy of *Highway 61 Revisited,* but she'd never seen the tattoo—or the muscle—up close and personal. Although he'd talked her into a date back then she'd realized pretty quickly over dinner she wasn't ready to date a guy whose life remained tightly tied to the business she'd walked away from. Still, she'd never forgotten the electric attraction she'd felt for a man who appreciated the classics.

"I need to talk to you." His arm braced the door open, keeping him in her line of vision.

Not that she would have shut him out anyway. She hadn't returned his last three phone calls, so she couldn't really blame him for seeking her out in person.

"It's a busy night here." Or at least it had been up until this moment. She couldn't be outright rude to him, but it wouldn't hurt to dole out a few excuses to avoid a conversation she didn't want to have because now he wasn't just looking for a date. His message hinted he wanted something she couldn't possibly provide. "I really don't have time."

"Your séance crowd just left, right?" He turned back toward the street that was now almost empty since her guests had departed. The Strip glittered two streets over, the neon lights casting a residual glow that made the streetlamps in front of her store unnecessary. "I've been trying to reach you for over a week now. Maybe I can help you pick up and you can at least hear me out."

Allow this delectable young musician inside her empty store lit only by a few candles? The idea struck her as unwise given that she'd been without a man in her life since forever. On an average day it didn't bother her too much that she hadn't taken a man to her bed in two years. But right now, staring at Graceland as it rippled in the dim light from a nearby streetlamp, Alyssa suddenly felt every moment of those sex-free years weighing on her. If Brett set foot in here now, she'd probably leave claw marks on that tasty young body of his.

Yeah, she needed to play it cool with him tonight.

"I don't need any help. And I'm sorry I haven't returned your calls but I'm out of the music business and I need to put some distance between me and my old life."

Some things were better off forgotten. Like how much she'd loved being the power behind the throne when it came to making stars. Like how many ways a man could screw you over—and not in the pleasurable way—when he possessed the potent combination of rock-god good looks and the soul of a poet. That kind of man had always had the power to make Alyssa weak-kneed.

"I'm not asking you to go back to your old life." He edged forward, propelling himself up the low step from the street so they stood on level ground. "I'm asking you to think about beginning a whole new one."

Brett watched Alyssa consider his words, her dark eyes uncertain. She was probably a couple of years older than his twenty-eight years, but her worn jeans and vintage concert T-shirt from an ancient jazz festival made her look about nineteen. Alyssa had been *the* talent manager in the rock business just two years ago. With her finger on the pulse of America's youth and an undeniable business savvy, she'd catapulted one unknown band after another into big-time radio play, and launched her sister Rosa's solo act.

She'd become a legend in her own time and then vanished from the scene when her sister hit a personal rough patch. She'd told him on their ill-fated date that she had no intention of returning to the music business, but he hadn't needed her help then the way he needed it now.

"Please." He hadn't planned on throwing in the personal appeal, but damn it, he needed all the firepower he could muster. "Just hear me out."

Her nervous gaze darted over him as he planted himself in her doorway, and Brett regretted having to impose like this. There'd been a current of attraction between them since the first time they'd met in a mutual friend's used record store, and he couldn't deny he'd always wanted to get to know her on a more intimate level. But she'd backed off.

He had respected that. Understood where she was coming from. Still, right now he needed her too much as a professional to allow his business to get mixed up with sex.

"Five minutes." She retreated a step to allow him inside, but she crossed her arms over her black T-shirt, not budging another inch. "That's all I can give you, and then you have to leave."

"I'll take whatever I can get and I'll thank you for it to boot." He flashed his best grin at her, the one that had probably landed him as many bar gigs as his music, but she simply lifted a haughty eyebrow. Waiting.

He wanted to tell her what a great place she had, to compliment her on the Good Luck Charm and the truckloads of memorabilia stuffed into every available corner. But she didn't seem in the mood for small talk.

"Look, I know you're not interested in representing musicians anymore, but—"

"I'm out of that business for good. It doesn't have

anything to do with talent. I haven't seen you on stage, but I've heard your demo and it's great. If you want to go out to L.A., I can give you a few names of people who might be willing to take you on."

It was more than she'd ever conceded in the past when she hadn't been willing to keep dating or share any thoughts on his career—even after she'd snagged a copy of his demo from him that first day in the music store. A few months ago, he might have taken the endorsement she was offering and run. But he couldn't afford to set up house somewhere else. He needed a break *now.*

"I appreciate that, but my days as a musician are numbered unless I get a break soon." When she looked confused, he leaned against the counter where she kept the register and moved straight to his bottom line. "I set up a savings account when I left my career as a financial analyst, and I allotted myself a certain dollar amount to use to pursue my dreams. That money is almost gone, so I'm going to have to call it quits."

Empathy warmed her brown eyes a shade darker. "I'm sorry—"

"That is, unless I can win the Elvis Legacy competition they're putting together at Golddiggers Resort and Casino this weekend."

"The Elvis Legacy? I thought they were going to hold that next January as part of a birthday bash for him. Isn't this some kind of *American Idol* rip-off where they crown a new king of rock 'n' roll?"

Brett suppressed a smile at her knowledge of the event despite her insistence that she ignored the local music scene.

"A new king or queen. And they decided to move it up and cash in on the popularity of those shows before the viewing public gets sick of them."

"And you want to win." She shifted her attention from Brett to a fat burning candle, its three wicks filling the whole store with the scent of cinnamon. She molded a bit of the hot wax around the rim, folding the candle down onto itself so that there would be less to impede its soft light.

"I've *got* to win, Alyssa. They're offering the winner a shot at a recording contract. This is my last chance before I go back to New York and kiss the dream goodbye."

"Why me?" She straightened away from the candle, shifting against the counter so that she faced him head-on. "Vegas might not be the music mecca of the U.S., but there are other talent managers here. Some of them have probably already approached you."

How could he explain the power of gut instinct that told him Alyssa Renato was the woman who could take him to the top? He'd heard her methods for attracting attention to her clients sometimes leaned toward the unorthodox, but how wild could she be to have garnered so much respect in the industry? Brett knew he could handle whatever she dished out, even if the idea of kooky séances gave him hives. He'd learned the hard way that talent wasn't always enough to propel a career.

"It has to be you." Time to lay his cards on the table. "I've just got a good feeling about us together. There's definite chemistry between you and me."

"Chemistry?" She suddenly seemed interested in a spinning rack of sunglasses near the register, her finger trailing over a pair of lavender aviator lenses while a tinge of color slowly crawled into her cheeks.

Or was the candlelight making him see things?

"Don't you think we've got a good rapport?" If the Good Luck Charm had belonged to anyone else, he might have been tempted to look around the place since he'd been an Elvis fan from way back. But not even the magic of scratchy old LPs recorded without all the high-tech sound gizmos that were now studio staples could lure his gaze away from Alyssa as she tried on a pair of pink rhinestone-studded sunglasses.

"We hardly know each other." Her words were as cool as the shades. "I couldn't say what kind of rapport we have."

"Come on, Alyssa. We've broken bread together. You know me. Besides, you're into all that intuitive stuff." He stalked closer, determined to make his point clear. Reaching for the pink studded frames, Brett slid the glasses off her face so he could see her eye to eye. "Don't you at least get a sense of how we'd be together?"

Her glossy dark hair shone in the soft flicker of the candlelight, thick waves tumbling to rest on her shoulders. He stared into those endless brown eyes of hers and told himself he couldn't be the only one feeling sparks fly.

"Just what kind of chemistry are we talking about here?" She narrowed her gaze, as if she could somehow see deeper into his motives if she looked long enough.

"Any kind. Does it matter what sort of chemistry we have as long as we're on the same wavelength when it comes to music?"

"It matters." She edged past him, the sleeve of her T-shirt brushing his arm as she busied herself straightening cubicles filled with ancient metal lunch boxes bearing images of everyone from James Dean to the *Partridge Family.* "Because I wouldn't be able to represent someone very well if there was any sexual chemistry involved."

"So in other words, you'd consider representing me as long as there's no sex?" It would be a tough bargain given what flickered between them, but hadn't Brett promised himself he'd put pursuit of his dreams first while he struggled to make it in this business?

He could ignore the attraction as long as he remembered Alyssa conjured dead celebrities for kicks. He'd been raised by an aunt who considered herself a psychic and drove their local Brooklyn police station insane with calls insisting she had visions related to every crime they investigated.

"That is absolutely not what I said." She settled a hand on one shapely hip and glared at him. All those long, tumbling curls of hers were undeniably feminine, yet her attitude broadcast a clear warning. She looked ready to take him out. "I was merely proposing yet another reason why I won't ever be representing you. Excuse me for being forthright while you're busy playing word games."

"No games intended." He held up his palms, surrender-style, surprised at her strong reaction. Apparently he'd struck a nerve, but he had the feeling it wouldn't be wise to investigate that terrain. "I just thought if we could talk face-to-face maybe I could convince you—"

"You can't." Some of the anger slid off her shoulders, and she ran one hand over a thick feather boa wrapped around a cardboard cutout of Marilyn Monroe before tossing the fluttery accessory around her own neck. "And I think your five minutes are up."

Damn. He was no closer to signing on with her than he had been when he'd walked into her store. If anything, he'd somehow pushed all her buttons and ticked her off instead.

Time to pull out the heavy artillery.

"Okay. I'm out of here." He backed up a step as if to retreat, and then lobbed his last bomb. "I just thought since your sister is performing at the Elvis Legacy, maybe you'd be ready to come out of retirement, too."

CHAPTER TWO

WAS THE GUY trying to give her a heart attack? In the flickering candlelight Alyssa stared back at Brett and tried to keep breathing. The feather boa slid off her shoulders to land on the floor.

"I'm sorry, I must have spaced out there for a minute because I thought you might have suggested my sister is performing somewhere and I know that can't be true." Hadn't Rosa promised not to compromise her health by putting herself in the limelight again? She'd been working at a flower shop for the past few months now that she had recovered. No way would she do something as foolish as sing in the Elvis Legacy contest. Still, Alyssa's heart thrummed faster with old fears. "Could you run that by me one more time?"

"Rosa Renato is on the docket to perform at the event." Replacing the boa around Marilyn, Brett edged closer to Alyssa. "I saw her name on the sign-up sheet with my own eyes."

He paused, as if waiting for her response. But Alyssa couldn't have been more stunned if he'd reached down to yank the circa 1974 lime-green shag throw rug out from under her feet.

"I assume you didn't know about this?" He gathered her hands in his broad palms. His warm, strong, sexy-as-hell palms.

Alyssa yanked her hands free even as she appreciated the sensual contact for snapping her out of dumb-founded shock.

"No, I didn't realize. Probably because Rosa doesn't want me to know." No wonder her sister had looked so salon-perfect with her new blond highlights. The twit was headed back to the stage without so much as a con-versation with Alyssa. A fine how-do-you-do consider-ing all they'd been through together. Didn't Rosa remember the pressure that had sent her swirling into a dark abyss? If she won this contest, she'd be launching a new career, a comeback that would thrust her right back into all the old problems they'd finally shaken off.

"You don't think she should perform anymore?" Brett leaned one arm along the top of the lunchbox dis-play, his numerous tattoos blending easily with the psy-chedelic swirl of patterns on the *Partridge Family* bus.

"She's…got issues." Alyssa couldn't even think about seeing her sister in the hospital hooked up to feed-ing tubes without experiencing major bouts of panic. Alyssa loved her adoptive family, but her connection to Rosa went even deeper.

"Maybe she feels ready to go back on stage. Maybe she misses the music. Hell, I know if I had to walk away from my career, I'd…"

His words died away as he seemed to catch the im-plication of her deliberately withering stare.

"I take it you're not interested in hearing her side?"

"I'm interested in keeping her alive and healthy." She moved through the store toward the register and picked up the telephone. Punching in her sister's cell number, Alyssa tried to think what she would even say to Rosa if she answered. At this rate, she feared her spinning head would only yank the phone cord out of the receiver.

But the line rang and rang until voice mail kicked in, leaving Alyssa frustrated and worried.

"Look, I'm sorry I mentioned the bit about Rosa performing." Brett had somehow gotten close to her again, his tall, lanky body in perfect ogling range while she fumed and fretted. "I guess I just hoped that if Rosa was making a comeback, maybe you'd want to make one, too. But I sure didn't mean to cause trouble for either of you."

He shook his head just enough to toss aside the hank of dark shaggy hair that had been covering one eye, treating Alyssa to the full impact of that mesmerizing gaze.

It was enough to distract her for a moment, the lure of his stare too potent to resist. Only one other man she knew had eyes that beautiful a shade of blue. And as she glanced up at the poster of the *Fun in Acapulco* album cover taped to the wall behind Brett's head, Alyssa had to admit Brett could give even Elvis Aron a run for his money.

Her sister would say such a thought was sacrilege, but hell, Elvis was still in poster form while Brett Neale stood before her in the sizzling hot flesh.

"It's okay," she admitted finally once she found her voice again. "I know you didn't mean to rile me, and you just might have given me the tool I need to prevent Rosa from hurting herself again."

It was a crazy plan, but it just might work.

No, it *had* to work since Rosa's life could depend on Alyssa's success. Besides, since when had Alyssa Renato backed away from something crazy?

"How can I do that?" Brett's brow furrowed before that dark hair of his slid over his eye again.

Alyssa's fingers itched to twine through that dark brown hair and brush aside the errant strands, but she reminded herself that her new plan would call for a more hands-off approach. She couldn't very well look at Brett as eye candy if she was going to form a professional relationship with him.

Pity.

Gathering her courage to do what needed to be done, she took a deep breath and shared her scheme.

"You can consider me your manager long enough for you to beat the pants off my sister in the Elvis Legacy contest."

"You'll represent me?"

"Just until I can be sure you win. After that, I'm making no promises."

Brett's grin could have made an ice princess melt. And Alyssa Renato had never been the cool and reserved type.

"Then I guess you really are my good luck charm." He offered her his hand to seal the deal. "I'm in."

That Graceland tattoo flexed along with a string of Chinese letters underneath. Alyssa dragged her eyes off his arm long enough to shake his hand and recognize she'd probably just lost her mind.

"You realize I've just agreed to represent you without ever seeing you perform live?" Decisions like that made for really bad business. But then again, her deal with Brett wasn't about business. It was about saving Rosa from herself.

"Not to worry. I've got a set at Planet Soul on Friday night. You can take in the act and figure out how we can tweak it for the competition."

Alyssa nodded. "Great. Friday at eleven?"

"I'm not in the eleven o'clock set." He shrugged like it didn't matter. "I go on at one."

"Not anymore you don't." Alyssa bristled, already looking forward to going head-to-head with the owner of Planet Soul. God, she'd missed this business. "We'll get you in the earlier set. And maybe before you take the stage Friday we can head over to Golddiggers and scope out the terrain for the competition? There's an Elvis-fest leading up to the main event."

"Sounds good." Brett smiled and backed up a step toward the door. "I can't thank you enough for working with me on this, Alyssa. You won't be sorry."

"You did me a favor by giving me a heads-up on Rosa. I'm going to call her now and see if I can talk some sense into her."

"But either way, we're still on for Friday, right? You're with me through the competition?"

"I'll be there. And win or lose at the competition, I'll make sure we get a few music execs on site to see your act." She could do that much for him. In fact, now that she'd warmed up to the idea, she had to admit it would be a pleasure to make a couple of phone calls on his behalf, catch up with some old friends.

After seeing him out, Alyssa ignored the leftover séance snacks and dirty dishes stacked by her register and started searching for Brett's old demo. She'd take notes and brainstorm how to improve his act right after she called her sister again.

Two hours later, ensconced in her queen-size, four-poster bed that was the sole piece of furniture she'd lugged from L.A. to Las Vegas, Alyssa finally got through on Rosa's cell phone. Alyssa flung aside her notebook and the portable CD player with a copy of Brett's original material as soon as the phone was picked up at the other end.

Too bad the voice that answered wasn't Rosa's but a southern-accented male's.

"Rosa Renato's phone." The speaker strung out the last syllable like a resounding note on a steel guitar.

"Um. Yes. Rosa Renato, please." Alyssa wracked her brain for the name of her sister's new man. Obviously a very significant new man if he answered her phone.

Shuffling noises sounded on the other end before Rosa's soprano took over.

"Hey, Night Owl. You ever look at a watch?" Her voice rasped with a sleepy note. "It's after midnight."

"Since when do you go to bed early?" When they'd been on the road together, they'd never gone to bed until dawn.

"Since I have a normal life. What's up?"

Seeing no sense in dancing around the issue, Alyssa dove right in. Subtlety had never been her strong suit.

"I hear you're singing again. Publicly."

A long pause followed and Alyssa remembered why

she and her sister rarely talked anymore. Anytime one of them brought up a sore subject, they ended up in an argument or shedding stupid tears that solved nothing. Not the most effective communication.

Finally, Rosa cleared her throat. Came up with an answer. "I thought you've always said you were okay with whatever I decided to do."

"Of course I'm okay with whatever you want to do, just as long as you don't get hurt in the process. Hell, Rosa, I thought you decided you shouldn't perform anymore." Alyssa remembered all the negative junk that had surfaced in her sister's therapy while she'd fought her way through recovery. The pressure of live performances and media attention had caused most of her problems. And since Alyssa had set up every last one of Rosa's gigs along with the demanding interview schedule to give her the necessary exposure to make it to the top, Alyssa took plenty of the blame.

"I need to do this, Lys. And you don't have to do anything for me this time. I've already got it all set up."

"So I'm out of the loop now?" Alyssa tried to ignore the hurt in her chest without much success. Didn't Rosa care about all they'd weathered together? "After everything we've been through?"

"I just don't want any pressure this time." Frustration threaded through Rosa's voice, her words going softer as Alyssa's grew louder.

"You think *I've* pressured you?" Alyssa considered pounding her head against the nearest column on her four-poster bed. "Rosa, I walked away from everything just so I could—"

"Alyssa?" The southern accent came back on the line sounding none too pleased.

"I really need to talk to Rosa." Her sister had a guard dog now? Her temper simmered as she thought of all the other times Rosa had bolted before they could resolve anything. "I didn't even get to tell her I'm representing someone else at the Elvis Legacy."

"I'll let her know. Don't worry about her, okay? She's doing really well."

Alyssa wanted to impress upon the guy—why couldn't she remember his name?—that Rosa couldn't perform next week, but before she knew it, she'd been politely shuffled off the phone.

Well, hell.

Refusing to feel guilty about taking Brett on as a temporary client when Rosa couldn't even be bothered to tell Alyssa that she was singing again, Alyssa pressed the play button on Brett's demo and went back to work. She would make sure Brett won the competition and the potential recording contract that went along with it because Rosa seemed to have developed amnesia about the detrimental effects of performing. Rosa could have her one night in the limelight, but no way would Alyssa allow her to get hurt again just because her new boyfriend thought she could handle a comeback.

Letting the sweet music of Brett's voice carry her away, Alyssa tipped her head back on the pillow to listen. She might only be reentering the music business for a short time, but damn it, she might as well jump in with both feet and enjoy herself. Her personal life sucked big time, so why not have a little fun in the profession she'd missed for two years?

And since fooling around with her sexy new client wasn't an option, she'd just have to keep them relentlessly busy and primed to take the number one slot at the competition.

BRETT HAD HEARD Alyssa's promotional methods were unconventional, but that knowledge hadn't prepared him for her maneuverings at the site of the Elvis Legacy shindig on Friday night.

He sat on a bench in the middle of the chaos in the casino's biggest reception hall and watched Alyssa argue with one of the hundred vendors setting up their wares in preparation for the weekend crowds. No doubt Alyssa was in the process of telling the ninety-year-old bald T-shirt salesman that his graphic renderings of her idol were all wrong. Brett had already heard her launch the same arguments with a leather goods merchant, an artist selling velvet paintings and two impersonators whose pompadours were too high and thin.

According to Alyssa, the King had exceptional hair.

All of which was well and good except that Brett couldn't see how a single one of her disputes had any bearing on his ability to clinch the Legacy title and a shot at a recording contract. With only a week left until the competition, shouldn't they be ironing out rehearsal schedules, discussing what to perform or even going over the basics of how to appeal to the judges?

Instead, Alyssa moved through the crowd on an endless mission to groom the King's image instead of

Brett's. Hell, he hoped he hadn't made a mistake by joining forces with her. He'd embraced the clear-cut rules and regulations of the financial world after his wacky childhood with his aunt the wannabe Miss Marple. And even when he'd left behind his neat world of organized columns of numbers to pursue music, he'd never aspired to live an over-the-top rock 'n' roll lifestyle.

Thinking he should have shared his mindset with Alyssa from the start, he was just about to rejoin her and suggest they head out to his gig at Planet Soul when a tall, frosty-looking blonde approached Alyssa. A clipboard in one hand and a sleek silver pen in the other, the woman glided to a stop in front of Alyssa, her white pleated skirt floating gently around her calves.

The event coordinator. Brett recognized her from when he'd signed up a few days ago. Maybe now Alyssa would get down to business and discuss the order of the performers on Saturday, or help finagle him a favorable slot on the schedule.

He rose to his feet and headed across the room to join them. Ducking under a wooden trellis covered in silk roses and a banner advertising weddings on the spot, Brett arrived at Alyssa's side just as the event coordinator was shaking her head.

"I don't know about sponsoring a séance here, Ms. Renato." The blonde wrinkled her nose, shifting her horn-rimmed glasses higher on her face. "Don't you think the event would be a little distracting for the people who were trying to make contact with…um…the other side?"

Crap. So much for Alyssa discussing his career.

She'd started off on a séance kick instead of promoting his music.

"I'm sure we can find some creative ways to work around that, Ms. Bristol." Alyssa whipped a business card from the back pocket of her jeans. "Just keep it in mind and we can talk more about it tomorrow."

After exchanging a few more pleasantries with the coordinator who surely thought Alyssa was insane, Brett's new manager steered them toward the door, her arms weighted down with shopping bags full of Elvis loot. A purple satin sleep mask embroidered with a Cadillac convertible propped on her forehead like forgotten sunglasses.

"Un-freaking-believable." Brett shoved open the doors to the reception room and led them through the main casino toward the entrance where he'd valet parked an hour ago.

"What?" Alyssa rummaged through a brown bag on her arm while Brett handed his valet ticket to a kid dressed in tuxedo pants and running shoes.

"You brought us here to shop for Elvis memorabilia and angle for a séance at the show this Saturday?" He watched the elaborate bob and weave of valets retrieving cars and hoped he hadn't made a big mistake gambling on Alyssa to save his music career.

"Of course not." She pulled a miniature velvet guitar out of her shopping bag and dangled it under his nose. "Isn't this cute? It's a purse."

She flicked a button of some sort to show him how it opened.

"Yeah. Cute." Gritting his teeth, he tugged the sleep

mask off her forehead as his car pulled up to the curb. He'd been intrigued by her offbeat personality when they'd first met, but he hadn't been relying on her business savvy when he'd asked her out. For that matter, she hadn't been conducting séances as a sideline back then, either.

She followed him to the vehicle, flashing a sexy smile at one of the other valets who nearly tripped over himself in his haste to open the car door for her. Brett helped her settle her bags in the back on top of his guitar before they pulled out onto the street toward Planet Soul.

"Okay, so I managed to fit in a little shopping while I was doing business. Is that a crime?" Alyssa rolled down the windows on his vintage Caddy, which was similar to the model on the sleep mask she'd been wearing. "Don't forget, you came looking for me to help you. Now that I've agreed to represent you the least you can do is cut me some slack on how I do business."

He knew she had a point. But, damn it, why couldn't they at least set some goals together so he could get a better idea of what they were working toward?

"And you think holding a séance while I'm performing will help me secure the recording contract?" He slowed down for another red light in stop-and-go traffic on the Strip. After living in Vegas for the past eighteen months, Brett knew plenty of shortcuts around the city but there weren't any that would help him reach Planet Soul faster.

"Just imagine what an impression you'd make if we conjure the King during your set." Alyssa grinned over at him, the reflected glow of neon lights playing over her dark hair and delicate skin. He hadn't noticed until now she wore snakeskin boots with her dark jeans tonight, the gray and white pattern gleaming from their perch on his floorboards.

Of course, he'd been making a concerted effort to honor their deal and not hit on her.

"Conjure Elvis? You can't be serious."

Apparently Alyssa Renato had lost her marbles during her hiatus from the music industry. How could she take him to the top of the charts when she seemed more apt to get them both committed to the nearest loony bin?

"Brett, you just remember who's in the driver's seat." She leaned across him to give the horn a quick honk. "Figuratively speaking, that is."

Yeah, she'd lost it all right. He shouldn't have been so quick to sign on with a woman who summoned dead musicians for fun. But he was going for broke, gambling everything he had on this one last chance.

He shrugged his shoulders at the guy glaring at him from the front of a white stretch limo in the next lane. Maybe limo drivers didn't take kindly to horn honkers.

"Can you expound on the driver's seat comment? Exactly how much control do you expect to wield in this partnership?" Sure, they were only bound to one another short term, but it was long enough to watch his fledgling music career go up in flames.

Or a puff of incense smoke while she and her crazy friends huddled over the Ouija board during the biggest performance of his life.

"Of course." Alyssa tossed the contents of her old leather pocketbook into her new guitar-shaped purse.

She sent wads of dollar bills, packs of cinnamon chewing gum and skinny tubes of lip gloss torpedoing from one bag to the other while he steered the Cadillac around a crowd of tourists snapping photos of the light display outside Bally's.

"With me at the wheel, there are no drugs, no drinking binges, no prima donna b.s. and no talking to the press unless I set it up for you. Simple enough?"

"Hell, Alyssa, I worked on Wall Street for five years. I'm not some twenty-year-old punk guitarist with more balls than brains." He'd jammed with plenty of guys who only played an instrument to help them score with women, but that had never been the point for Brett. "I'm not in this for the rock 'n' roll lifestyle, you know."

"Yeah, well, neither was Elvis Aron and look what happened to him." She waved out the window as they passed the Elvis wedding chapel and a couple kissing just outside the front door.

"Friends of yours?"

"No. Just sending good karma toward the newly-weds. With fifty percent of marriages ending in divorce these days, couples need all the help they can get."

"Especially when they marry on the spur of the moment in Vegas." Brett moved to the right lane as they neared the turnoff for Planet Soul. "And I think I heard that it's up to fifty-eight percent now."

"Shoot. Now a wave doesn't seem like nearly enough good karma to send their way. You think we ought to go back and honk our horn at them?" She flipped open a compact from her purse and slicked on a layer of shiny lip gloss that smelled like bubble gum from clear across the car.

At least she didn't seem serious about honking the horn.

"Does that mean you're a romantic?" He slid the car into a parking spot on a side street near the back entrance of the popular nightclub where he'd be taking the stage in a few minutes since Alyssa had pulled a few strings and maneuvered him into the coveted eleven o'clock set.

She had done that much at least, and she'd made it happen as fast as she'd promised. Maybe he needed to relax a little more and let her take the lead, but he'd never been the kind of guy to give up control easily.

"Not really a romantic. I just think those souls who are either foolish enough or brave enough to try for happily ever afters deserve the support of the people around them." She toyed with the strings on her velvet guitar and then met his gaze. "It's hard enough to stick to a monogamous relationship without the people around you trying to tear it down."

He sensed a story behind those words, but knew he didn't have enough time to ask about it. Still, he wondered if Alyssa had been in a relationship like that before. Somehow he could picture her being both brave *and* foolish, and he hoped she hadn't been hurt for her trouble. Alyssa might be a little wild, but now that he thought about it she'd followed through on her promises so far, even giving him a few hints on improving his demo that he thought might work well.

Time to hold up his end of the bargain and give her the

kind of performances she needed from him in order to further his career. He cut the engine, ready to go in the club, but Alyssa leaned across and flicked the key forward to the accessory function and clicked on the radio again.

He rechecked his watch. "It's almost eleven o'clock. I should really get inside."

Alyssa shook her head. "You might not be able to play prima donna with me, but it's a good idea to turn on the celebrity behavior for Fast Mike."

"You know the owner?" He'd never gotten a good read on Mike Kinecki, the guy who ran Planet Soul.

"I *own* the owner." She tilted her chin and drawled the words in Marlene Dietrich style. "And I guarantee he'll respect you more if you waltz in there late. I already told him you're the next big thing, and I think he'll fall all over himself tonight to book you for the next month in the prime-time slot."

Brett's spirits would have lifted considerably if he hadn't suddenly pictured Alyssa flirting with Fast Mike. The guy was twice her age.

"Do you have something going on with Mike Kinecki?" He hadn't planned to pry, but he realized he really hated the idea. Alyssa's business methods might confound him, but he couldn't deny the attraction.

Whereas her unorthodox ways chaffed his hide professionally, her free-spirit willingness to try anything sparked an automatic male reaction. Alyssa was pure fantasy.

"Bite your tongue." She frowned at him, her shiny lips plumped into an enticing pout. "I just know how to play him. You understand your guitar, I understand club managers. And this guy is impressed by star quality. Haven't you ever heard the old adage, 'fake it till you make it'?"

"That's not me." Since when did you score points with your boss by not showing up at work on time? He would have been booted on his ass ten times over if he'd pulled that crap when he worked as a financial analyst. "I'm not much for playing games."

"Then let me play them for you. This business is all about games."

"I don't know." He'd seen that to a certain extent over the last year and half, but he'd always told himself he wouldn't go that route.

"Well I do." She leaned close to make her point, her body looming near in the confines of the car. "Trust me."

She probably hadn't meant the move as a come-on. Hell, he knew damn well she hadn't because she looked just as surprised as he felt when the heat ratcheted up a few degrees in the intimate space.

And as she lingered there, suspended in her surprise, Brett realized she knew all about the chemistry between them that she'd denied two nights ago. Feminine awareness lit her dark eyes from within in the scant moment before her gaze fell to his mouth.

If there had been any other tune in the world on his car radio, Brett might have stood a chance at pulling away. But as the strains of "Can't Help Falling in Love" filled the vehicle, the music seemed to weave around them and draw them closer still.

Or maybe that was just his long-denied libido roaring for a taste of this woman's bubble gum-scented lips.

Either way, he couldn't help taking just one lick.

CHAPTER THREE

RETREAT.

Retreat!

Alyssa's common sense screamed the warning in an all-points bulletin to her body. But her fingers weren't listening as they feathered a touch across Brett's sculpted jaw. And her legs sure weren't paying attention since they failed to move so much as an inch away from Brett's thigh.

And *bless my soul,* but her lips seemed to lead the charge in the other direction since her mouth wasn't having any part of a retreat. They parted on contact as this delicious man she barely knew kissed her.

So much for being a professional. Alyssa clicked off the annoying voice of her conscience and allowed herself to enjoy just this one kiss. She was only representing the guy for a little while anyhow. Did it matter if she broke her own rules about manager-client relations?

Besides, she didn't remember kissing being such an all-consuming experience. Sure it had been a long time for her, but could her memory be failing that badly?

Twining her fingers through Brett's hair, she pulled him closer for a more thorough taste. Just to jog her memory, of course.

His tongue slid over hers in sensuous rhythm like a

man accustomed to making music with every part of his body. Alyssa had never been able to carry a note, but that didn't staunch her sudden urge to start singing.

Moreover, if the man was this adept with his tongue...

She shivered alongside him at the thought, realizing he hadn't even touched her yet. All that sensual want from just the stroke of his lips over hers, the dance of his tongue in her mouth.

There was no telling what might have happened next if the deejay hadn't interrupted Elvis's tune with an overenthusiastic segue into the news and weather. But she knew one thing for sure. In all her thirty-two years, she'd never been kissed that way.

"Bad idea." She figured she'd say it before he did. And no matter that her hormones were now firing through her with a fresh sense of purpose, she still recognized kissing him had been a mistake. "I'm sorry about that."

"I'm not." His voice drifted around her as he switched off the car radio. "I told you we had chemistry."

"I thought you said that was work-related."

"I think good chemistry works on a lot of levels if you let it." He covered her hand with his and Alyssa panicked.

If he started touching her, she might forget every smart intention she'd ever possessed. She'd been majorly attracted to him six months ago. Now it seemed that fascination hadn't gone away. It had simply slid over to a backburner and simmered.

"So what do you think?" His thumb skimmed over her palm. "Should we let it?"

"No." She snatched her hand back before she fell victim to her sex-deprived senses again. "Definitely not. If we have an award to win we need to spend our time focusing on achieving the goal instead of seeing how fast we can fog up the windows, right?"

She reached for the car door handle, ready to bail.

"You ought to know musicians don't separate work and pleasure like that. Sex and rock 'n' roll go hand in hand."

His expression remained so serious she couldn't tell if he was joking.

"Are you messing with me?"

"Hell no." Slowly, a grin crawled over his face. "But keep in mind that I'd like to."

Muttering under her breath, Alyssa threw the door open and welcomed the still heat of the dry air after the sultry confines of Brett's Cadillac had scrambled her brains. She needed to think about steamrolling over Fast Mike with attitude, not steaming up the car windows. And to do that, she needed to adjust her mindset. If she wanted the rest of the world to believe Brett Neale was all that, she had to believe it first.

Casting her glance backward toward the car, she saw him haul his guitar case out of the backseat before sauntering over to join her.

"Are we late enough by now?" He steered them around to the propped stage door exit in the back.

Planet Soul was a Las Vegas institution for live music. While it lacked the glitz of the casinos and their floor shows, the club had no parallel for great stage acts, a kicking sound system and the best margaritas in town.

Before they reached the steps of the unadorned private entrance, a burly doorman shouldered his way through, doling out a grin for Brett.

"Hey man, you're late," he shouted over the muted roar of the crowd filtering through the back door along with a dim blue glow.

"You're right on time," Alyssa assured Brett, winking at the doorman as she sailed past him like she owned the place. She'd learned a long time ago the key to quick access was to never doubt you belonged at the hot spot in question.

Anticipation bubbled through her as the familiar buzz of nightlife kicked up all around her. The dark hallway was technically a backstage area but that didn't prevent plenty of club goers from filling the narrow passage. A hum of excitement ignited the crowd as Brett entered the building behind her. Definitely a good indication of his popularity.

Although if the trampy twosome in matching "Ready" and "Willing" tank tops thought they were going to get their manicured claws on Brett, Alyssa would send them and their thong-bearing hot pants back to their tables.

Alyssa allowed the old familiar sounds and smells of a juke joint to sink in while she watched the club's owner pace outside his dinky office a yard away.

When he realized his talent had arrived, Fast Mike, a sweet-natured Mexican-American who couldn't have stood more than five foot six, greeted her with open arms.

"Hola, chica!" He unleashed a torrent of Spanish that Alyssa couldn't understand. Just because she'd apparently been born in Tijuana didn't mean she spoke the

language. But Mike never remembered this until he'd rattled on for a few minutes, finally slowing down long enough to switch to English.

"You're representing this guy?" He looked Brett over with a critical eye before slowly nodding his head. "The girls seem to like him, eh?"

"He's going straight to the top," Alyssa confided with the practiced tone of a trader giving an inside tip. "I'd be surprised if he's in town much longer."

Mike's eyes widened predictably before his gaze flew back to Brett. "You'll play here exclusively this week, eh? You do the eleven o'clock sets and we'll put you out on the marquee. Maybe do some ads?"

"Sounds good," Brett agreed before Alyssa elbowed him discreetly.

"We'll see," she supplied evenly, unwilling to get locked into Mike's club for too long. With any luck, Brett would be on his way to L.A. after the Elvis Legacy. "You can put him in through next Friday and then I'll get back to you about any further gigs."

While Mike nodded and looked worried, Alyssa turned to Brett. The Ready and Willing chicks were giggling and sidling close to Brett but not touching him. Damn lucky for them.

"You ready to go on, Brett?" She couldn't wait to see this man's live performance for herself. If he could sing anywhere near as well as he could kiss, they were all in for a treat.

He edged past the groupies with a smile and then nudged Alyssa down the hall with a guiding hand at her waist.

"Hell yeah, I'm ready. You remember what I told you. My work is always a pleasure."

AND SO WAS SEX.

Brett wondered if Alyssa remembered that part of their conversation later that night as he finished up his set. She'd watched most of his performance from a back corner table and even now he'd lost sight of her in the crowd, he sensed she was still out there. Watching him.

The woman sizzled.

He'd known it from the moment they'd met, but back then she'd been more distant. Unattainable.

Tonight it was like something inside her clicked and she had left behind that remote inaccessibility, morphing into a vital woman brimming over with life. Could it be the music? The reconnection with the profession she'd ditched out of worry for her sister?

She was definitely in her element here. Brett's eyes found her in the crowd as he ended one number and geared up for his last. He liked to finish his sets with an update of the Elvis standard "Too Much." The tune contained a raw sexual energy that transcended any performance style. Brett's version wasn't all that different from the original, allowing plenty of guitar to rev the lyrics.

Alyssa wouldn't want to miss this one. As a die-hard Elvis fan, she'd appreciate the nuances of Brett's cover of the song. He met her gaze across the dim, smoky bar as his fingers danced over the chords of the opening riff. Her hand wrapped around the bottled water given to her by a passing waitress, Alyssa edged closer to the stage, body swaying to the music as she moved.

Men's eyes followed her as she wove through the crowd but her gaze never left Brett's. She settled into a spot at the edge of the dance floor in front of the stage, hips swiveling in perfect time to the twang of bluesy rock. His fingers stroked the chords deftly, hands moving easily over the instrument that inspired such an appealing sway to Alyssa's curves.

He sang to her. Played for her. Ate up her undivided attention. When he got to the line "I like to hear you sighin' even though I know you're lyin'," her lips curved in a sexy smile. He couldn't wait for his set to be over so they could take up where they left off with that kiss.

She might regret the personal connection in a professional relationship, but he didn't. He knew he was delivering his best-ever rendition of "Too Much" and it had everything to do with watching her obvious pleasure in his music, from her shimmying shoulders to the seductive roll of her hips.

If he could unleash that kind of heat with a song, just imagine what he could do with his hands on her instead of on his guitar. The possibilities titillated.

Alyssa Renato might be a little too wild with her penchant for séances and her unconventional approach to business, but how could he complain when she was his ticket to success? She intrigued him in a way no other woman ever had. And damned if she didn't inspire the best performance of his life.

Tomorrow he'd figure out a way to convince her to back off the public conjuring display at the Elvis Legacy competition. For tonight, he only wanted to act on the heat between them because he had no intention of letting Alyssa go home alone.

ALYSSA WAS still mesmerized by Brett's performance an hour later as he drove her home. The city lights glowed in all their glitzy glory, the Strip humming with activity even at 2:00 a.m.

There'd always been an awe-factor when it came to her clients since, first and foremost, she counted herself as a music fan. If anything, her proximity to the music-making business made her all the more susceptible to a great act. She knew better than most people how much hard work and raw talent went into a kick-butt delivery.

And Brett's had been…transporting. She'd never forget that magical moment watching him on stage. She'd felt as breathless as a starstruck teenager, as giddy as those fans in Elvis's heyday who'd fainted at his shows.

Add to that a heady dose of a mature woman's sexual appetite and *zing!* she'd been electrified.

"You haven't said much about the performance." Brett's words recalled her from such intimate thoughts.

She was still a professional, damn it. Surely she could pull her starry gaze back to earth for a few minutes. Every artist deserved honest feedback and a certain amount of ego stroking. She knew how difficult it could be to put yourself on the line night after night in front of fickle crowds who may not appreciate what you were trying to accomplish.

"You've got a dynamite voice and a killer stage presence that you're marketing all wrong." She'd learned the best way to deliver criticism was to front load it with compliments. The positive words helped take the sting out of the need for improvement. And bottom line, she knew Brett was willing to make any necessary changes.

"What marketing?" He frowned, apparently unswayed by her praise. "Isn't that your job now?"

"I mean your packaging." Her gaze slid down to his jeans which reminded her that his package was actually quite admirable. Flustered, she forced her eyes back to the road. "I mean your material isn't showcasing your strengths as well as it could. I think we need to revise the playlist."

His side of the car remained quiet for so long she finally turned to peer over at him.

"Do you have a problem with that?" She gathered up her bags as they turned down her street. "I have to say I'm a little surprised at your resistance to my methods considering how much you lobbied for me to take you on."

She kept the words light, but she hadn't forgotten the sting of his disapproval over the public séance. How could they form a solid working relationship if he thwarted her at every turn?

He pulled the car up to her building in the quiet street. Not many people chose to live over the small shops in a neighborhood still given to occasional crime, but Alyssa had simply installed bars over the downstairs windows and made herself at home. She liked the morning commute of one flight of stairs.

"I'm not resistant." He switched off the car engine and took her bags out of her hand. "In fact, I'm very open to discussion. Maybe I could come up for a few minutes to talk about the playlist?"

"It's almost 2:00 a.m." She couldn't let Brett set foot in her lonely apartment. She'd been kicking herself for kissing him all evening, so it only made sense that she'd *really* regret sleeping with him.

"That's when I think best." Before she could argue, he slid out of the car to open her door, appearing on her other side to offer his hand to help her. "Come on Alyssa, I'm still keyed up from being on stage. I won't sleep until I at least understand where you're coming from about the playlist. Can't we talk through your ideas for changing the music?"

Of course they could talk. If she was sure that's all they would do, Alyssa would have no problem inviting him in to go over his set. It was the undercurrent of sex that concerned her.

She had to admit to being a little keyed up herself.

Finally, she took his hand and stepped out of the car.

"Okay. But no kissing." She should be able to restrain herself as long as they had that much clear before they went upstairs. "Is that a deal?"

She dug through her guitar purse for her keys while he seemed to consider the proposition.

"Fine. I promise not to instigate any kissing." He shoved open the door as soon as she unlocked it, holding it for her while she went ahead and switched on a light in the store.

Did he think *she* would be instigating the kissing? She knew better than that, damn it. Even if Brett happened to be a world-class kisser.

The perpetual scents of cinnamon candles and vanilla incense floated around them as they picked their way through the crowded memorabilia shop toward the back room that led to her apartment upstairs.

On second thought, why invite trouble by putting themselves within diving distance of a bed? They could talk down here where the atmosphere was less intimate and less comfortable. And she would be much more unlikely to instigate any kissing.

"I didn't have a chance to mention it the other night, but your store is great." Brett scanned the wall of scaled-down movie posters. "You've got a better variety of merchandise here than the twenty vendors put together at the Elvis fest."

She could feel her guard slipping as she warmed to his words. How could a woman ignore all those tattooed muscles and masculine charm, too?

"That's because most places selling memorabilia are only interested in the stereotype. The vendors were all showcasing Hawaii Elvis instead of Heartbreak Hotel Elvis, or Army Elvis. And God forbid they highlight Gospel-singing Elvis." She flipped on the light to the wide hardwood stairway leading to her apartment but was careful not to step any farther in that direction. "But he remains a legend because he was all of those things. An Everyman to five decades of music fans."

"You should have been his manager." Brett pulled out a chair for her at the table where her séance group normally gathered.

Relieved and possibly a little disappointed that his promise not to pursue any kisses seemed genuine, Alyssa slid into the seat while he grabbed another chair and flipped it around to straddle it backward.

"Actually, I consider the King an honorary client." She didn't need to impress Brett, so if he wanted to think she was a nutcase, that was his problem. Ever since her sister's battle with anorexia, Alyssa had vowed not to let other people's expectations dictate her behavior. "When I see his image being reduced to a stereotype, I feel compelled to point it out to people and make them remember he had more going for him than sideburns and aviator sunglasses."

His chin resting on his forearms along the back of the chair, he seemed to consider that for a moment, his thumb drumming a soft beat against his lips as he thought. Her gaze strayed back to his Graceland tattoo, and she reminded herself to ask him about it sometime.

"I'm sure he would have been grateful for the positive promo." His hypnotic blue gaze reminded her of those moments when he'd been onstage and seduced her with his music.

She suppressed a shiver at the memory, skin tingling with awareness.

"But what about me, Alyssa? Do you think I've got something going for me besides a few guitar riffs?"

She spent a few minutes outlining her thoughts on his playlist, about trimming out the ballads and concentrating on the hottest, most upbeat songs. He needed a hit, and his best option would be something with lots of rip-roaring guitar.

But as every good manager knew, the musical talent was rarely enough on its own.

"And you've got a few other things going for you." She forced herself to plow ahead since he deserved her honest professional assessment, a full accounting of his strengths and weaknesses. Yet all she could think about right now was how personal his performance had seemed.

"Such as?" He rocked forward on the chair slightly, his feet keeping him balanced on the floor even as he tipped closer.

Her breath caught in her throat at his sudden proximity. She could feel the heat of his body, smell the musky male scent of his skin.

Had she really said no kissing? Just now the ban struck her as a monumentally stupid idea.

"Such as your delivery," she managed finally, her voice hitting a throaty note to make Kathleen Turner proud. "You have a strong stage presence."

"Strong?" He unfolded his arms from their perch on the chair and for a minute she thought maybe he'd touch her. Kiss her anyway and consequences be damned.

Instead he just hooked his thumbs around the seat's wooden spindles. "You mean strong as in memorable?"

"Strong as in commanding. You looked like you belonged there, and that's not a quality that comes naturally to many performers."

"Alyssa likes commanding." He seemed to be committing the news to memory. "Got it. Anything else I should keep in mind?"

She recalled the strength of his last number and the way she'd sizzled for him from the moment he'd opened his mouth.

"More sex."

"Alyssa wants more sex?" A sly smile lifted one corner of his mouth.

Her pulse pounded hard enough to make her dizzy. Or maybe that sudden light-headed feeling was just another side effect of Brett Neale's major sex appeal.

"Not just me. Every woman wants more sex." She applauded herself for deflecting the conversation from her personal wants. There wouldn't even be any kissing tonight, so she sure as hell couldn't see the point in thinking about sex. "And as you pointed out yourself, the best rock 'n' roll delivers. If you can recapture the hot intensity of your last song, I guarantee you'll win Saturday night."

"That could be a problem." He threaded his fingers through his dark hair and frowned.

"Why?" Imagining what it would be like to smooth away his foreboding expression with her fingers, Alyssa toyed with the hem of the linen cloth on the table and realized she'd be thinking about sex tonight no matter what they talked about.

"The sex in the last song came from you, not me."

CHAPTER FOUR

THE ONLY SOUND Brett could hear in the moments after his declaration was the ragged breathing of his sexy new manager.

Inhale.

Exhale.

He swore he could feel the light puff of her breath on his cheek, the scent of her as distinct to him as the fragrance of cinnamon and incense in her conjuring room.

At first, he hadn't thought it would be wise to sleep with her, but the more time they spent together the more he understood the inevitability of sex. He hadn't formulated one thought tonight without the image of Alyssa overshadowing it. In the course of the past week, she'd completely taken over his brain. Ah hell, who he was kidding? He'd been gone on this woman ever since he first laid eyes on her six months ago.

"I don't know what you're talking about." She tried to dodge him, but he noticed she lowered her lashes, not even looking at him while she lied through her teeth.

"You know exactly what I'm talking about." He reached for her chair and pulled her seat closer. Maybe instead of fighting this attraction so hard, they just needed to give in and explore it. Take it wherever it might lead. What would be left to tease his imagination and distract him from his music once he'd indulged in this overwhelming need to taste Alyssa again? "The heat between us during my last song was so thick you could scoop it up with a spoon."

His gaze roved over her, absorbing every inch. Her dark purple T-shirt had been washed so many times the soft fabric molded comfortably to her skin, outlining compact curves and feminine strength.

No doubt about it, giving in looked better with every sizzling second.

"That doesn't mean we should act on it." Twisting a silver and turquoise ring around her finger, she didn't look half so self-assured now as she had back at Planet Soul where she'd been utterly at home.

The attraction made her uneasy.

"I know I said we could keep this under control." Curving his hand about her nervous fingers, he squeezed her palm. "But I didn't expect one simple kiss to knock me on my heels and take my performance in a whole new direction. You have to know I've wanted you for a very long time."

"Combining sex with business is a bad idea." Her dark eyes contained an anguished mix of desire and doubt. "I would never want to be responsible for doing anything to mess up your career—"

"You said you didn't want to be my manager after next week anyhow." The more he thought about them being together, the more sense it made. "What does it matter if we follow this where it leads, Alyssa?"

Her name on his lips made a kind of music all its own. She stared up at him like a woman in a trance, gaze fixed on his eyes and then lowering slowly to his mouth.

He hadn't consciously decided to move closer, but he knew he must be venturing nearer when her eyes drifted shut, lashes fanning out along her cheekbone like those of an exotic doll.

Their lips met on a mutual sigh, the tenuously agreed-upon kiss feeling like a mini-orgasm since it wrought such thorough satisfaction. A sense of rightness flooded through him, as if he'd waited forever for this kiss, this woman. She tasted like no confection he'd ever sampled before, the perfect blend of sweet entice-ment and sensual fulfillment. He'd never get enough of the erotic flavor of her.

A muffled hum of pleasure eased from her mouth, the sound more a vibration than a noise. And it seemed to echo clear to his toes.

"Alyssa." Her name breathed from his lips, and all through his senses, as if he couldn't soak up enough of her essence just by being near her. He wanted to ex-perience her every way a man could have a woman. She could be his muse. His inspiration…

And then her arms were winding around his neck and he knew there would be no turning back. Heat surged to his groin, firing the most primal of needs. There'd be time enough to sing to her, to write odes to her later. For now, he simply needed to touch her.

She pressed closer, her breasts grazing his chest as she leaned into him. The softness of her fueled his hun-ger, propelling his hands on a quest to explore more of those supple curves. Tunneling fingers through the silky mass of hair at her neck, he skimmed down through the strands to trace her spine. Like a roadmap to places unknown, the course led him to the pleasing roundness of her rump, the flare of feminine hips.

Delicious.

His fingers cupped her, dragged her to the edge of her chair, anxious to touch more. Taste more. Like a drug to his senses, the feel of her in his arms chased away all worries, all doubts. She was his own personal Doctor Feel-Good.

He broke their kiss long enough to stare at her again, to try and get a fix on this woman who struck him as simultaneously so sharp and so wild. A heart-stopping smile kicked up her lips, a wicked glint shone in her eyes.

"I'm way too old for you, sugar." She slipped her hands under his shirt and walked her fingers up his chest. "You just might be out of your depth with a foxy broad like me."

Whipping his shirt over his head, he hauled her out of her chair as he rose to his feet.

"You might know more than me about the music business, but you can bet your last pair of rhinestone sunglasses that I know more about singing." Lifting her high, he laid her tempting body out on the round table in front of him.

His private feast.

"Singing?" Her eyes widened for a moment as she found herself staring up at him from the tabletop. "And just what does that have to do with anything, my sexy young stud?"

"You'll see when I help you hit the sweetest high note of your life in about ten minutes." Stepping between her thighs, he stretched out over her, elbows bracketing her shoulders.

Her gaze dipped down the length of him before she hitched a finger into the waistband of his jeans. "Ten minutes? That's the problem with you young guys. Always in a hurry. Haven't you learned the key to a good performance is longevity?"

"Spoken like a true manager." Bending over the smooth column of her neck he nipped her ear and then pressed a kiss into the delicate skin behind her lobe. "But what you don't realize is that the first ten minutes are all part of the warm-up act. You haven't seen anything until the headliner performs."

Her neck arched along with her back, giving him all the more access. A soapy scent mingled with some kind of clean lemon fragrance she must have worn behind her ears. Or was that coconut? Something awfully tropical for a Vegas woman.

"Nothing wrong with a little brash confidence, I suppose." She slid against him, teasing his erection with a barely-there wriggle of her hips. "But if you're going to talk smack, I hope you're prepared to back it up. You don't want to disappoint your audience."

"Not a chance." To prove the point he eased back to align their hips. Press his advantage over her. Against her. Damned if he didn't feel mighty impressive right about now. "I can definitely deliver."

"Oh." She flexed her fingers along his abs, reminding him how much power she had over him if she moved her hand just a couple of inches to the right. He pressed harder, leaned into her more heavily and her hand slid away as she sighed with soft pleasure. *"Ooh."*

"Are you okay with being in here?" Not sparing another glance for the back room of her store, he stared only at Alyssa, wanting to make this perfect for her. He'd invested plenty of time in talking her into representing him, but now that she'd only agreed to a couple of weeks, Brett realized he wanted a hell of a lot more. There was something almost tangible drawing him to her. Instinct. Karma. Animal lust?

He couldn't pinpoint it exactly, but he recognized a connection that wouldn't be denied.

"I like it in here." Her head swiveled around to take in more of the room. "There's a lighter on one of the chairs if you want to light the candles."

For the chance to watch the reflection of candlelight over naked Alyssa, Brett couldn't move fast enough. Stepping out of the vee of her thighs he retrieved the lighter and set flame to one wick after another around the room.

A red triple-wick candle bloomed light and spicy fragrance followed by a chain of white pillar candles in brass holders spaced at even intervals around the walls. The soft glow gave the mountains of Elvis throw blankets and inflatable seat cushions an air of refinement, a pop culture shrine in the middle of the Nevada desert. But right now, he only wanted to think about recreating the sexy rhythm of her hips that he'd first witnessed at Planet Soul. Watching her move to his music had been more seductive than any foreplay.

"This place looks ready for a little conjuring." Alyssa propped her elbow under her cheek as she pivoted to look at him from her place on the table. "You want me to invite a ghost for a three-way?"

"I think you'll be more than enough woman to keep me entertained." Dropping the lighter back onto a seat cushion, he tugged Alyssa up to a sitting position and contemplated how he wanted to unwrap her. Fast and furious so he could have immediate results? Tempting, but not wise after her crack about young men being in a hurry.

Bending low, he tugged at the neckline of her T-shirt with his teeth before kissing his way down the front of the cotton, making sure to exhale a warm breath over the curve of her breasts.

"What about me?" She shivered lightly as he worked the fabric up just enough to expose a narrow strip of skin at her waist. "Maybe I'd like a little extra male entertainment and you'll welcome the opportunity for someone to come to your rescue once I get a hold of you."

He flicked his tongue along the patch of bared skin, the taut flesh warm and fragrant. "Now who's talking smack?"

Her abs tightened and tensed for a split second before she lay back, fingers twining through his hair to draw him closer.

"Just trying to hold my own with you around." Her voice faded to a husky whisper, her whole body relaxing into a kind of sensual torpor as he used his mouth to edge her T-shirt slowly up her body. "Want help?"

Her fingers slipped under the hem of her shirt as if to lift it off for him.

"What happened to taking our time? Moving slow instead of racing to the finish?"

"Maybe there's something to be said for a little youthful enthusiasm on occasion," she admitted, yanking her shirt over her head and flinging it clear across the room.

He hoped it hadn't landed on a candle, but not for all the world would he turn his head right now to look.

Alyssa's breasts were cupped by two black satin record albums, the nipples covered with pink lace labels bearing Elvis's name.

Alyssa knew her breasts were nothing to write home about, so Brett's lingering attention sent a shiver of pleasure all the way to her toes. Until she remembered her bra, that is. The custom-made, double album lingerie could stop traffic out of sheer novelty.

Damn her unique fashion sense.

"What's the matter? Never seen a copy of the *Essential Sixties* double record?" The lace suddenly itched her tender skin. She'd much rather have Brett's lips on her than one-of-a-kind lingerie.

"Not quite like this before." His gaze never left her cleavage as he traced the tops of her breasts exposed by the fabric. "Best album packaging I've ever seen."

His words soothed her ego even as his touch stirred so much more. Smoky heat curled through her, the warmth flowing deep in her veins. She wanted his hands all over her. Now.

"I'm more concerned with the *un*packaging, if you please." She traced the muscles of Brett's shoulders with her palms, unable—no, unwilling—to remember the last time she'd touched a man. It seemed like it had been forever. And no one else had ever felt like *this* man who hadn't let the rock 'n' roll lifestyle turn him into a strung-out mass of skin and bones. Brett was steely strength and muscle, vitality and good health.

All of which boded very well for what she had in mind.

"So impatient for the woman who wanted to take her time." He accommodated her by flicking a black satin strap off her shoulder before kissing the skin where the fabric had rested.

"Screw taking your time." Shivers tripped through her one after the other now, and she realized the taut tension inside her had been building since their thwarted date six months ago. All of a sudden it had become too much to bear and Brett was the only man who could fix it. She wrapped her leg around the back of his thigh and pressed herself against him.

Screw it, indeed.

Her words clearly reached him because he unhooked her bra with less finesse and more raw need. His hard hands—musician's hands, complete with callused fingertips from years of plucking guitar strings—roamed over her with new purpose. He cupped her breasts and plumped the soft mounds, tweaking the nipples into aching peaks.

Yes.

Every chord inside her hummed in tune to the sweet music he wrought with his touch, her hips already swaying beneath him. She wrapped her arms tighter about his shoulders to bring him down on the table with her, but he scooped her up and carried her to a worn-out old sofa she'd moved down from her living room.

He lay next to her on the thick cushions, the eighties oversized styling leaving plenty room for two. Still, she pulled him closer, on top of her, so she could feel the whole length of his sculpted male body against her soft curves. The rigid press of his erection nudged her belly and sent a surge of exquisite longing to her core.

Her fingers dug into his shoulders, desperate for more. She'd occasionally craved sex in the last two years since she'd been dumped by a rising star drummer shortly before Rosa's illness. But Alyssa hadn't really missed it enough to risk her heart and sanity on a man. Until now.

While she planned to keep her heart safe, her sanity was completely up for grabs. And her body? That *so* belonged to Brett tonight.

His hands spanned her waist, cradling the slight curve of her abs before sliding down the zipper of her jeans. He skimmed the band of her satin panties, sending heat waves through her whole body. Toying with the strings on her low-rise bikini, he tugged and pulled until he untied the bows at her hips, rendering her naked beneath the denim.

"Wicked man." She nipped his shoulder as she wriggled under him, every inch of her craving more of his touch. "Those are some very clever hands."

"I told you I'd have you singing for me tonight." Propping himself up on one elbow, he stared down at her as his other hand continued to wreak havoc between her thighs. "All you have to do is tell me where you like to be touched."

Tell him?

She couldn't speak with his fingers tracing intimate circles along the inside of her uppermost thigh. And she couldn't even *move* once he pressed his thumb to the throbbing heat of her clit. How could she possibly say what she liked best?

"What do you think, Alyssa?" Brett kissed her mouth with a slow swirl of his tongue in a way that mimicked the movement of his fingers. "Do you like this?"

Her heart galloped so loudly that his voice seemed a million miles away. And then his finger slid deep inside her, pressing hard against the taut knot of her G-spot until she cried out from the tight throb of pleasure.

"Oooh!" The note sang out of her like an aria, the waves of her orgasm carrying her deep into uncharted sexual terrain. And *bless my soul,* but it rocked her world.

She clutched Brett's shoulders, clinging to the solid weight of him to anchor her in the stormy tide of liquid heat. Her voice rang in her own ears, echoing right up to the rafters. She'd summoned spirits in this room before, but she'd never conjured up pure magic.

Brett bent to kiss her neck as he held her in the aftermath, his words whispering over her ear. "I told you we had chemistry."

"Maybe there's a little," she admitted, not even sure if she knew her own name anymore. Her breath came in hiccuping gasps, her voice scratchy in the wake of her primal scream. "And you've got quite a technique… for a young guy."

He levered back to look at her, blue eyes surprisingly intense.

"What are you, all of five minutes older than me?" With slow deliberation, he unfastened her pants and dragged them down her legs. "I just made you come without even undressing you, woman, so I think I've got more going for me than a good technique."

Pleasure hummed through her at his words, her every cell agreeing with him.

"I'm thirty-two and wise enough to know raw talent when I see it." Her thighs quivered as his knuckles grazed her legs and the air conditioner blew cool gusts over her warm skin. She wouldn't be able to rile him for much longer since any second she was going to pass out from bliss overload. "You really think you've got what it takes?"

When he stood up long enough to unearth a condom from his wallet and shed his pants she got a view she wouldn't soon forget. Totally *smoking*. This man delivered a hunka, hunka burning love.

"Definitely." He crooned his assurance into her ear. "I think you want me bad."

Judging by the way she nearly hyperventilated at the feel of his naked thighs against hers, he probably had a point. Fingers twitching with impatience, she stroked her hand over his face, his stubble scraping her palm.

She lowered her mouth to his, hungry for another taste of him. His kisses flooded her consciousness, robbing her of any other thought but the feel of him on her lips, the scent of musky man and smoky incense making her dizzy with longing. A keen pang of sensual hunger tightened in her belly, forcing her to tug the condom out of his hand.

"You're right. I do want you bad." The foil packet

crinkled as she tore it, her coordination impaired by lust. "Let me."

"Impatient…" He sighed the complaint as she rolled the condom over him, even though his throbbing length confirmed he loved every minute of her touch. It pleased her to think she could spark just as much pleasure in him as he gave her.

He felt too good. Too perfect. Too marvelously big.

Swinging up to her knees to straddle him, she steadied herself on his shoulders. Their gazes locked for a long moment, his blue eyes not missing anything. He studied her with a kind of soulful tenderness only a musician could comprehend.

An unsettling thought for a woman who never liked to overanalyze anything but Elvis.

Quickly closing her eyes again, Alyssa retreated to the world of sensation where she could connect with Brett on a more comprehensible level. She lowered herself over him until his erection nudged her most sensitive flesh.

This, she understood.

Liquid warmth flowed through her veins as she swayed downward, hips rocking subtly to appreciate every inch of the luscious invasion. She wanted more, but he eased her along carefully, slowly, taking his time. He guided her hips with his hands, holding her off when she moved too fast, letting her press forward when he was ready.

She'd thought she was in the dominant position? Even beneath her, Brett ran the show. A fact which might not sit well with most managers, but considering how superbly gifted he'd been with his fingers, she was willing to see what he could do with his…package.

So far, so yummy.

Goose bumps broke out over her skin, an erotic shiver dancing through her as he took his own sweet time. And when at last he filled her, stretched her, satisfied her so thoroughly with that incredible body of his, he only allowed himself to stay a moment. Then the whole agonizing—okay, fantastic—process started all over again.

She could get into this groove. The rhythm he set forced her to slow down. Indulge. Enjoy. He wouldn't let her take the fastest course to the goal, instead he showed her how to squeeze sweet gratification out of every moment along the way. The heat inside her built and built, tension coiling so tight she thought she'd explode and still he took her higher. Higher.

When at last he allowed himself to drive deep with long, steady thrusts, Alyssa flew apart in a million directions. She floated high on a wave of pure orgasmic satisfaction, body convulsing so sharply she thought the aftershocks would never stop. Brett's hoarse shout mingled with her cries, their yells more powerful than any impassioned séance pleas ever spoken in this room.

As she slumped over his beautiful body, Alyssa was almost afraid to analyze why she'd been quick to give in to the attraction of Brett today when she'd held other men at bay for so long. Ever since she'd given up her management business, as the matter of fact.

Too bad a little voice inside her kept repeating what the King would say about the situation if he ever reigned over this room like she'd often dreamed.

Some things were meant to be....

CHAPTER FIVE

IT WASN'T UNUSUAL for Brett to wake up with a tune in his head. For one thing he was a musician. And for another he'd always been a pretty well-adjusted guy with his priorities straight.

As he kicked off the purple velvet comforter from Alyssa's bed late that morning, he told himself it wasn't even all that unusual for him to wake up singing an Elvis tune. Since his mother had been a major fan, he'd inherited a definite respect for the King.

But in all his twenty-eight years, he'd never woken up with "Can't Help Falling in Love" humming through his brain. And it scared the crap out of him that he'd been half singing it in his sleep this morning while Alyssa snoozed beside him. Not that he had anything against love and romance. They were nice ideas for one day in a far-off future after he'd chased his dreams down an uncertain path. Yet even in that distant tomorrow, he never pictured himself with someone as unconventional as Alyssa.

Peering across the blankets, he watched the steady rise and fall of her chest where she curled on her side, one hand tucked beneath her cheek. The dark hair that kinked and curled wildly around her face while she was awake lay in a tame swath behind her, the glossy locks calling him to stroke his fingers through the strands.

No doubt about it, she was a beautiful woman, her jaw so perfectly sculpted she looked too lovely to touch as she slept. But when awake, her quirky enjoyment of music and collectibles made her approachable, her down-to-earth sense of humor and willingness to conjure celebrity spirits setting her apart from anyone he'd ever met before.

Sure Brett might be attracted—okay, so he was superattracted. But that didn't mean he wanted to wake up whistling mushy songs every morning when she was around. This woman could launch his career. She knew the ins and outs of the business he craved. He wouldn't screw up a good thing by reading too much into a night of great sex. To do so would be shortsighted, and might actually offend Alyssa who seemed to pride herself on a healthy dose of independence.

Staring up at a ceiling cluttered with tiny, star-shaped mirrors, Brett hoped she wouldn't regret their night together. His subconscious might be weaving impossible scenarios of sex and rock 'n' roll, but maybe he needed to give her a little breathing room first. Enough space to reestablish a working relationship before he wasted his final bet at the big time. If it didn't work out, he would go back to his life as a financial analyst and at least he'd always know he gave it his best shot. But he wouldn't give up on his dream until he'd gambled his every last dime to make it happen.

He debated how immature it would be to steal one

last peek at Alyssa naked beneath the blanket before getting up when the phone beside her bed rang.

Any hope of seeing Alyssa naked again died as she blinked her way out of sleep and reached for the phone.

"Hello?" Her scratchy voice played over his senses, sending a cheap thrill to an erection that showed no signs of disappearing.

He started making plans for their morning, wondering how he could get out of bed without actually putting all that blatant sex drive to use. Then again, maybe if Alyssa really wanted to, it wouldn't hurt if they...

"Count on us," Alyssa spoke into the phone, bolting upright in bed and jarring him out of wicked fantasies. "We've already got the séance plans in motion and I can personally promise it will make for a very entertaining event."

Funny how the word "séance" could deflate the best-laid sex plans. Brett shoved aside his lust to focus on the rest of Alyssa's conversation, which involved crystal balls, tarot cards and ghosts. He couldn't stave off the flashbacks to a childhood that had been peopled with poltergeists. Every time his Aunt Marsha turned around she was either squealing in terror over the presence of an unfriendly spirit or counseling a well-bred phantom on how to cross over to being peacefully dead.

Other kids had memories of Boy Scouts, campfires and ghost stories. He'd had *Night of the Living Dead* in his own backyard. By the time Alyssa hung up the phone, he didn't need to ask what was going on. The grin on her face told the story.

"We got the go-ahead for the séance at the Elvis

Legacy competition." She clutched the velvet bedspread to her chest but didn't quite manage to hide the subtle curve of her breasts. "You're going to have the best show Golddiggers has ever seen, and that includes the unicycle-riding twins who lit their bike on fire while pedaling over an alligator tank two years ago."

Brett blinked, trying to process words that sounded more like a carnie trying to sell him on a local circus act.

"What do you mean you got the go-ahead for a séance?" She surely hadn't been serious about showing up at his performance with all her mantra-chanting friends? "You signed on to represent me at least through the competition. You can't ditch me during the contest to play with your crystal ball."

Her fingers fisted deeper into the bedspread as her grip tightened. "On the contrary, I plan to use the crystal ball in an effort to *help* you."

"I thought you were just yanking my chain last night about summoning spirits." Then again, maybe he'd just heard what he wanted to hear. "Hell, I thought at very worst you were trying to organize some kind of event for your spirit-seeking friends. But *you're* going to be a part of this ghost-calling exercise?"

"Me personally." She reached for some garment hanging off the bedpost and wrestled her way into it—actually a sleep shirt with an ancient Jimi Hendrix album cover ironed on the front. "I'm going to oversee the whole thing because I told you that I would help you win this thing Saturday and I stand by that. The séance is going to attract a boatload of media attention and fan interest, and then it's up to you to capitalize on it and impress the judges."

She yanked the telephone—a classic princess style in shiny silver metal—onto her bed and gripped the receiver.

Brain still spinning from her insane plan that had nothing to do with his talent or his guitar riffs, he plucked the receiver from her hand and replaced it in the cradle.

"Wait a minute. Do you care to tell me why we can't make a go of this contest without a lot of theatrics? If you think I don't have the talent to win this on my own, I'd rather know straight up now so I can find a manager who believes in me more than some half-fried plan to hypnotize the judges into thinking I'm Elvis reincarnated."

She slid out of bed, her sleep shirt only covering half of her thighs as she stomped toward a built-in bookcase at one end of her bedroom. Daylight streamed in through the blinds, the creamy-colored metal slats not all that effective at keeping out the noonday sun. When he'd brought her up to bed as the sun was rising, he'd asked her if anyone else could open the Good Luck Charm for her in the morning, and apparently she had help who worked the early shift.

Now, she pulled out one three-ring binder after another from the bookshelf and tossed the heavy volumes onto the bed at his feet.

"Here are a few mementos from my former life as a talent manager. Just the highlights of other 'half-fried plans' I've had in my career." She pitched a framed photo of her with her sister at the Video Music Awards, followed in quick succession by a silver-framed picture of Alyssa at a press conference with a country music singer surrounded by Grammy Awards, then a promotional photo signed by a teenage pop star whose dedication to Alyssa read, "I owe you the world."

"You represented Cassie Styles, too?" He ran a finger over the teen idol's photo, wondering if the young woman's career would have stayed on track longer if Alyssa hadn't left the business. Cassie had burst on the scene with major octave range and endless ambition, but she'd gotten derailed when she eloped with a fading movie star who introduced her to drugs.

"Yes I did, back in her good days. And you know what? No matter how many octaves the princess of pop could hit, I always made sure to cover her nonexistent ass with a solid promotional angle, too." Alyssa's cheeks flushed pink, her lips pursed in a tight little frown of disapproval. "You're the one who asked for my help, Brett. It seems you're awfully damn critical when you're the guy who propositioned me."

He flipped open one of the binders she'd thrown at him, humbled more than a little by the pages and pages of awards, letters and press photos she'd accumulated over the years. She'd saved personal notes from music industry headliners, producers and some lesser-known studio bands that wouldn't be immediately recognized by the general public, but whom Brett knew to be major behind-the-scenes players.

No doubt about it, Alyssa Renato was big time. And he'd just figured out how to really piss her off.

Nice morning-after move, Casanova.

"You're right." Shoving aside the binders, he slid out of bed and stepped into his pants. He followed her out of the bedroom and into the living room where he caught her by the arms. "I'm sorry."

Turning her to face him, he remembered the kisses they'd shared. The sex. And something more. They'd shared something incredible and he'd repaid her by being a jackass.

"I just don't know why you have to jump all over the séance idea." Her clipped tone didn't sound like she was all that ready to forgive him, but at least she didn't shove him away, either. "This is Las Vegas, Brett. You can't just put on a show here and expect people to love you for your talent alone. You need to be over the top. And since we can't build you your own private amphitheater, and I don't want you performing with Siberian tigers, we need to find something else that's big and showy and will land you the attention your act deserves."

Even pissed off, she could be damn convincing. Remembering the way she'd worked over Fast Mike last night, Brett suspected Alyssa could maneuver her way into most anything she wanted.

A good skill for his manager. A frightening talent for the woman he'd just slept with. But damned if he didn't want them both.

"Okay." He still didn't like it. The thought of a séance made him want to run for cover. But he wouldn't impose his past on Alyssa and read something into her actions that wasn't there. "I just wish this could be more about the music. Elvis had a guitar. Nothing else. No conjuring magic. No bells and whistles."

"You think he didn't have an angle?" She shook her head, curls spinning in every direction. "Ed Sullivan would only film him from the waist up, Brett. You know how ingenious that was? Every teenage girl in America wanted to know what was going on below the belt. He couldn't have asked for a better publicity stunt."

He softened his grip, knowing he needed to smooth over his knee-jerk reaction to her idea. She deserved better from him today after what they'd experienced last night. And no matter what else happened between them, he didn't have any intention of giving up his dreams.

"You're right." He was man enough to admit it. Just selfish enough that he still didn't like it. "Maybe I'm not looking at the big picture here. But I'll leave publicity up to you as long as when it comes to you and me, I've got equal say."

ALYSSA BLASTED one of Brett's new demo tapes three days later as her "Meet the Presleys" group began arriving at the store to practice for their first public performance. She could feel herself getting drawn back into her old lifestyle as the guitar hummed right through her, the music calling to her soul as surely as the rock 'n' roll lifestyle she adored.

She *sooo* shouldn't go there.

But the recording session with Brett two days ago had been inspired. They boosted each other creatively, pinging ideas around the recording booth so fast they'd ended up with some incredible new material. Brett had even jotted down some ideas for another new song.

Now, as she shut off the overhead lights in the store, Alyssa's thoughts drifted from their professional successes to their night together. It had been beyond incredible. Not just because the sex with a studly younger man made her knees weak and her toes curl. No, she'd loved the shared moments of conversation about everything from their mutual admiration of Elvis to the hazards of greedy club managers and drunken fans.

Loved?

Okay, so that was overstating the case. Maybe. Either way, she'd had a blast remembering what it felt like to live in the moment, with no worries about the past or future. God, it had been too long since she'd been able to just be herself. She was always so careful not to talk music around her sister. And because she and Rosa shared the same friends and same séance group, that meant Alyssa didn't talk music with anyone these days.

Until this past week, she hadn't fully appreciated what a hole that had left in her life.

She flipped the Closed sign on the front door of Good Luck Charm, eager to conjure up her idol tonight in an effort to find the elusive sense of inner peace that had been missing since she'd asked her sister—and herself—to walk away from the music business. Elvis, patron saint of the Renato sisters, somehow had the answer.

A crazy superstition? Maybe. Alyssa preferred to think of her conjuring obsession as a way to maintain a strained friendship with her sibling, a common interest to bring them together after so many other shared pursuits were no longer an option.

Just color them dysfunctional. At least Rosa was still alive.

Now, as Alyssa lit a vanilla bean-scented incense

stick on the checkout counter, Laura Grimaldi danced past her.

"Alyssa, honey, this man's voice is sex in stereo." Humming along with Brett's chorus, Laura grooved in time to the music as she juggled a plate of strawberries dipped in white chocolate.

She thought his *voice* was sexy? Laura hadn't even seen the man's hip swivel. Alyssa got hot flashes just thinking about it.

"He's great, isn't he?" In fact, Alyssa had been distracted with thoughts of how wonderful he was for three days straight. They'd worked together on some interviews she'd set up today, their preparation schedule so busy they barely had any time to discuss what was happening between them. That worked just fine for her since she wasn't ready to dissect all the feelings he'd stirred inside her. He'd only left a few hours ago to pick up some new guitar strings before his set at Planet Soul, but they'd made plans to see each other Friday—their last day to rehearse before the competition.

Only a few more days and he'd be out of her life. Damned if she should be thinking about him so much when he'd be making tracks to pursue a major career so soon.

"This is the man whose act you want to promote on Saturday with the séance?" Laura set down the tray of strawberries beside the cash register now that Good Luck Charm had closed for the day. Pulling out her turban, she carefully positioned the prism medallion of her headwear over the place on her forehead she referred to as her third eye.

"I figured it would be good for your business and his, too." Alyssa admired her friend's easy commitment to a career some people considered kooky. The fact that Laura could find personal healing as well as humor and fun in contacting spirits only elevated her in Alyssa's eyes. "The press will eat it up and the Meet the Presleys group will have a chance to be on TV."

"They'll love it." Laura popped a strawberry in her mouth while the two of them supervised the preparations for the séance.

Alyssa's gaze fell on Hester Schwarz, the little old lady from somewhere out in the middle of the Nevada desert who swore Elvis came and danced with her in her backyard on late summer evenings. She never missed a chance to contact him with the rest of the group.

Too bad Rosa wouldn't be here. Alyssa hadn't been able to get in touch with her all week despite numerous phone calls and messages. Was Rosa angry? Hurt? Alyssa hated not knowing.

Laura waved the plate under Alyssa's nose, tempting her with chocolate. "But I have to say I'm surprised you're representing this guy after the number of times you've sworn up and down you'd never go back into the music business. Rosa must be so happy for you."

Alyssa nearly gagged on her strawberry. Whenever she hadn't been thinking about Brett's hip swivel, she'd been imagining how upset her sister must be that Alyssa was representing her toughest competitor at the Elvis Legacy.

"Actually, I haven't had the chance to talk to her about me representing someone else again." Her sister's new boyfriend seemed to be keeping her pretty busy. "But that's just because her boyfriend hurried me off the phone last week when I tried to discuss it with her."

One of Brett's original recordings ended and his cover of "Too Much" rocked the speakers, sending the small gathering into an uproar. Laura twirled around with a squeal while Mrs. Schwarz clapped her hands together in delight. The group's only male member—Jesus Vargas who still wore his hair in a ducktail at seventy—bowed in front of Hester before asking her to dance.

All around, approval of Brett's rendition seemed pretty amazing considering this group of Elvis fans was hard-core. Alyssa fought off the old shiver of anticipation she always used to get when she listened to a musician destined for the top. Brett would be one of those people—if he found a good manager willing to put the time in to make it happen.

And much as she might secretly hope otherwise, it wouldn't be her. Couldn't be. How could she ever go back into the business permanently when Rosa—who adored music every bit as much—could never take the stage again without a serious threat to her health?

"So he just showed up here last week and said he wanted you to represent him?" Laura opened the front door for two more séance stragglers, the last of the group they were expecting for the practice run tonight. "I'm surprised you finally took the plunge."

"Why?" Defensiveness crept through her as she snatched a handful of strawberries and fired them into her mouth one after another. "Brett is incredibly talented."

"No kidding." The prism on Laura's turban winked

in the lights as she pointed to Hester and Jesus tangoing their way around the séance table. "He's fantastic if he can make those two finally get together after all the months they've been circling each other. I'm just saying it's good to see you getting back into the music industry after all this time."

"I'm not going back into the business." She'd keep her promise to Rosa, damn it, no matter how much she'd enjoyed this brief return to music. That part of her life was over. "Elvis is the only guy I'm promoting these days."

Brett's song faded away on the stereo, filling the room with an empty, uncomfortable quiet. Kind of like her life would be once he hightailed it out of Vegas to strike it big in L.A.

She lurched toward the stereo to click on the radio, determined to make that resounding silence go away. Her life was not empty—not now, and not when Brett left. She had a terrific shop with a steady business that supported her very comfortably. Plus, she still had enough clout in town to secure tickets to any show she chose. Too bad it wasn't quite as fun to hear the new acts now that her memorabilia shop kept her ten steps removed from her old life.

"Why?" Laura watched her so closely, Alyssa swore the other woman used her third eye, too. "Why aren't you returning to music when we all know how much you love it? The store is cool, but I always thought it would be just a temporary stop for you until you were ready to go back to your true calling."

"True calling?" Alyssa told herself that, despite Madame Stargazer's trappings, Laura was no fortune-teller.

She couldn't know how much Alyssa loved her old job. "I'm a woman of countless skills, my friend. Talent management is simply one among many."

A few yards away in the back room, Alyssa could see their group starting to set the mood by lighting candles around the table. She moved toward them, only too glad to sidestep this conversation.

"Wait." Laura's hand snaked out to hold her back. "I'm serious. Why not sell the shop and live your dreams again now that Rosa is better?"

Blinking back the unexpected pain that came with the thought of not living her dreams, Alyssa paused. Remembered a time that caused her a hell of a lot more pain than a few outdated career ambitions.

"Why? I'll tell you why. Because when Rosa wavered two steps from joining Elvis on the other side of the pearly gates, I promised her I would get out of the business for good if she would only get better." She'd promised everything she could think of, in fact, her panicked ramblings had been frightening for a woman who until then had made her living on slick business maneuvers. "I knew it hurt her to walk away from the spotlight, but I made her do it to save her life."

Those months had been such hell. Watching her sister waste away had eaten away parts of Alyssa, too. They were sisters—the only blood connection Alyssa had ever known. And until she'd been faced with the prospect of losing her best friend, her one real ally in the world when even their mother had abandoned them, Alyssa hadn't realized how much that bond meant. "I'm *not* going back on that promise."

Laura's grip softened as she tugged Alyssa farther back into the privacy of the storefront while the others remained caught up in their own conversation.

"I know how sick Rosa was back then." Laura had met Alyssa for the first time in the hospital cafeteria when they'd both reached for the same packet of sweetener. Laura's mother had been recovering from a plastic surgery mistake the same month Rosa had been fighting for her life. "Are you sure she even remembers you making this promise? Or that she even cares now that she's got so much going for her?"

"A new boyfriend and a job arranging flowers? No offense to the bouquet designers of the world, but deciding when to use carnations and when to reach for chrysanthemums doesn't seem like the kind of work that would satisfy a woman who'd once entertained millions of people."

Kind of like how hawking Elvis memorabilia wasn't quite the same as promoting the most talented musicians in the world to bottom line-oriented venues who wouldn't know creativity if it fell in their laps. There had been a challenge Alyssa could really sink her teeth into without pretending to be an uptight corporate type. No one in the music world ever blinked when she carried a guitar-shaped purse into a meeting.

"I think she's a lot happier than you give her credit for. I only wish I could say the same about you." Scooping up the plate of chocolate strawberries, Laura switched off the radio and headed toward the séance table. "But who knows, maybe this new guy will be just the thing to put a twinkle back in your eye."

Gliding into the back room with a swish of her floor-length purple cape, Laura left Alyssa to wonder if she'd just stepped into the *Twilight Zone.* Rosa the depressed was content with arranging flowers while Alyssa the chronically well adjusted needed a fortune-teller to explain how a man could make her eyes twinkle?

She'd call Rosa again tonight. Try harder to mend the gulf between them and patch up a relationship held together only by their occasional séance meetings and Alyssa's continual fear something would happen to Rosa if she didn't keep an eye on her.

Huffing out a sigh, she followed her friends into the séance circle and prepared to conjure the King for real this time. In order to heal this rift with her sister, she needed his royal wisdom now more than ever.

But not even a dispensation from Elvis Aron would free Alyssa to follow Brett on the road to fame, fortune and something even more shimmering and elusive… something she dared not name.

CHAPTER SIX

"YOU'RE TELLING ME you contacted Jim Morrison?" Brett strummed a little riff from "Come on Baby, Light My Fire" on Saturday morning, hoping to cheer the woman who would be his manager for a mere two hours more unless he could change her mind. "For real?"

They'd spent the night together, but somehow they hadn't gotten around to talking about her séance earlier that week. First they'd ripped their clothes off. Then he'd played a few songs for her so they could say they'd done some work. Then they had sex again. And again.

Hell, yeah, he was crazy about this woman.

He also happened to be riding the most creative wave of his life with new songs exploding into his brain every time he turned around. Alyssa was the best thing that ever happened to him—personally *and* professionally.

"Apparently he faked his own death, only to kick the bucket in a bar fight a few years later over the validity of The Doors' music." Alyssa had been on edge all morning as they prepped for the competition, her clipboard and her cell phone hardly leaving her hands.

"Your Ouija board told you all this?" Brett still wasn't sure how he felt about her close encounters with dead people, but at least she didn't seem to take it too seriously.

"Heck no." She peered around the ballroom the convention had reserved for the performers to warm up in and stow their equipment. All around them, musicians tuned instruments ranging from bass guitars to bagpipes. Every act west of the Rockies seemed to have congregated at Golddiggers Casino today for the chance of media coverage and a recording contract. "Madame Stargazer was temporarily inhabited by Jim's spirit. She talked for him."

"Madame Stargazer sounds very…imaginative." His fingers picked out a chord from the Elvis hit "Good Luck Charm" that he wanted to perform today in honor of Alyssa—his personal ticket to the big time. She'd nixed his idea in favor of "Too Much."

"We prefer to think of her as highly intuitive." Still Alyssa didn't look at him, her eyes locked on the double doors leading into the ballroom.

"No sign of your sister yet?" Brett knew Alyssa had been thinking about Rosa, her old fears for her younger sibling robbing her of the pleasure she might have taken in a competition Brett was determined to win.

He hated to see her mired in those old hurts since it was obvious to him she belonged in L.A., wheeling and dealing and inspiring other musicians to new creative heights. Although he'd be damned if she would motivate anyone else quite the way she'd stirred him.

"No." Dragging her gaze away from the entrance, she swiped a restless brush of her hand over the back of his shirt, removing lint he knew wasn't there. "And I know she had to have gotten my messages the last few days. I don't know if she's mad at me for representing you or embarrassed that I found out she signed on for this event—" Shrugging, she made a *tsk*-ing sound under her breath. "I don't know. We seem to suck at communicating these past couple of years."

Laying a palm over his guitar strings, Brett quieted the vibrating chords. "Alyssa."

"Yeah?" A furrow creased her brow, worry etched into her heart-shaped face.

Her eyes were so endless, so full of the capacity to love and give. He couldn't imagine what it might be like to have that kind of caring and concern pointed toward him. Ever since they'd connected in the steamy heat of his car a week ago, he couldn't deny thinking about her pretty much every waking moment.

In his life as a financial analyst, he'd played it careful and safe. But he was a musician now, if only for a few more hours. And Brett the guitarist didn't care about playing it cautious. He was falling for Alyssa—Ouija board and all.

"Who are you representing today?" He traced the delicate curve of her cheek with his thumb, his fingers sinking into the silky fall of her dark hair. "Me or your sister?"

She rolled her eyes. "I can't ever *not* represent my sister. She's a Renato, you know?" A hint of a smile curved her soft lips. "She's walking around with my nose and eyes, even if she's got much better boobs."

His eyes involuntarily tracked over her chest.

"Definitely a matter of opinion." Pulling his focus

back to her face, he reminded himself that he needed to have this out with her now, while he still had a shot at convincing her to stick with him. "But what I mean is—don't check out on me now when I need you so damn much."

"I'm totally prepared." She reached behind her to retrieve her clipboard off his amplifier. She'd been carrying around notes all day as she ran between the ballroom where he warmed up and the convention hall where the initial acts were already performing on stage. "I've got two music execs in the audience just salivating to see you. The séance kicks off in an hour, right before you take the stage. I'll get things started, but then I'll let Madame Stargazer run the séance on her own so that I can stick close to you and—"

"That's not what I mean." Lifting his guitar off his lap, he propped it against the amp and set aside her clipboard so he could hold her. "I just don't want you to let Rosa's performance rattle you. If she signed on to sing after all she's been through, she must really need to be here."

"That doesn't exactly make me feel better." She whispered the words into his shoulder as he held her. "She's so desperate to get back into the career I denied her that she'll go behind my back?" A small shiver trembled through her, so subtle he wouldn't have even known it if he hadn't been touching her. "I don't have any choice but to feel guilty."

Not having a clue how to answer her fears, Brett let the chaos of the backstage areas swirl around them while he held her, wishing he knew what to say to set her free from her old promise. And not just for his sake, damn it, although he'd be lying if he said that wasn't part of it. He wanted her to see that for her own happiness she needed to fix things with Rosa.

Inhaling the cinnamon incense scent of her, a permanent fragrance around her shop that followed her wherever she went, Brett slowly became aware of her fingers trailing over his shoulder.

His Graceland tattoo.

"I never asked what made you decide to imprint Graceland here." Inching back enough to look up at him, Alyssa tossed a lock of dark hair out of her eyes. "You're a fan from way back?"

"Actually my mom was the fan in the family." He didn't have many memories of her, a single mother, but he could still hear her singing an Elvis Christmas tune in his head while she decorated an early holiday tree. "Cancer took her right before my fifth birthday."

Her hand stilled on the tattoo for a moment before she leaned close to place a gentle kiss on his shoulder. "I'm sorry."

"My aunt told me afterward that my mother always wanted to go to Graceland but she never made the time to just get in the car and go." He was sure a woman so young would have had a lot of other things she wanted to accomplish in her lifetime, but that unfulfilled wish was the only one his aunt had shared with him. "It always bugged me she didn't take that trip. Realize her dream."

Alyssa edged back again to glance up at him, her gaze wary. Speculative. "We can't always accomplish everything we dream about."

· "We can sure as hell try." The needle burned that

message into his flesh the day the tattoo artist imprinted Graceland on his arm. "I got the tattoo the day I left the financial world to go after a music career. And whether I make it big or not isn't the point. But I won't go back home until I give this everything I have."

For once Alyssa the brash, bold talent manager who conjured spirits and protected the Presley image, didn't have a single thing to say. Brett took the opportunity to press home his point. Tugging her closer to his heart, he cinched his arms tighter around her.

"Chase your dreams with me, Alyssa."

He didn't know if his words had made an impression or not because just then, the double doors to the back-stage area swung wide and a excited rumble went through all the Elvis Legacy wannabes.

Rosa Renato had just entered the building.

BRETT'S TEMPTING request still ringing in her ears, Alyssa instinctively moved out of his arms toward her sister, knowing she'd never consider his offer without talking to Rosa first.

God, how could she even be thinking about taking this up with Rosa after all her sister had been through? Alyssa needed to at least tell her face-to-face that she'd only agreed to help Brett because she'd been scared spitless Rosa would fall back into self-sabotage once she stepped on stage again.

Of course, Alyssa hadn't counted on how much it would hurt to walk away from Brett and all he seemed ready to share with her now. It seemed she was doomed to being scared no matter what she chose.

"Rosa!" Alyssa shouted over the throng growing around her sister, who could still attract a crowd when she went into rock star mode.

And in a backstage area crammed with musicians who would give their eyeteeth for the successes Rosa had already seen, Rosa pretty much ruled the room.

"Make way! A-list talent manager coming through." Elbowing her way through the Rosa Renato groupies, Alyssa shouted for her sister again.

Eventually, she cleared herself a path. Faced the sister who'd been through so much with her.

A sister who kept a white-knuckled grip on a tall, lanky guy wearing a Celtics shirt and a sporting an auburn crew cut that was only slightly less fifties' looking than Jesus Vargas's ducktail.

"This is your new boyfriend?" Alyssa regretted the surprise in her voice because the guy was actually very good-looking, he just—didn't look like the rock 'n' roll type Rosa usually went for. But judging by the way Rosa leaned in close to him, it was obvious she thought the world of the Irish professor.

"Sean, meet my ever-tactful sister, Alyssa. Sis, make nice with my new husband, Sean Halloran."

A few cheers broke out among the musicians still clamoring for a little of Rosa—Mrs. Halloran's?—attention.

"You got *married?*" Alyssa couldn't decide if she felt betrayed or happy. Pissed off at being left out of the loop or thrilled her sister had found The One.

"Don't be mad." Rosa moved deeper into the protective circle of her new husband's arms, a gesture that startled Alyssa half out of her sneakers.

Did Rosa think she'd be mad?

A lightbulb flashed on so bright in Alyssa's brain she suddenly identified with her clients who complained about the blinding lights of the stage. Of *course* Rosa worried Alyssa was mad. And with good reason since Alyssa had half debated being upset just now.

What if all the time Alyssa had been trying to protect her sister, Rosa had been as intimidated as anyone by her sister's admittedly bulldog tactics? Not all that hard to believe since Alyssa always had a knack for wheeling and dealing. Getting her way.

Oh hell.

Regret whistled through her in the empty space that had once been a great relationship with Rosa.

"I could never be mad about you being happy." She leaned in to hug her sister. Gently. Tenderly enough to not annoy Sean, who despite his skinny frame looked like he wouldn't let anyone mess with his new bride. "You are happy, aren't you?"

Alyssa ducked back, reassessing the pair together again. An odd match, her exotically beautiful sister and the ghostly pale professor. But their twined hands, so strong and united together…that told Alyssa all she needed to know.

Rosa rolled her eyes and ignored the question she seemed to think was too obvious to answer. Her husband backed up enough to shoo away some of the musicians, giving the sisters a little room to breathe.

"Sorry I didn't return your calls the past few days," Rosa whispered, still clinging to her new husband. This total stranger she'd fallen in love with while Alyssa had been absorbed in her own worries that maybe were…a little over inflated?

"I was afraid you were upset with me because I'm representing Brett." Alyssa had tried explaining her motives on her sister's answering machine a few nights ago, tired of waiting to talk to Rosa in person.

She pulled Rosa behind a wall of electronic equipment and monster-size speakers that had a devil's face painted on them in red spray paint.

"Upset?" Rosa's gaze flicked over Alyssa's head to someplace behind her where Brett probably waited. "I'm just so grateful you're getting back into the business. I've felt like crap for the last two years about falling apart on you. I know I haven't been the best sister, and I know I was such a disappointment—"

Tears stung Alyssa's eyes as she realized how much she'd failed the woman who meant more to her than anyone in the world.

"You have *never* disappointed me. Ever. I thought you were mad at me for making you quit the business because it seemed like you went so quiet every time we talked. And I didn't want to upset you any more since I knew the eating disorders could be triggered by stress and—ah, hell, Rosa, I'm so sorry."

They hugged and cried, ignoring the whole rest of the world around them, although Alyssa's new brother-in-law did a pretty good job of keeping everyone at bay.

Alyssa babbled about the promise she'd made to Rosa and all the reasons why she'd worried her sister resented her. Rosa rambled about the pressure she put on herself to be successful and the way therapy and flower-arranging were both helping her to accept herself.

"But, if you're in the competition today you want to get back into singing, right?" Alyssa vowed to clarify everything with her sister from now on, determined never to rely on her faulty sibling radar again.

First and foremost, Alyssa planned to put the brakes on her séance trick for Brett today if her sister really thought she could reclaim her old success as a singer. Would he understand?

Alyssa's gut clenched, knowing he would gladly accept the challenge of performing without any gags or stunts. He was a good man. An honest, fair-minded guy with great principles.

Which was why he needed a crafty manager so damn badly.

But not at Rosa's expense.

"Oh my God, no. I'm not here to win." Rosa pulled over Sean who winked down at her before planting a kiss on top of her head. "My therapist suggested I face my old demons now that I've made a lot of progress, just so the past doesn't ever rule me again. If I can sing today in front of a crowd without passing out, I'm going to volunteer to lead the church choir. Be normal. Use my voice for something that won't make me crazy."

Holy crap.

Rosa really didn't want to win. Her sister had just cleared the path for Alyssa to claim every dream she'd ever imagined. *Graceland, here I come.*

But first, she needed to talk to Brett.

"Rosa, do me a favor and don't leave after your per-

formance today, okay? I've got a friend who might need
a little help from Meet the Presleys today."

She just hoped he wanted it. And even more, she
hoped he still wanted *her*—high dysfunctional quotient
and all.

CHAPTER SEVEN

FOR SEVEN DAYS in a row, Brett had woken up to "Can't Help Falling in Love" playing in his head. Coincidence? Not a chance.

Sad he'd been too boneheaded to see it until the strains of Elvis's most famous love song gave way to an endless mental loop of "Heartbreak Hotel" resounding between his ears. His whole relationship with Alyssa was going down in flames in Golddiggers Resort and Casino, all because he hadn't put himself on the line when he'd had the chance. He could have told her he was crazy about her. That he'd fallen in love with her so fast it made his head spin, and his brain cycle through old Elvis hits.

But no. He'd been the biggest chickenshit of them all. And he'd accused *her* of not living her dreams?

Picking up his guitar, he wound through the backstage area, needing to talk to her before his performance. But between the fans filtering into the ballroom and the party atmosphere rapidly taking over the place, Brett couldn't make any headway. The M.C. had announced Rosa Renato by the time he made it to the other side of the room where he'd seen Alyssa and her sister talking earlier.

Damn.

Knowing Alyssa wouldn't miss her sister's act, Brett slipped closer to the main stage. Searching. Scouring the crowd for a sign of her. He ducked around roaming waiters toward the folding chairs set up in the middle of the convention center, circumventing the booths packed with memorabilia Alyssa would argue didn't fully showcase the King's abilities.

Hell yes, he'd fallen in love with her.

Finally he spotted her off to one side of the platform, her dark eyes locked on Rosa along with the rest of the room. Well, everyone but him, who only saw one Renato female.

She must have sensed his gaze because she turned just then. Stared back at him.

Call it intuition. Karma. Animal lust. Hell, call it all of the above and more than that, too. This had been love at first sight, even though he'd been too blown away by her to realize that's what had happened the moment they met.

He wanted to talk to her. Needed to tell her then and there she was more important to him than any competition, prize or music career. But as soon as he reached her, she splayed her fingers over his mouth to silence him before he could say a damn thing.

"I have something important to say that can't wait." Still, she waited anyhow, as if giving him a chance to argue.

He nodded instead.

"I'm not one hundred percent sure if you can win strictly on your performance today, Brett." She arched up on her toes to whisper into his ear, her words meant for his ears alone while her sister crooned her heart out on stage nearby. "But either way, I need you to know that I believe in you. And I am one hundred percent sure we can build you a kick-ass career on the West Coast with or without a win today. So it's up to you how you want to chase your dreams."

Floored, Brett angled back to look at her. Found only gorgeous sincerity in her eyes.

"You're serious." The love he'd been feeling in his heart burst so damn big he thought it would crash right through his rib cage. She believed in him. Wanted to come to L.A. with him. "You want to represent me?"

"I want to do much more than that with you." Smiling, she trailed her fingers over his cheek. "But being your manager is as good a place as any to start."

Thunderous applause broke out through the audience, and for a moment, Brett thought the whole world cheered his good fortune. What a lucky, lucky man he was to have a woman like Alyssa by his side.

For good, damn it.

"Hell yeah, I want to win." He joined the applause for Rosa a little late, his attention taken up with Alyssa and what was happening between them. "But only if it won't mess anything up with you and your sister."

Her smile was her only answer before she sprinted off toward the back of the room. What on earth?

And, as he scratched his head and tried to figure out what she was about, the M.C. announced Brett's performance. Making him realize he *still* hadn't managed to tell her he loved her.

No time like the present.

Vaulting on stage, Brett warmed up his fingers on the guitar strings. Who was he kidding? He was warming up for the rest of his life with Alyssa.

He had no clue what had come over her to make her put so much faith in him, but the financial analyst in him would figure it all out and add things up later. Right now, his inner rock star was going to leave it up to fate.

And music.

"This one's going out to Alyssa Renato, the woman I can't help falling in love with." He heard the squeal in the crowd and wasn't sure if it was from random fans responding to his corny Elvis impersonation, or a certain woman who might enjoy that bit of news.

For now, he just planned to give the best performance of his life since he'd dedicated it to the most special woman in his world.

ALYSSA SWOONED right along with every other woman in the crowd at Golddiggers as Brett Neale, rising star, launched into a rendition of "Too Much" that would make any female weak at the knees.

And "Too Much" was only the beginning.

His dedication of love still echoing in her ears, Alyssa gave the cue to Laura "Stargazer" Grimaldi to take the séance into high gear at the back of the room where only a few dedicated media members lingered since everyone else in the place had tuned into Brett. All of which was according to plan since Laura's crystal ball conjured the coolest electronic holograph—an image of Elvis singing, projected up on stage right alongside

Brett. They'd slaved away all night on the parlor trick and it couldn't have worked any better.

The whole place erupted in spontaneous applause. Out of the corner of her eye, Alyssa saw both music executives on their cell phones, each frantically trying to give her a thumbs-up sign. No doubt, Brett would have two solid recording offers by nightfall.

A media frenzy that even Alyssa couldn't have predicted swarmed the Meet the Presleys members while flashbulbs popped nonstop all around Brett. And although Alyssa knew Brett cared more about his art than the fame, she couldn't help but rest easier now, knowing he'd always be able to play the music he loved thanks to his assured success.

"That's one hell of a stunt, Sis." Rosa appeared at Alyssa's side, her face glowing with excitement. She'd dodged the circling reporters around the séance table to join Alyssa on the fringes of the spotlight.

A place that made sense for Rosa, now that Alyssa finally understood her better.

"He's one hell of a guy." Alyssa flung her arm around Rosa's shoulders, ready to celebrate so many good things in her life. A new man. A new brother-in-law. A sister who looked happier than she could ever remember seeing her. "You realize that almost thirty years after our orphanage days, Elvis is still taking care of us?"

"Looks like he's taking pretty good care of Brett Neale, too." Rosa pointed to Brett, who currently fended off journalists and photographers, TV cameras and a hundred swooning women as his song ended.

Alyssa felt the familiar adrenaline kick in. She

adored the music business, only this time the thrill was tinged with so much more, a swell of love for the man at the center of it all.

And this time, she didn't mean Elvis.

Brett's eyes met hers across the room. Searching. Finding. Communicating the love he'd announced to the whole convention center.

"Guess I'd better go help him out." Leaving her sister in the capable hands of Sean Halloran, Alyssa launched through the crowd toward the man of *her* dreams.

The rest of the room faded away as she threw herself into Brett's arms, giving him her heart and soul in a kiss captured by a sea of flashbulbs. Oh yeah, she was definitely living her dreams. And it was only going to get better.

Brett broke away to look into her eyes, pulling her into a booth selling velvet paintings where they could grab a few stolen moments behind a life-size canvas of the King.

"I hope you realize I'll never be able to go back to being a financial analyst now that you've got me pouring my heart out on stage and falling in love at first sight." He stroked his fingers through her hair, twining a curl around his finger. "No one who works with a calculator for a living could ever be that irresponsible."

She could have fallen right into those incredible eyes of his. Elvis might have gorgeous baby blues, but Brett was the real deal—a living, breathing embodiment of a lifetime of fantasy. And even through the rapid-fire beating of her heart she could hear the M.C. of the Elvis Legacy competition getting ready to announce their winner.

Not that she had a doubt in her mind who that would be.

"Well lucky for you, we girls who play with crystal balls for fun don't exactly play it safe either. I'm crazy in love with you, Brett Neale."

"Crazy enough to come to L.A. with me?" His hands trailed down her sides, dragging her hips against his.

"Honey, I'm crazy enough not to bother packing." She nipped his shoulder, dying to get him alone to tell him how grateful she was he'd talked her into being his manager. His lover. Maybe one day, a whole lot more.

But right now the velvet paintings all around them were shaking as reporters tried to invade their hideaway. Up on stage the winner of the day's competition was being named. Still, Brett took his time brushing a kiss across her lips.

"Who needs clothes when you're living on love?" His hand slid under her shirt, just enough to graze her bare back. Remind her of the heat between them.

A wave of pleasure cruised through her veins despite the growing shouts of camera-wielding journalists asking if Brett was going to come out on stage to accept his award.

Bless my soul, he'd won the Elvis Legacy.

Alyssa squealed her pleasure as she flung her arms around him and squeezed. She'd push him toward the stage in a minute so he could accept the honor and all the fun that would go along with it. But first she couldn't help whispering one final thought....

"You realize tonight I'm finally going to have an honest-to-God icon in my bed?"

Everything you love about romance...
and more!

Please turn the page for Signature Select™
Bonus Features.

Bonus Features:

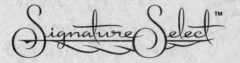

BONUS FEATURES

Love So Tender

"Finding Romance in Elvis Tunes"
I WANT YOU, I NEED YOU, I LOVE YOU... by Joanne Rock

EVER NOTICE SOME OF THE MOST romantic men wield a guitar? For the past century, the guys we would have once considered poets are finding homes in music, giving a voice to feelings and emotions through songs they write or sing. Consider Johnny Rzeznik's "Iris" that gives us shivers when he croons lyrics of love. The man knows a thing or two about romance.

One of the most versatile singer/songwriters of the past hundred years has to be the one, the only, the King of Rock 'n' Roll. Elvis Presley tapped into enough romantic themes that he could have been perfectly at home in any of the Harlequin/Silhouette lines. He started his career with steamy, sexy songs. After a stint in the army, he traded in some of his raw, sensual style for more dramatic, emotional fare. Just for fun, let's take a spin through some of Elvis's hits for a few examples of his romantic savvy...

1) If "Love Me Tender" had been a book, it would be the quintessential Harlequin Romance. Warmhearted and tender, the title says it all.

2) "Big Hunk O' Love" has Blaze written all over it. No interpretation needed there!

3) "Suspicious Minds" delves into the more mature relationship that's compelling but fracturing. This is the same kind of emotional punch we see in Harlequin Superromance, a series devoted to complex relationships with real-life drama.

4) What about classic romance plots featuring Mr. Right? This is Silhouette Romance's terrain and Elvis proves he can appeal to the softer side of love. In "Don't Be Cruel" he urges his sweetheart to take a trip to the altar and say, "I do."

Q: Which Elvis single reached quadruple platinum status?

A: "Hound Dog/ Don't Be Cruel," his 1956 release was the only single prior to 1985's "We Are the World" to achieve this status.

5) The King of Rock 'n' Roll even knew how to capture romance that's sparked by danger and fueled by passion—the same kind of suspenseful adrenaline ride that we expect from a Silhouette Intimate Moments. His hit song "It's Now or Never" conveys this do-or-die urgency.

6) Songs like "Surrender" talk about hearts on fire and seem to have Silhouette Desire written all over them.

> **Q:** What famous musician had this to say when Elvis died—"The King is dead. But rock 'n' roll will never die. Long live the King"?
>
> **A:** John Lennon

7) But Elvis's sexy side didn't take away from a deeply spiritual facet that permeated his music from the very beginning. He's the only artist with two multi-platinum gospel or inspirational albums, and he shows a keen understanding of how faith and love intertwine in songs like "You'll Never Walk Alone."

8) For more action and adventure, check out Harlequin Intrigue–style tunes like "Trouble." Elvis does a pretty convincing tough guy.

9) Thanks to Elvis's many feature films, his repertoire includes plenty of songs with exotic settings and glamorous, international passion. Songs like "Vino, Dinero Y Amor" capture the mood of Harlequin Presents along with "Guadalajara" and "You Can't Say No in Acapulco."

Q: Who was Elvis's silver screen idol?

Hint: *This "Rebel" shot to fame shortly before Elvis.*

A: James Dean epitomized the kind of brash, tough image Elvis projected in his music.

10) Silhouette Special Edition introduces the real-life challenges of love and family, but at the core of this popular line is still a strong romance. Elvis's take on commitment is clear in romantic staples like "Can't Help Falling in Love." Is there a better way to begin a happily-ever-after than a walk down the aisle?

11) Winding up our musical trip with a fun detour through Silhouette Bombshell, we find a heroine-driven line featuring strong, savvy women saving the day. Surely Elvis Presley couldn't relate? Maybe not entirely, but he admired strong women, devoting plenty of songs to females who were bold and brash. Check out "Hard Headed Woman" or his cover of "Maybelline" about the driver of a pink Cadillac who wouldn't back down from a Ford when she wanted to race. Sounds like a Bombshell in the making!

THE SCOOP
How I Met Mr. Right
by Jo Leigh

I met my own personal Mr. Right when I was
twenty-one. Lawrence was tall and gorgeous and
smart and just a bit dangerous. We met at a local
bar, Sloans, in West Hollywood. I was working at
Fox Studios and he was a recording engineer. We
were mad for each other, but we were also crazy
and still finding ourselves and our relationship
was anything but smooth.

And then there was our work. I was utterly
driven to make movies, which I'd wanted to do
since I was ten, and he was a busy engineer,
working into the wee hours of the morning at a
small recording studio in Hollywood. We didn't
sleep much, but then again, we didn't need to.

After about a year, we had our first real test. I,
by some miracle, landed a job on a location
shoot. It was a movie called *The Deer Hunter*, and
I flew across the country to a little town called
Coreopolis in Pennsylvania. Talk about
exciting! I got to hang out with Robert DeNiro,

8

Meryl Streep and Christopher Walken. But I missed my guy. Toward the end of the shoot, some of the cast and crew went off to Thailand, but I remained in Cleveland to wrap things up there.

Lawrence flew out to join me for a long weekend, and we drove to New York. It was incredible. We had drinks with Al Pacino, stayed with Rip Torn and his girlfriend Amy. Got lost in Brooklyn and saw a free concert in Central Park.

It was the last of the really good times.

When I got home, we fell apart. I'm still not sure why, except that we were young and insecure, and while I still loved him beyond reason, he pulled away. We broke up. Well, actually, he broke up with me, and I tell you, it nearly killed me.

I never truly got over him. I dated, but no one compared. I got lost in my work, traveling all over the country on location, making movies for television and the big screen, meeting fascinating people, learning about screenplays and the fundamentals of story structure. I worked for most of the major studios at one time or another, and had amazing teachers. It was a real dream come true. Professionally, at least. Personally, year after year went by, and Lawrence was still there in my heart. The pain had diminished, but had never disappeared. I tried to banish him, but I couldn't. I didn't know how.

In the late '80s, I was back in Los Angeles, working for a small production company and deeply involved in The End Hunger Network, a volunteer organization putting together a telethon to raise money for Hunger charities. The night of the show, I didn't feel well. And I didn't feel well for a long time after that. Enter phase two of my professional life.

It turned out that I had a rare autoimmune disease, kind of like lupus, but not. What it meant was that I could no longer do my job. I couldn't stand for longer than ten minutes. I was on a lot of serious medication, and frankly, it sucked. I had to find another way to make a living, and I couldn't depend on my body to support me.

And that's when romance came into my life. Again, professionally, not personally. I took a class in L.A. on writing romance novels. I figured it would be a piece of cake. Ha! It was very difficult, and very different from writing the screenplays I'd been used to, but I persisted, and thankfully, sold my first book to Meteor Books. Shortly after that, I sold a book to Silhouette, and that was it for me. I had found a way to be creative from the comfort of home, to tell stories about love and adventure and happy endings.

The irony wasn't lost on me. How could I write about happy endings when I'd never had one of my own? So many years had gone by, and while I'd been with some terrific guys, there hadn't been that *something,* that magic. None of them were Lawrence.

I had no idea what had happened to him. I wasn't even living in Los Angeles anymore. I'd moved to Houston for a few years, and then I'd moved to Las Vegas.

But I wasn't moping about. I loved writing, and I had fabulous friends, mostly writers. I taught story structure in workshops all over the country. I was lucky enough to write for a lot of lines—Intimate Moments, American Romance, Temptation, Intrigue and Blaze. I was happy, and I'd made peace with the idea that writing about true love was going to be as close as I'd get to those happy endings. But it was okay. I wasn't lonely or bored.

Then in March of 2001, I opened an e-mail from an address I didn't recognize. My heart pounded in my chest as I read the brief note.

See, it started out with the salutation Jake. Only one person in the world had ever called me Jake.

Lawrence.

He'd found me on the Internet. From my books. From my writing. He congratulated me on my success as a writer, and hoped I was doing well and that I was happy.

I shook as I typed the response.

He called a couple of days later, and oh, I may be a writer but I don't have words to express my feelings during that phone conversation.

He told me he'd never forgotten me.

That he had few regrets in his life, but the biggest one was that he'd lost me.

I cried a river of tears, and felt my dormant heart come back to life.

Two months later, we moved in together.

It's been almost three years now, and what can I say? My books are different now, because I'm different. I know a whole lot about true love, and not from books and movies. I know everything about happy endings, because, after twenty-three years, I'm living mine.

How's that for romance?

The Writing Life
A Day in the Life of an Editor
by Laura Shin

Ever wonder what an editor does all day? Read on to find out about one day in the life of this editor! A day in the life? That suggests there's such a thing as a typical day. No such beast. But I'll try....

Monday, June 7, 7:12 a.m.: Get off elevator with lunch and a manuscript. Turn on computer, take a quick look at the message light on the phone (no red light—yay!) and make tea while computer warms up. Check mailbox (21-page fax from author—her changes to the printout/galley). Return to office, open e-mail program and see what awaits...

I have 17 messages. Delete without opening four encouraging me to obtain free drugs from Canada. Read and delete the two jokes from friends. Accept two meeting requests (one for a cover "post-mortem" where Editorial, Art and Marketing get together to look at covers and sales results to see if any trends can be seen and another to approve the October covers). Three queries from authors about publication dates/ISBNs/titles/covers (answer what I can). Two from editors asking about publication dates/ISBNs/titles/covers (answer what I can). One e-mail from an author containing changes to a line edit (print and put aside for later). One from an author with changes to a printout (print and put aside for later). One from the legal department asking about a request from an author who would like to make a small adjustment to the contract (new delivery date—send agreement). And the final one contains photos of an author's new puppy (smile).

Take deep breath and a swig of tea and pull to-do list close.

* Editorial meeting (via videoconferencing) 10:30.

* Sign off on September "prelims" (proof and approve look of everything that goes before Chapter One in the book).

* Sign off on November "black and whites" (proof and approve cover copy).

* Add author changes to printout for October books.

* Deflag (look at copy editor's work and also deal with any queries she has flagged) for November book.

* Draft responses to questions asked for magazine article.

* Line edit due for January book in three weeks.

* Work on revision letter for book read two weeks ago (must find time to write letter!).

* Call U.K. office (before noon) to discuss cross-line series with shared author.

* Call Australian author (after 5:00) to discuss cross-line series with U.K.

* Revise manuscript that arrived last week.

* Read for approval two proposals (3 chapters + synopsis), three long synopses and two short e-mails (to see if ideas will fly before full proposal developed).

* Art information due to Art and Marketing next week—check with editorial assistant to see which books have complete art info sheets.

* Title April and May 2005 books, finalize
  schedules and schedule the rest of 2005
  (currently about half done).

Catch up with fellow editors and find out if
there are any questions or issues that need to be
resolved. (Show photo of author's puppy.) Spend
a few minutes discussing title options and a new
in-series promotion. Work on prelim package, get
halfway through and hear e-mail message come
in. Note from French office requesting
information on books that contain a particular
subject matter. Get out schedule and start to
compile list. Check with other authors to ensure
complete, put list down and head to editorial
meeting. Discuss series business, hear what
books have been bought .

11:15 a.m.: Get back to office, inhale breakfast,
pick up list for France, hear computer announce
arrival of another message. Ignore it. Finish list
and e-mail. Open newest message from Direct
Marketing requesting clarification about our
program. Start to answer and realize that I need
clarification from executive editor. Run to next
office to ask, get waylaid by editor asking about a
tricky plot point in an unrevised manuscript.
During discussion, receive flash of insight into a
plot problem on the completely unrelated
manuscript read two weeks ago. Head back to

office. While eating lunch, type response to Marketing with one hand.

12:50 p.m.: Hit Send and get out of office before any more messages (or people) arrive. Meet co-worker at prearranged spot and go for walk in park across the street. Chat about books and life in general, enjoy the sunshine and warm temperature, watch a woodpecker search for grubs and fly back to its nest, arrive at the end of the trail. Turn around and do it all again for the return journey.

1:33 p.m.: Back in office. See red light on phone blinking. Creative art editor needs details on setting for chosen scene that will be depicted on a January book. Go down hall to ask assigned editor to check with author. Give opinion about a "slush" manuscript that has solid writing but many problems with characterization. (Suggest it be rejected but that the problems be outlined.) Discuss e-mail that author sent regarding a possible trilogy. Read first draft of speech that editor's writing to be given at a conference. Return to office, look at to-do list. Smack forehead at realization that phone call to U.K. did not take place (office now closed). Vow to do it first thing next morning. Check e-mails—request (with exclamation mark) from single-title-program editor for information about books that haven't been written yet so that freelance copywriter can create back cover copy. Add it to list and send e-mail to author. Finally return to pre-lims. Proof, check copyright, booklists and edit reader letters for length. Return package to Production, chat with editor about a recent business presentation she gave, get called into another office for a demo of the electronic database that I'll be testing, fill water glass, check printer and mail-box (revised ms has arrived), ask editorial assistant if she has a head count for national RWA conference. Clarify question about company policy for her.

Make it back to office. Let author know that her manuscript arrived. Look at clock—3:40. Decide to proof black and whites now that things are quiet. Proof for 20 minutes. Read one of the e-mailed "ideas." Make notes and debate sending them right now. Opt to do so and then begin to deflag manuscript. Get message from author re: character descriptions that raises another question. E-mail it to her, notice that it's now 5:05. Decide to deflag until 5:30. Thirty minutes later, get 89 pages into the 311-page manuscript and decide to at least get halfway.

Accomplish goal, make new list for tomorrow, drop off black and whites to Production and head on home with three chapters in hand to read on the bus.

Whew!

Here's a sneak peek...

LEARNING CURVES

by
Cindi Myers

Available from Signature Select October 2005

Shelly Piper is a size-twelve woman in a size-six world. And in network news, where thin is in, Shelly is relegated to behind-the-scenes reporting—until Jack Halloran hires Shelly as his new co-anchor. It's Shelly's dream job, and Jack's her dream man. But when the ratings prove viewers want a slimmer Shelly, she's determined to fight the ratings rather than lose a dress size—or her job.

CHAPTER 1

SHELLY PIPER studied her reflection in the unforgiving glare of fluorescent lighting and mirrors on three sides and didn't know whether to weep or puke. The pale green chiffon bridesmaid's dress stretched across her sturdy frame like a misplaced canopy for Barbie's dream bed. She forced a finger underneath the band of one puffed sleeve, hoping to restore blood flow to her arm. The designer of this thing obviously never met a ruffle, pouf or fribble she didn't love, since the yards of billowy fabric were liberally decorated with every frill and fribble imaginable. "I look like a Jell-O mold," she said.

"Oh, now it's not that bad." Her best friend and bride-to-be, Yvonne Montoya, tried to smooth the full skirt of the dress, which ballooned over Shelly's hips. "I think it's just darling."

"A darling Jell-O mold." She frowned over her shoulder at the bow perched on her backside.

"No, you look beautiful," Yvonne protested.

Only a bride, vision fogged by love and the

prospect of her own white satin splendor, would think this. Shelly caught the eye of the salesclerk. The woman's smile was strained. "I'm sure the effect of all the bridesmaids together will be wonderful," she said.

Liar. Shelly tugged at the ruffled neckline, trying to pull it up over her cleavage. The designer apparently hadn't considered that some women had real breasts, either.

"Emma and Stacy loved the dress," Yvonne said.

Emma and Stacy were liars, too, Shelly decided. They were also sizes four and six respectively. They needed all these ruffles to give the illusion that they were more than shining hair and good cheekbones.

"Perhaps if I ordered the dress in a larger size." The salesclerk frowned at the bow. Or maybe she was frowning at Shelly's butt. Shelly was tempted to give a belly dancer shake for the clerk's benefit.

"The size isn't the problem." She reached for the zipper and began to pull it down. "This isn't the sort of dress for my body type." Shelly was a well-endowed size twelve. One hundred percent natural curves. She'd learned long ago to avoid ruffles the way a dieter avoids cheesecake.

"Shelly, please!" Yvonne hurried after her as she headed for the dressing cubicle. "This is my *wedding!*" She said the word as if it was an occasion upon which life and death depended. Who knows, for Yvonne, maybe it was.

Six years ago, on a particularly maudlin evening

shortly after her twenty-fifth birthday, a weeping, slightly inebriated Yvonne had vowed to be married by the time she turned thirty. When she'd missed that deadline, she'd plummeted into a months-long funk that had lifted only when she'd won the coveted proposal from Daniel Dunnegan, a commodities broker she'd known all of three months. Still, the man—and the upcoming wedding—made Yvonne happy, so Shelly was determined to keep her that way.

"It's going to be a beautiful wedding." Preparing for her role as maid of honor, she'd been practicing saying this repeatedly, a calming mantra for the stressed-out bride.

"But you have to be in it. And you have to wear that dress. It's the perfect dress."

Perfect for what? But she really already knew the answer. Since they were kids, Yvonne had harbored dreams of the perfect Cinderella wedding, complete with ruffled dresses, a four-tier cake and a white satin gown with a train five yards long. Having finally won that prized proposal, she had poured twenty years of pent-up longing into creating the absolutely perfect dream wedding.

It was a testament to their friendship that Yvonne hadn't let her less-than-perfect choice of a maid of honor cloud her vision one bit. "I didn't say I wouldn't wear the dress," Shelly said, watching her face in the mirror as she spoke. Same pleasant smile, same calm expression. This is what years of training to be on television will do for you. You could say the most alarming things with a straight face. Fifty homes destroyed by a tornado? Mass flooding in the southern valley? World's worst bridesmaid's dress proudly worn in public? That calm reporter's demeanor never changed. "Of course I'll wear the dress," she continued. "It's going to be a beautiful wedding."

"It is, isn't it?" Yvonne's voice sounded dreamy, as it did too often these days. She drifted away, leaving Shelly to change clothes in peace.

Five minutes later she emerged from the cubicle, herself again in a neat black pantsuit with a beaded top that drew attention to her face and a long jacket that skimmed her hips. After years of dieting, exercise and various desperate measures, she'd celebrated her thirtieth birthday last year by embracing the fact that she was a size-twelve woman in a size-six world. She was healthy, she was strong and she was beautiful, even if not everyone appreciated her beauty. *She* appreciated it, and to hell with the rest of them.

Of course, there were still days when she looked at pictures of size-two models in magazines and wanted to slit her wrists. After all, years of brainwashing couldn't be banished overnight. But she'd come a long way since the times when her mood for the morning was dictated by numbers on the scale. She had a whole new wardrobe of classy, flattering clothes and a new appreciation for her own sexy curves. And she'd discovered there were more than a few men out there who appreciated a woman with a woman's shape.

Now if she could only convince her bosses at First For News to appreciate her as much. After years of slaving away behind the scenes, she'd finally earned a tryout for a weekend on-air reporter's position. But that had been weeks ago. The powers that be were certainly taking their time making up their mind.

"Will that be check or charge?" The salesclerk greeted her at the front register.

Shelly handed over her charge card and tried not to think about how much she was paying for a dress she would wear once and then banish from her closet forever.

"I'm going shopping for stationery this afternoon, want to come?" Yvonne came to stand beside her. "You can help me pick out thank-you notes."

Oh joy. Shelly shook her head. "Sorry, but I have to get back to the station. I'm hoping to catch Darcy by surprise and make her tell me what the higher-ups have decided about the reporter's job."

"You mean they *still* haven't told you?" Yvonne planted her hands on her hips and looked outraged. Or as outraged as a curly haired blonde with big brown eyes can look. "No one's worked as hard to get that job as you have. Why can't they just give it to you?"

"This is television." Shelly shrugged into her coat, then draped the dress bag over one arm. "Qualifications don't necessarily have anything to do with whether or not you get a job." But dammit, she *had* worked hard to prove herself. She'd volunteered for every shitty schedule, worked overtime turning in award-winning copy and had taken hours of classes to hone her skills in front of the camera. Going by seniority alone, she was next in line for a promotion. There was no good reason the job shouldn't be hers.

She kept reminding herself of this on the drive from Cherry Creek to downtown. Though six inches of snow had fallen over the weekend, most of it had already melted away. The streets were clear and the sun shining through the windshield made it feel warmer than the thirty-eight degrees showing on the Republic Bank sign. A typical January in Denver.

As the elevator ticked off the passing floors on its way to First For News' offices at the top of the Republic Plaza Building in downtown Denver, she rehearsed the spiel she'd give her boss, Darcy Long. *It's been three weeks. They told me from the first I was one of the top candidates. When will they make a decision?* A polite, firm request for action. The key was to act professional and think positive.

As she stepped off the elevator, she caught a glimpse of a woman in a pink blouse and gray slacks darting down the hall. Darcy. And the hallway led to her office. A feeling of triumph surged through Shelly as she hurried after her boss.

She cornered Darcy in her office at the end of the hall. Darcy's eyes widened as Shelly swept in after her and closed the door. "I don't have time to talk,

Shelly," Darcy said, making a show of shuffling papers on her desk. "I have a meeting with Roger in five minutes." Roger was Roger Murphy, executive producer of First For News.

"Then you have five minutes." Shelly settled into the chair across from Darcy's desk. "This won't take even that long, I'm sure."

Darcy's face looked pinched, though a series of Botox injections had made it impossible for her to actually frown. "What do you need?" she asked as she dropped into her chair.

"It's been three weeks since my tryout for the on-air reporter's spot," Shelly said. "Have you heard anything?"

Darcy wrinkled her nose. (The only part of her face she *could* wrinkle, Shelly supposed.) "I really don't have time to discuss this right now. Maybe later…."

"How much time does it take to tell me yes or no?" Shelly struggled to keep a pleasant look on her face. Her stomach was doing the backstroke and she was wishing she hadn't eaten that chicken sandwich at lunch.

"All right then, no." Darcy avoided her eyes.

Shelly swallowed hard. "No you haven't heard anything, or no I didn't get the job?"

Darcy sighed. "No, you didn't get the job."

"What? Are they crazy?" She sprang to her feet, every calm, professional word she'd rehearsed burned from her brain by red-hot anger. "They told me I was a top candidate. That I did great in my audition. I've worked here ten years. My piece on homeless women won an award last year."

"Tamra Smothers won an award for reporting that piece," Darcy said.

"Yes, but *I* did the work. And everyone here knows it." She paced back and forth, fists clenching and unclenching, before she turned on Darcy again. "What did they say? Why did they turn me down?"

Darcy shuffled papers again. "Oh, they weren't specific. They apparently feel they've found someone else who will connect with viewers better."

The words set off warning bells in Shelly's brain. "What do you mean 'connect with the viewers better'? Who did they hire?"

"I believe her name is Pamela Parsons. Very good credentials, I'm sure."

"Pamela Parsons!" Known in local circles as Perky Pam, Parsons was a bleached-blond beauty queen whose main claim to fame was posing in a bikini in ads for Honest Cal's Used Cars. The ads were plastered all over town, insuring that everyone knew who Pam was— "She's not a journalist. She's a model."

"She has a journalism degree from the University of Colorado." Darcy stood. "Look, I really have to go now." She offered a patently fake smile. "Don't worry, I'm sure there'll be another chance for you soon."

Right. Just as soon as I bleach my hair and lose

forty pounds. "They thought I was too big, didn't they?"

Darcy stumbled on her way out the door and turned to stare at Shelly, her face blanched white. "I didn't say anything like that."

"You didn't have to." She took a deep breath, holding back the black mood she could almost see at the edge of her vision. "I've heard it before."

"You'll never prove anything if you try to sue."

"Oh, the station would love that, wouldn't it? Did they tell you that? 'Don't let her know the real reason she lost the job. We don't want a lot of publicity about size discrimination.'" Darcy's wild-eyed look told her she'd scored a direct hit.

"You wouldn't try to do that, would you?" Darcy asked. "You'd ruin your career before it even started."

She nodded. The news business was amazingly insular. Get a reputation as a troublemaker and you were history. Besides, she'd have to spend a boatload of money and time she didn't have trying to fight something that would be pretty tough to prove. "I don't know what I'm going to do right now," she said. "But I'll let you know."

She managed to hold a hint of a superior smile on her face until Darcy gave her one last angry look and left the office. Then she sank into a chair by the door and let out the breath she'd been holding. "So what has all this positive thinking done for you lately?" she mumbled under her breath.

***

"Jack, before we start the interviews, I need to run some ideas by you for the promo spots." Executive producer Armstrong Brewster cornered Jack Halloran outside the KPRM conference room after lunch.

"Sure." Jack checked his watch, a classy but modest Tag Heuer his father had given him last Christmas. "I've got about fifteen minutes before the first candidate arrives."

"It won't hurt them to wait a little bit on a star." Armstrong punched the keys of his PalmPilot. "Now what do you think of some footage taken at one of the area ski resorts—maybe Loveland, since it's closest? Put you in a sharp-looking ski suit, surround you with snow bunnies."

Jack made a face. "No one wears ski suits these days. And no one calls women skiers snow bunnies. It's sexist."

"Right. Well, if you don't like that one, how about filming you at the gym? Maybe on one of those rock climbing walls? Play up the whole physical fitness thing and show off your muscles. The viewers love that kind of thing."

"What does any of that have to do with the news?"

Armstrong heaved a sigh and fixed Jack with a pained look. "It might be the news, but it's still entertainment. You have to catch people's attention. And in this case, *you're* what will capture them and, we hope, make them tune in to look."

The idea grated. Surely the kind of people who

tuned in to watch his show would be more intelligent than that. "This is a serious news magazine. About issues."

He started toward the conference room where the job candidates were waiting. Armstrong fell into step beside him. "You think because this is public television we don't have to compete for viewers? We have to get them any way we can. So if sex appeal sells, then we give 'em sex appeal."

"This kind of thing is exactly why I left the networks." He'd lost count of all the times he'd put in long hours, working on gritty, investigative pieces, only to find himself pushed into promo fluff pieces that made the station look good. When he'd learned that his last position as prime-time anchor had come not because of his journalistic chops, but because he scored highest with the target market group of twenty-five to thirty-seven-year-old women and men, he'd resigned and vowed to find a place where he could be more than just a pretty face stuck behind a desk.

He glanced at Armstrong, who was stabbing a stylus at his PalmPilot like a man trying to spear eels. "There's more to life than looks, you know."

"Tell that to a man with a full head of hair." Armstrong slotted the stylus back in the case and looked at Jack. "Now which of the promo ideas do you like best?"

"None of them." They reached the conference

room and stopped outside the door. "Let's finish this discussion after the interviews."

"Maybe I should get Mr. Palmer to decide on a promo spot."

"May I remind you that my uncle is providing the financing for the show—he doesn't want to be involved in production. That's your job."

Armstrong snapped shut the PalmPilot. "In that case, I say we do the spot at the gym. It'll appeal to women *and* men."

Jack shook his head and opened the door to the conference room. He wasn't done discussing this yet, but right now he had to choose a coanchor for the show. From the first he'd agreed that having two people to present the news was better than making this a one-man show. Adding a woman provided another prospective on issues, as well as appealing to a different demographic.

He might resent that television was ruled by audience numbers, but he wasn't naive. The trick was balancing reality with the way he wanted things to be.

"Hello, everyone. Sorry to keep you waiting." He took a seat at one end of the conference table while Armstrong sat in a chair against the wall. "I'm Jack Halloran and this is the producer of the show, Armstrong Brewster."

Jack studied the four candidates and mentally matched them with the curricula vitae he'd studied earlier. A tall African-American woman with a cascade of braids and a model's high cheekbones smiled at him. Angela Lawson. Early-morning anchor at a network affiliate in Tulsa. Only four years out of the University of Oklahoma but rising fast.

To Angela's left was a petite woman with a lion's mane of blond hair. Mindy Albertson. Blue eyes and peaches-and-cream perfection. She looked like the cheerleader who'd lived next door. The one who'd been the most popular girl in every high school in America. But she wasn't a dumb blonde. She'd graduated with honors from NYU and had been weekend anchor at a large independent in Rochester.

Veronica Sandoval was the third candidate, a native of San Antonio whose black hair was fashionably disheveled—a look he would bet took hours to get so perfect. At thirty-four, she was the most experienced in the group, and the oldest, though she looked at least five years younger than the graduation date on her CV indicated.

He turned to the last candidate, a honey-blonde in a well-cut blue suit. Unlike the others, she wasn't beaming at him with an impossibly wide smile. Instead, she was watching him. Studying him. As if this was all quite serious business to her.

He folded his hands in front of him on the table and addressed the women. "I'd like to start by having each of you talk about why you think you're the best candidate for this position. Angela, why don't we start with you."

The African-American woman sat up a little straighter and glanced around the table. "No offense

CINDI MYERS

to anyone else here today, but it's obvious I'm most likely to appeal to a young, hip demographic. Public television has a stodgy image. You can pull in viewers by overcoming that."

In the background, Armstrong was nodding his head. He liked the way this woman thought.

"But you have to give people more than fluff."

The woman on his right, Shelly, had spoken. Angela looked annoyed. "Hey, I can deliver serious news." She smiled. "But I can also look good doing it."

Armstrong chuckled. Jack turned to Shelly. He gave her points for speaking up, but she was in the hot seat now. "Ms. Piper, is it?" he asked.

34   She nodded.

"Why do you think you're best suited for the position?"

"I've got ten years of experience in broadcast journalism. Five of those have focused primarily on investigative reporting. I've lived in Denver for twenty years. I know what's what and who's who in the state and local government. I'm hard-working and tenacious when it comes to tracking down information." She paused and took a deep breath, her eyes still fixed on Jack. "And I care about the stories I do."

He blinked. Her last words were startling. Most reporters he knew went out of their way to affect an attitude of detachment. They prided themselves on being objective and dispassionate. To profess an emotional investment in your work seemed old-fashioned, even unprofessional.

Certainly the other two candidates didn't make that mistake. Veronica stressed her ties to the Hispanic community and her experience as a political reporter. Mindy played up her on-air experience and added that she was "A lot of fun."

Not something he'd thought about as a requirement for a reporter of serious news, but Armstrong nodded in approval. Jack wrote *fun* next to Mindy's name on his list.

He consulted his notes once more. "Now I have a sample scenario for you to consider. Suppose a state representative has a key vote on a pressing issue to be decided soon in the legislature. He's refusing all requests for interviews through normal channels. How would you go about learning his views on the issue?"

The women looked serious, brows furrowed, lips pursed in thought. Mindy was the first to speak. "I'd make friends with his secretary or administrative assistant. They know everything and she could give me the inside track to her boss."

He nodded. Not a bad tactic. "Veronica?"

"I believe persistence pays off," she said. "I'd call and visit his office daily until he agreed to talk to me."

Nagging could sometimes be effective, he would admit. He turned to Shelly. "What would you do?" he asked.

"I'm assuming this is a representative from this

district," she said. "Both Tom Murphy and Pete Ro-
driguez are big skiers. If the session is really tense,
with a big issue up for debate, by the weekend they're
going to want to take a break on the slopes, so I'd follow them there and maneuver myself to ride the
chairlift up with them. Then I'd strike up a conversation. You can learn a lot riding the lifts."

He nodded. "Very creative."

"You ski?" Mindy's tone was scornful.

Shelly's expression tightened. "Yes, I ski. As I
said before, I've lived here for twenty years."

"You certainly don't look like a skier." Mindy
looked down her nose. "I mean, you don't look very
athletic."

"You mean I'm not skinny."

This remark was met with chilling silence. The
women avoided looking at Shelly, though they ex-
changed conspiratorial glances with each other.
Shelly held her head up, and turned to address Jack.
"Something else I should have mentioned earlier.
The average woman in this country is a size twelve.
I know how important demographics are in these de-
cisions, so you might think about that."

The atmosphere was a trifle tense after that, and
Jack cut the interview short after only a few more
questions. "You'll be hearing from us in the next few
days," he told the candidates as they filed out. "Thank
you for coming."

When he and Armstrong were alone, he turned to
the producer. "Well?"

"I liked that Angela woman the best. Though Mindy's a close second. They're both young, smart and gorgeous. The viewers would love them, and the two of you together would be dynamite."

It was what he'd expected Armstrong to say, but he was still disappointed. "I liked Shelly Piper the best," he said.

Armstrong frowned. "She was okay."

"She was more than okay. Didn't you hear her answer my question about landing an interview with the legislator? She's obviously a creative thinker, and her knowledge of the city could prove really valuable and would balance out the fact that I'm so new here."

"Yeah, but she's a little…chunky."

"Chunky?" He frowned. "She wasn't skinny but she looked okay to me."

"Well yeah, she looked okay for a woman on the street, but the camera adds ten pounds."

"What does that have to do with anything? She sounds like a good reporter."

"I'm just telling you what people are going to say. People expect women on TV to be skinny. You put her on and you're going to get calls. Besides, if we went with Angela or Mindy we could do promo spots with you two beautiful people and we'd have viewers turning in just to look at the two of you."

Which was exactly what he *didn't* want. "That's not the audience I'm going for."

"Then hire Veronica. At least she'd get us the Hispanic viewers. And she's nice looking, too."

He shook his head. His mind was made up on this one. He wanted someone he could work well with. Someone who would get what he was trying to do here, covering solid news stories with a depth the networks couldn't manage. "We're going to hire Shelly," he said.

Armstrong shook his head. "You're making a big mistake."

"No, I think I'm doing exactly the right thing." Jack rubbed his hands together. He and Shelly Piper were going to be good together, he knew it.

...NOT THE END...

Look for LEARNING CURVES in bookstores October 2005!

Signature Select™

THE FORTUNES OF TEXAS:™ Reunion

In September, look for...

Lone Star Rancher

by *USA TODAY* bestselling author

LAURIE PAIGE

Fleeing a dangerous stalker, model Jessica Miller retreats to Red Rock, Texas, to Clyde Fortune's ranch... the last place on earth she expects to find love. But when Clyde opens his home to Jessica, the brooding loner also finds himself opening up his heart for the first time in years.

Silhouette®
Where love comes alive™

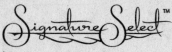

COLLECTION

**From three favorite
Silhouette Books authors...**

CorNeReD

Three mystery-filled romantic stories!

Linda Turner

Ingrid Weaver

Julie Miller

Murder, mystery and mayhem are common ground
for three female sleuths in this short-story collection
that will keep you guessing!

On sale September 2005

Where love comes alive™

Bonus Features:

**Author Interviews,
Author's Journal
Sneak Peek**

SCC

MINISERIES

National bestselling author

Debra Webb

FILES FROM THE COLBY AGENCY

Two favorite novels from her
bestselling Colby Agency series—
plus Bonus Features

Love and danger go hand in hand for two
Colby Agency operatives in these two
exciting full-length stories!

Coming in September.

**Bonus Features
include:**

**The Writing Life,
Trivia
and an exclusive
Sneak Peek!**

Where love comes alive™

If you enjoyed what you just read,
then we've got an offer you can't resist!

Take 2 bestselling
love stories FREE!

Plus get a FREE surprise gift!

Clip this page and mail it to Harlequin Reader Service®

IN U.S.A.	IN CANADA
3010 Walden Ave.	P.O. Box 609
P.O. Box 1867	Fort Erie, Ontario
Buffalo, N.Y. 14240-1867	L2A 5X3

YES! Please send me 2 free Harlequin® Blaze™ novels and my free surprise gift. After receiving them, if I don't wish to receive anymore, I can return the shipping statement marked cancel. If I don't cancel, I will receive 6 brand-new novels each month, before they're available in stores! In the U.S.A., bill me at the bargain price of $3.99 plus 25¢ shipping and handling per book and applicable sales tax, if any*. In Canada, bill me at the bargain price of $4.47 plus 25¢ shipping and handling per book and applicable taxes**. That's the complete price and a savings of at least 10% off the cover prices—what a great deal! I understand that accepting the 2 free books and gift places me under no obligation ever to buy any books. I can always return a shipment and cancel at any time. Even if I never buy another book from Harlequin, the 2 free books and gift are mine to keep forever.

151 HDN D7ZZ
351 HDN D72D

Name	(PLEASE PRINT)	
Address	Apt.#	
City	State/Prov.	Zip/Postal Code

Not valid to current Harlequin® Blaze™ subscribers.

Want to try two free books from another series?
Call 1-800-873-8635 or visit www.morefreebooks.com.

* Terms and prices subject to change without notice. Sales tax applicable in N.Y.
** Canadian residents will be charged applicable provincial taxes and GST.
  All orders subject to approval. Offer limited to one per household.
® and ™ are registered trademarks owned and used by the trademark owner and/or its licensee.

BLZ05   ©2005 Harlequin Enterprises Limited.

Signature Select™

COMING NEXT MONTH

Signature Select Collection
LOVE SO TENDER by Stephanie Bond, Jo Leigh and Joanne Rock
Why settle for Prince Charming when you can have The King?
It's now or never—Gracie Sergeant, Alyssa Reynolds and Ellie
Evans can't help falling in love...Vegas style! Three romantic
novellas that could only happen in Vegas.

Signature Select Saga
SEARCHING FOR CATE by Marie Ferrarella
A widower for three years, Dr. Christian Graywolf's life is his
work. But when he meets FBI special agent Kate Kowalski—a
woman searching for her birth mother—the attraction is
intense, immediate and the truth is something neither Christian
nor Cate expects. That all his life Christian has been searching
for Cate.

Signature Select Miniseries
LAWLESS LOVERS by Dixie Browning
Two complete novels from THE LAWLESS HEIRS SAGA.
Daniel Lyon Lawless and Harrison Lawless are two successful,
sexy and very sought-after bachelors. But their worlds are about
to be rocked by the love of two headstrong, beautiful women!

Signature Select Spotlight
HAPPILY NEVER AFTER by Kathleen O'Brien
Ten years after the society wedding that wasn't, members of
the wedding party are starting to die. At the scene of every
"accident," a piece of a wedding dress is found. It's not long
before Kelly Ralston realizes that she's the sole remaining
bridesmaid left...and the next target!

Signature Showcase
FANTASY by Lori Foster
Brandi Sommers doesn't know quite what to do about her
sister's outrageous birthday gift of a dream vacation to a
lover's retreat—with sexy security consultant Sebastian Sinclair
included as the lover! But she soon discovers that she can do
whatever she wants....

STEPHANIE BOND

was seven years deep into a computer career and pursuing a master's degree at night when an instructor remarked that she had a flair for writing and encouraged her to submit to academic journals. Once the seed was planted, however, Stephanie immediately turned to creating romance fiction in her spare time. She sold her first book in 1995, and two years later left her computer career to write full-time. She now writes for the Harlequin Temptation and Harlequin Blaze lines, having gained notoriety for her spicy romantic comedies, such as *Too Hot To Sleep*, and *It Takes a Rebel*. Stephanie lives with her husband in Atlanta, Georgia, her laptop permanently attached to her body.

JO LEIGH

The author of over thirty novels, **Jo Leigh** grew up in Southern California and dreamed of making movies. At eighteen, she began work at 20th Century-Fox and for the next fifteen years she worked on location shoots all over the country. During that time she fell in love with writing, and she sold a series idea to Cinemax. She also has written several screenplays. She started writing for Harlequin in 1994 and hasn't looked back. She currently lives on a mountain in Utah with her own personal hero. She loves to hear from readers at www.joleigh.com.

JOANNE ROCK

RITA® Award-nominated author **Joanne Rock** has kept busy since her first sale, writing at least five books a year for various Harlequin series. A Golden Heart winner, she has garnered multiple awards as a published author, including a *Romantic Times* W.I.S.H. Award and a Blue Boa. A former college teacher, Joanne has a master's in English from the University of Louisville and started writing romance when she became a stay-at-home mom, deceiving herself that she'd have more time. Twenty books and three kids later, she lives with her husband and sons in the Adirondacks, committed to mass chaos and happily-ever-afters.